WICKED COURT

KETLEY ALLISON

WICKED COURT PLAYLIST

Dolls - Bella Poarch

Crazy - Natalie Jane

Don't Blame Me - Taylor Swift

I'm Her - Natalie Jane

Not to be Dramatic - Zoe Clark

The Things I Do For Love - bludnymph

Beggin' - Chris Lake, Alan

Blood//Water - King Kavalier Remix - grandson, King Kavalier

Dirty Thoughts - Chloe Adams

BOYTOY - Halle Abadi

Listen to the rest of the playlist on Spotify:

A NECESSARY INTRODUCTION

Hello butterflies, Cav here.

Let's get the formalities out of the way, shall we? If you're looking for a gentle preamble or a soft landing into our world, I'm going to have to disappoint you. I'm not one for mincing words or sugarcoating the reality of what lies ahead.

If you're the type who likes surprises and prefers wandering into a story blind, then this is where you should probably skip ahead and just start reading. Trust me, there's a lot waiting for you on the other side.

Our tale, while firmly planted in the here and now, brushes up against some themes and scenarios that, while enjoyable to us, may not be as thrilling for you. Some triggers include dubious consent, multiple partners, and discussions about past child abuse. They're part of the story's fabric, part of what made us who we are.

And since I've got your attention, let's clear up one more thing. Our story circles around an accused witch, but keep your wands and broomsticks at bay—there's nothing paranormal or supernatural going on here. We're keeping it contemporary, rooted in the kind of reality where humans create magic with their hands and minds, not spells.

So, why am I giving you this little warning? Because I care, believe it or not. We want you to be ready for the ride, to understand that while we're inviting you into our chaos, we're also mindful of your mental health.

Our journey is intense, filled with moments that'll have you on the edge of your seat, maybe even questioning what you'd do in our shoes. But it's also about finding light in the darkness, about the power of connections that defies the odds.

If you're up for it, if you feel that thrill at the prospect of a story that challenges as much as it entertains, then by all means, turn the page. We're ready for you. But if any of what I've mentioned gives you pause, then consider this your sole heads-up to proceed with caution, or maybe even check out another book, that's more your speed.

Either way, you've been warned. Welcome to our world.

PROLOGUE

ELARA

I kneel blindfolded in a sea of hushed anticipation, acutely aware of the weight of unseen eyes upon me.

My heart races, a captive animal within my chest, betraying my feigned calm. Auburn locks cascade over my shoulders, a stark blaze against the shadowed quiet, marking me as different, as other, despite my longing to blend in.

Then, there's a shift in the air, charged with a tension that tightens like chains around my wrists.

"Elara," comes a rasp from the darkness, a sound that shouldn't reach me but pierces straight to my core.

A shiver traces my spine like a lover, born not of cold, but of a terrifying recognition.

The voice carries a mixture of desire and anger so potent it feels as though a storm is about to break over my head.

I shouldn't be here. I'm not one of them. Yet, here I am, caught in a ritual I barely understand.

Footsteps descend the staircase, each one echoing like a gunshot in the charged silence, drawing nearer.

I tilt my head, the slightest movement, as he approaches, as if part of me can still hear the continued whisper of my name, feel the intensity of someone's unwavering focus.

A large, calloused hand cradles my chin, tilting my face upward. A gasp escapes me, surprise and a flicker of fear mingling with the certainty that my time has come.

"Hello, butterfly."

CHAPTER 1
CAV

THREE WEEKS EARLIER

Engraved in blood and ink, our motto reads: *Veritas in Umbris*. Truth in Shadows.

An apt reflection of our existence.

As the Consul and second-in-command to the three Sovereigns of the Cimmerian Court, I'm given power and influence that only the dark arts could match.

You wouldn't know it at this moment.

I'm on my knees before the three Sovereigns. My shirt was ripped off while being dragged through the woods and marched underneath the Great Hall on campus down a hidden stairway, my wrists bound by torn shreds of my bedsheets. The others were used to blind and gag me.

I don't need to see or speak to understand my current predicament. My ears may be bleeding from the unnecessary boxing I received when being woken up by one of my so-called 'brothers,' but I can hear just fine.

A hushed murmur ripples through our ranks, circling my bowed form, laced with reverence and an eerie fear. I assume I'm near the dais where the Sovereigns enjoy holding court, their elder faces obscured by porcelain masks and their thousand dollar suits covered by velvet cloaks of deep crimson, with runes and other symbols woven through by gold thread.

There's a shuffle to my left and then my right.

"Kaspian?" I mutter through split, bloody lips. "Axe?"

"Here," a voice rumbles on my left, said with such reluctance it's as if we're attending homeroom and the teacher is going through the attendance roster.

"Yeah," a low voice confirms on my other side.

So, Kaspian Valenti and Axton Devereaux, my brothers-in-arms, were also thrust in front of our leaders at fuck o'clock in the morning.

"Don't forget, I am also excited about our Court's version of an alarm clock," comes another familiar voice. "How's everyone doing this lovely morning?"

My shoulders stiffen. They also got to Wilder.

The reason for our mandatory arrival is becoming ever so apparent.

Fuck.

"Did I give you permission to speak?"

The throaty voice comes from the front. One of the Sovereigns, then. Of the three, two enjoy hearing themselves talk and order us around. It's the Sovereign that doesn't speak, *never* speaks, that unnerves me.

While each represents the pillars of the Court, he's the one who gets to enact strategy and enforce punishments. And his idea of torture is always … unique.

Footsteps follow, the sounds of expensive treads hitting concrete, complimented by dripping water nearby.

"Apologies, Sovereign."

I lift my head as I say it, jutting out my chin. I can never precisely *bow* to authority—not in the way they want.

Rough nails slice through my lashes as two unforgiving fingers dig under the strip of cotton that obscures my vision, threatening to cut my corneas before tearing the fabric away.

I blink through the sweat now free to run into my eyes, squinting and surveying my surroundings as quick as possible after being blinded for over an hour. Strands of damp, black hair stick to my forehead and curl into my eyes, but I can't do anything but jerk my head to clear the view.

We're beneath the dim, crimson glow of our emblem. The chamber, an architectural masterpiece of Gothic grandeur that only the elite could think to carve under Ivy League buildings, boasts intricately carved stone pillars dancing amidst the haze of countless candles. The air is heavy with the lingering scent of incense, an aroma that clings to the dark velvet tapestries that hang from the walls like banners of mourning.

"You failed us, Cavanaugh."

The Sovereign who tore off my blindfold stands before me, apathetic behind his plain white mask.

"You were meant to retrieve the ruby Heart for us and instead, you've given us silence." He adds, "Did you not think we'd come for you?"

"I knew Mommy and Daddy would be mad," I say through a clenched jaw, "so forgive me for delaying your sadism."

Though it's impossible to tell, I'm confident his eyes narrow behind the black hollows of his mask.

"Insolence, too? You've forgotten your place."

"I know it well." I keep my voice steadfast. "And I'd simper and beg for your forgiveness to your heart's content, but for the surprising revelation that even you, sire, couldn't predict that the Heart doesn't *exist*."

Silence, but for the fidgeting of the other thirty freshmen and sophomore initiates of the Court surrounding our circle, also cloaked, but wearing half-masks of porcelain.

Kaspian, Axe, and Wilder remain bound and blind by my side, though their chins are up like mine. All have blood and dirt marring their features. And when I came back with the news, I convinced each of them that there is no Heart, the largest ruby in the world rumored to have been lost somewhere in Titan Falls.

One we were desperate to find.

They are my loyal brothers of the Court. We'd die for each other. Kill for each other.

The Sovereign inclines his head. The other two Sovereigns remain seated on their ornate stone thrones, gloved hands gripping the arms.

"You seem so confident in your answer, Cavanaugh," the standing Sovereign continues. "It gives me such great delight to inform you that you're wrong."

My answering smirk freezes on my face.

"It exists," the Sovereign says. "The Heart isn't the myth that many would like you to think it is. It's the pulse of our power, soaked in a history you've barely scratched the surface of. Our possession of it will rewrite the past and open us to alliances and power-plays that have shaped the world's elite for centuries. I'm shocked by your irreverence, Cavanaugh, considering your family's unshakeable belief that it will cure their curse of misfortune that has been ruining your ancestors for hundreds of years."

It pains me to do it, but I sputter, "That can't be true—"

"*Do not question your Sovereign.*"

Spit flies out of the small hole of a mouth in his mask, followed up by a *crack* across my face.

I keep my profile where it is after being whacked to the side, my lip curling, my vision turning red with actual blood along with the rage.

The Sovereign doesn't give me much time to stew. "Consider this mission your crucible. The Heart's recovery can redefine our Court's standing and your places within it, since you've all been demoted to a level below even the initiates. Failure is not an option. *Defeat* means death."

I meet his statement with silence, since I assume that's what he expects.

"As punishment for your current blunder, I want you to take our disappointment out on one of your favored brothers."

I still don't turn my head, but I swallow against the thickness in my throat.

"Choose, Cavanaugh, which one will suffer for your ineptitude."

Out of the corner of my eye, the other two Sovereigns stand and come forward. They split off on either side of the first one, pulling the blindfolds from Kaspian, Axe, and Wilder.

Someone from behind yanks me to a stand by hooking under my arms. In a single swipe, they free my bound hands, but instead of coming to blows with the Sovereigns—*because they're right, I failed*—I fist them at my sides, clenching and unclenching, bringing blood back to my fingers and keeping my expression stoic.

I have to remain unaffected, even as one initiate steps forward with the Court's ritual knife, an antique silver blade sharpened by centuries of kills.

He hands it to me hilt first, the small rubies on fire by the surrounding candlelight.

Axe, Kaspian and Wilder remain on their knees. No one moves to help them up or untie them. They could slip out of their bindings and get up themselves. We're all finely honed weapons, but they don't.

They're under orders.

"I'm losing patience, Cavanaugh," the Sovereign says.

I stare down at the backs of my brother-in-arms' heads—dark auburn, tarnished brown, ash blonde—none of us can claim a single, pure strand on our scalps.

And I don't know which one to choose to maim for my sins.

This isn't supposed to be difficult. I torture and manipulate for fun. I'd braid intestines while my victim was still alive to watch as a hobby if I could.

My throat tightens. I must punish one of them, to prove my unflinching loyalty to the Court.

But I won't do it without facing them. And they won't take it without holding my stare the entire fucking time.

Walking a path around them, I meet Kaspian's slate-blue eyes first, his jaw set. We share a history, have trusted each other with our lives countless times.

Axe kneels silent and steady, granting me his stoic permission with a slight nod. He would endure this trial without complaint.

Wilder's deceptively large, hazel eyes are defiant, burning with that familiar hunger. Our rivalry runs deep, fueled by the desire to be first at everything. I know he'd relish this chance to prove himself above the others.

It's Axe's quiet resignation that decides it.

"Axe," I say, my voice echoing in the vast chamber.

Axe's lips curl into a smirk. In a single, lithe jump, he rises, striding to the center of the sanctuary. He allows the initiates to force him into the engraved ceremonial chair with his legs widened to accommodate the back of the chair he leans into. His hands curl around the chair, his muscles undulating between his shoulders. There's a resignation in his bowed posture that makes my grip tighten around the hilt of the knife, the sharp prongs holding the rubies cutting into my palm.

I lift the ancient blade, its edge glinting in the firelight.

This is my duty. I will not flinch.

Its blade gleams ominously. The first incision has to be precise, a symbol of our fealty to the Court above all else.

As the tip touches Axe's marred skin, there's a palpable shift in the room. I press down, carving the first line of the X —next to the other three.

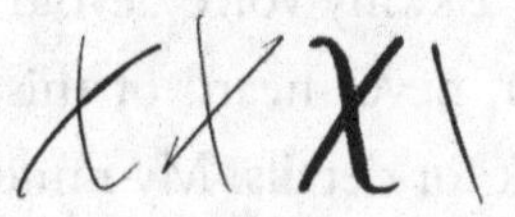

Axe's body tenses, but he doesn't flinch as I carve another rune across his shoulder blades. The Sovereigns may not outright confirm their love of the occult, but we do enough to sense their belief in dark magic.

The feel of the knife hitting his bone is unnerving, though the only reaction I give is the regular thump of my heart.

I complete the first line and start the second, my movements steady. Blood beads along the wound, a stark contrast against all the pink scar tissue mottling his back.

When I finish, the X is a stark, brutal mark, a symbol of punishment and a reminder of our ruthless creed.

I step back, knife dripping at my side.

Axe rises slowly, his movements deliberate. There's no anger in his eyes, only a deep understanding of the sacrifices we make, the costs of our allegiance.

The Sovereigns nod in approval, their expressions unreadable behind their masks. The initiates watch in silent judgment, the ritual a grim reminder of the price of failure.

"Well done, Cavanaugh."

The First Sovereign comes to my side, exchanging the bloody blade for a folded piece of paper.

I open it without question, reading the name written in elegant script.

Elara Wraithwood.

"My next kill?" I ask, my voice devoid of interest.

I don't know her, never heard of this person and do not need to defend or ask for details. My mind races with the *why*, though. Rarely do we target females.

"I've received evidence that her family may have information on the Heart's location," the Sovereign answers cryptically before drawing away. "Do not disappoint me this time."

I don't watch him depart.

I focus half of my attention on Axe as he prowls out of the room, his back painted with rivulets of bright red blood.

The other half stares at her name.

CHAPTER 2
ELARA

"They're back again."

I hold my phone between my shoulder and ear as I shove my cognitive psychology books in my bag. "Who is, Mom?"

"You know. Them."

Her tone is husky, rattled. I can barely hear her over the noise of other students gathering their things and shuffling out of class.

"We've discussed this, Mom." I match her muted tone. "The gardener comes on Thursday mornings. He drives a navy pickup truck. Is that what you're seeing?"

There are a series of taps on the other end.

I try not to sigh. "Yes, I still understand that two taps mean yes, and one tap means no."

"Good. I need to make sure I can communicate if he comes in and tries to rape me and I can no longer talk because he's gagged me."

"Mom—" I grit my teeth against any admonishment. I

should be thankful that her scenario is short today. I say lightly, "Leonardo's worked for us for years. You do background checks on him every week. He's not a threat."

"You promise? It only takes a second to stab someone."

"I promise you he hasn't killed anyone."

Slinging my bag's strap on my shoulder, I join in the line leading out of the classroom. "But why don't you ask Micah to drive into town and get your favorite dish from that French spot? Have lunch in the parlor and lock the door. By the time you're done, Leonardo will have finished with the gardening."

Mom hums in thought over the line. I wait her out and push through the main doors of the science building.

The first brush of sunlight spills through the towering oaks of the campus, igniting my hair into fiery tendrils that fly into my face as the wind picks up.

Then, two taps into the phone sound out.

My shoulders relax at her acquiescence and the tension releases in my neck. It helps that I've been massaging the back of my nape for the last five minutes. "Great. How about I come visit this weekend—"

"Elara, over here!"

The shout slices through the morning bustle, and I swivel, the weight of my books snug against my hip.

"Hey, Jonah," I call back, my voice rising effortlessly above the chatter of students.

He's flanked by a couple of sophomores whose names escape me, but their eager smiles are familiar enough.

Charisma—it's not something I learned, more like a birthright I've had to draw on every time I leave my home.

"Your presentation on gothic literature yesterday was

mind-blowing, El," Jonah says, his hand sweeping through his hair in a nervous gesture. "You have a way with words."

"Thanks. Words are easy. It's the silence between them that's tricky," I say, giving him a wink before going back to my phone. "Mom, I have to go. I'll call you tonight."

"Okay, but make sure it's before sunset. If you don't by then, I'll assume you're hurt, or maimed, or beheaded—"

"I miss you too, Mom," I say brightly as my roommate and best friend approaches. "Love you."

I hang up, swiftly tucking my phone into the snug back pocket of my worn jeans.

"Hey, Sasha," I greet as we fall into step together, navigating through the buzzing crowd in the main quad.

"Are you going to the Summer Solstice thing tonight?" she asks, her question tinged with hopefulness.

Nods and *hey you!*'s sound out, and we acknowledge each one. Anyone who catches my eye gets a smile from me, creating a familiar rhythm in my morning routine.

"Wouldn't miss it," I reply, though my mind races with the thought of the tight spaces, the press of bodies. I push aside images of my mother, trapped within the walls of our home, her fear of the outside world like a living thing. "You?"

"Duh. It's the event of the season!"

Her enthusiasm is infectious, but a part of me wonders if she senses the performance in my answering grin.

Not that anyone ever does.

"Let's get ready together," she suggests. "Meet in our room at, say, six? I'll grab a bottle of vodka from Erik when I see him after class."

"Still using him for his access to contraband, huh?" I tease with a genuine smile this time. "Does he have any idea what cute, tiny little you is up to whenever you grace his room with your presence?"

My delightful roommate possesses the delicate features of Tinker Bell but wields a mouth—and mind—like a garbage truck, and I wouldn't have her any other way.

Sasha's face lights up as she laughs.

"It's not just the booze. Or the 'shrooms," she amends. "He's also eats me out on command."

"*Sash!*" I shove her shoulder. "If he ever realizes you've been using him for sex and drugs, he'll be utterly heartbroken."

"*Pff,*" she scoffs, dismissing the notion. "Like he didn't do the same to me throughout our freshman year. He'll get over it."

"So long as quality tongue comes with top-shelf vodka," I reason.

"You think I'd accept anything less?" she quips before veering away, her long ebony ponytail swinging with each step.

I continue my walk to the arts building with my smile in place, waving and acknowledging everyone I come across and promises to meet up later.

To the athletes, I'm the fiery supporter. To the academics, a peer with a sharp mind. To the artists, a soul that appreciates their craft, all while my phone incessantly vibrates in my pocket with my mother's concerns.

Students part for me, making way for whatever they think I am—or perhaps who they hope I might be.

My last class before lunch is across campus, a lecture on ancient civilizations that I find utterly captivating. The professor, Dr. Harlow, with his tweed jacket and passion for

Mesopotamia, often lingers on my thoughts longer than the subject itself.

I am an unabashed history nerd. It's part of what got me to attend Titan Falls with its rich history of accused witches in the 1700s and a missing treasure alleged to be hidden by them before they died. Ancient, missing artifacts are particularly captivating.

Well, that and Titan Falls University was supposed to be my brother's alma mater. I always wanted to follow in his footsteps, even when he tried to ignore me and called me his invisible friend to his buddies.

Thoughts of my brother quickly spiral into worries over my mother, so I staunch them before they become so overwhelming, reining in my emotions with practiced control. I switch my mind over, like the flip of a page in an old, well-used book, and return to campus life.

Slipping inside the lecture hall just as Dr. Harlow begins his discourse on the Sumerians, I strive to keep my attention focused despite the persistent prickling at the back of my head. Dr. Harlow usually grabs my attention easily, regaling the class with tales of gods and kings, of love and war.

Yet, despite the allure of ancient civilizations, my stomach churns and twists at the mere thought of who sits in the back row, staring down the class like kings themselves.

I'm loved and accepted by everyone on campus.

Except for them.

CHAPTER 3
CAV

The scent of decay permeates the ancient lecture hall as Elara Wraithwood's soft laugh slices through the professor's monotonic drone.

There she is, the sacrosanct campus darling.

Sprawled in the back row, my boots lazily propped on the chair ahead, I watch her every move with an intensity that borders on obsession. Alongside me are the boys, my loyal comrades, equally captivated by her presence.

If only she knew the lengths we're willing to go to make her scream. She'd never laugh that softly again.

Ever since a Sovereign handed her name to me on a piece of paper, Elara's image has haunted not only my dreams but also my waking hours. Her light, freckled skin and thick, reddish-brown hair have etched themselves into the depths of my mind, but soon she'll see us as more than just the bored kings of campus.

We've been given a toy.

A possessive hunger stirs within me.

"She's like a walking campus brochure," I comment quietly to Kaspian, Wilder, and Axe. A hint of contempt laces my voice.

They smirk, knowing I speak the truth. Elara's popularity, the way she prances around TFU like she belongs here, her *niceness* and inclusion of everyone, makes me want to ruin her. She's like a politician without a black, corrupt heart. Her upbeat nature makes me want to gag.

There's a flit of movement to my left, distracting me, and I look down and to the side.

Wilder's busy fisting his cock under his chair's fold-up desk, his stare locked on the back of Elara's head.

"Are you that starved of pussy?" I murmur.

"Nah." He grunts, his jerks coming faster. "I love them peppy. You'd be surprised how much of that school spirit is used to suck cock. I'd shove my dick so far into her pretty mouth, she'd cry happy tears all the way through."

Wilder stiffens then groans as he bends forward, owning his public cumming by continuing to stare at her through his lashes and hissing through his teeth. Tendons pop into his forearm as he rubs his dick raw.

"Now how the fuck are you going to clean that up?" Kaspian asks idly on my other side, his fingers flicking across his tablet while he reads more about Elara.

With his quick mind and unsettling focus on tasks he deems worth his time, he'll dig up every single detail in this girl's life, right down to a lice breakout in her daycare when she was three.

My stare narrows on Kaspian's tablet while in my periphery, Wilder pulls his hand out of his pants and reaches behind me to rub it on Kaspian's shirt.

With a growl an alpha wolf would be proud of, Kaspian retaliates by lashing out and pressing a nerve near Wilder's ear that incapacitates and makes him resemble sitting on an electric chair.

All this happens behind my shoulders while I gaze at Kaspian's screen with growing concern.

So much of her is available online. Elara's active on social media and an avid philanthropist, supporting any charitable cause, especially ones involving puppies. Kasp and I could pinpoint her monthly cycle, for fuck's sake, but there is virtually nothing about the ruby Heart.

What was the evidence the Sovereign received that convinced him she possessed something of such value? After what I endured months ago, I was certain there was no ruby, no hidden treasure worth billions. I enjoyed dangling the possibility to those who were desperate for it, but Sarah Anderton's fortune isn't the legend everything thinks it is.

At the growing commotion in our row, Elara glances back at us, her amber eyes meeting mine with abject disapproval for daring to interrupt her A++ ass-licking of Harlow's hairy chocolate starfish.

I meet her stare head-on, eyes flat as a piranha while chewing on live flesh.

For a second, uncertainty flickers across her face before she whips around again, coppery strands swinging.

Good. My reputation precedes me.

Kaspian reaches into Axe's bag and pulls out hand sanitizer, spraying it dramatically on his hands and up his forearms. "You're nauseating, Wilder."

Despite all this activity, Axe hasn't let his attention stray from Elara, his eyes like steel-gray traps awaiting the chance for her to step into his teeth.

His clenched jaw speaks volumes. He leans forward, unwilling to press his tender back against his seat.

I quickly glance away.

Wilder recovers from the nerve-pinch, breathing through his nose and glaring a promise at Kasp to cut his cock off and have him choke on it later.

Ignoring the threat, Kaspian asks under his breath, "Wilder doesn't have a half-bad idea. Can't we play with her a little before getting what we need from her?"

"That depends," I say. "How much longer do you want to wait to save ourselves and our families?"

He frowns at that.

I study the back of her head. Loose waves adorn her perfect, eggshell skull. Elara Wraithwood possesses what most, if not all, of humanity covets: Beauty. She is a princess carved from a fairy tale, a mythical goddess, a rare creature of contradictory traits. Her hair, a natural copper, contrasts wonderfully with her buttery amber eyes. She's pale, with the tip of her nose constantly flushed with red—from cold, from the sun, from attention, who knows.

Coupled with her oval face and plush, heart-shaped lips, Elara stands out. Even her *name*, for God's sake, exudes perfection.

It grates on me.

She doesn't know what genuine power looks like.

Then, she turns and smiles at her neighbor again.

Bright, fluttering, beatific. A butterfly too close to our web.

We dismissed her as easily as I'd crumble those papery wings to dust in my palm.

Kaspian, Wilder, Axe and me ... well, butterflies don't fly at night for a reason.

Unfortunately, we now don't have a choice.

"Are you sure she's the one?" Wilder muses, drumming his fingers on the desk, his satiation at an end. "What could she possibly have to tell us about this mythical jewel?"

"If the Sovereigns say she has it, then she has it." A sinister grin pulls at Kaspian's lips. "I bet she's not as perfect as she seems. Everyone has their breaking point."

She faces forward now, her shoulders a straight line, the tension clear in the stiffness of her spine.

She knows she's being watched.

I add, "If not her, then someone in her family has the answers. Either way, we have use for her."

"*Use* means fuck," Wilder muses, leaning back in his seat and threading his fingers at the back of his head, "and that I would gladly do with my hand around her throat. But I refuse to make conversation. She probably eats rainbows and fairy dust for breakfast."

"Whereas you'd make better use of a bloodied unicorn carcass," I hear Axe mutter.

Wilder grins at him. "You assume I'd wait until it's dead."

I hold up a hand to shush them, and not because Professor Harlow's eyes keep darting towards us, debating whether to call us out for chatting in class. Or jerking off.

He won't.

I've told them to shut up because Elara raised her hand in answer to the professor's question regarding the Titan Falls witch trials.

How frivolously predictable she is. Of course she knows the details. Little teacher's sidepiece finishing her homework on time so she can blow him later.

I raise my voice while she waxes on about fear and superstition targeting those who don't fit society's mold.

"That's a naïve take."

Elara, the professor, and everyone else cranes their head at me in surprise. It's unlike me to take part in class other than to ace the exams. Even Axe cocks a brow at my willing participation.

I continue, "Those trials were less about fear of the unknown and more about manipulation. It was all a power play by those in charge."

Elara rests an arm on the back of her neighbor's chair, the warm color of her eyes regarding me coolly. "No, fear was the tool. It's easy to control people when they're scared."

I scoff, my upper lip curling with disdain. "So you agree. It all comes down to a game of control." I lean forward, my voice low, but clear, in the hushed room. "Isn't that your game, too? Smiling, being everyone's friend—it's your way to manipulate, to fit in. Have you ever considered that you're playing at the same thing they did? Just with a cuter face?"

Elara sucks in a breath, but her response is unwavering. "There's a difference between genuine connections and inciting fear. I don't hide behind a mask, unlike some people."

"Now, don't pretend you're above us all."

I sneer. *Break, Butterfly.*

"We all wear masks, including ones as pretty and insubstantial as yours."

The professor stutters, "Now, Cav—"

"Do you get some kind of sick pleasure from putting people down?" Elara asks sharply.

I rise from my seat, Kaspian and Axe shuffling to give me room without bothering to hide their curiosity. "I just enjoy exposing weakness when I see it."

A ripple goes through the class. Out of the corner of my eye, I see Wilder leaning forward and licking his fingers, eager to witness the fallout.

Elara doesn't miss a beat. She watches my movement toward the aisle, targeting *her*, her expression calm. "Exposing weakness? What a revealing hobby you have, Cavanaugh."

My full name on her pert lips tickles me in places I'm not happy about.

"But since we're into reflections," she continues, "maybe you're the one who's scared. Scared that beneath all that smug superiority, there's nothing of substance. Just a micro-dick guy afraid to face his own flaws."

The room stills. Dr. Harlow stifles a gasp, genuine terror shining through his spectacles.

I hear Kaspian let out a low, surprised whistle, "Well, she's fucked."

The lecture hall shifts into an airless vacuum with a rush in my ears, blackened corners, and a simpering, red-headed target at the center.

I move down the aisle, snaking down the stairs, those in aisle seats shrinking away as I pass.

Elara follows my path with an unblinking stare and notches her chin when I reach her seat and lean over her buddy beside her.

It's a shock to my system when her scent invades my space, a vanilla musk so unlike the usual cupcake-vanilla most of the girls on campus wear. It's startling, unnerving, but I flick it aside and keep my expression flat when I steal her air. She tenses, but doesn't back down.

"Tell me, Elara," I purr, "what does someone so popular and well-behaved always have to hide?" I lean in to whisper conspiratorially, "A deep, dark, priceless secret. And how I love to eat those up and spit *you* out."

Her composure finally cracks, shock flitting across her face. The class murmurs.

"Cavanaugh Nightshade, I insist you get back to your seat!" Harlow demands.

My smile widens. I decide to wait on "following" his orders, choosing to step on Elara's shadow instead.

Elara pushes to her feet. I languidly arch back to provide her space. I'm sad to say I narrowly avoided those perfect breasts of hers from squishing into me by mere inches.

She's not perfect. She's nothing.

Elara glares at me, tears lining her eyes, her entire body trembling. "No wonder your name is such a mouthful. Your parents gave you a douchebag name because you're an asshole. A *fucking* asshole."

She hurries from the classroom without a backward glance.

I fold my arms, triumphant.

And feel the familiar thrill of the hunt rising within me.

CHAPTER 4
ELARA

After the first cut, someone lets out a shriek, followed by a nervous giggle.

The freshman making those contradictory sounds clutches her forearm, red droplets seeping between her fingers as she spins to her cluster of friends, the steaming cauldron behind her containing her blood and greatest wish for the summer before it begins.

"Why did I come here again?" I ask under my breath, not expecting anyone to answer, including my own good sense.

"Because it's entertaining to see the fresh blood *spill* their blood over a cute guy in a skull mask, thinking dead witches will grant their wish." Sasha, dressed in as a sexy Victorian duchess beside me, sighs. "That used to be me. Oh, how fun and naïve I was."

I make a face at her, scrunching my nose with unamused disdain, but deep down grasping for innocent nostalgia, just like she is.

The organizers invite all freshmen at TFU to the summer

solstice party in the woods surrounding TFU campus. It used to happen only once a year, to kick off first semester, but students enjoy it so much, it now happens twice a year, in case that first wish didn't take. It sounds innocent. The invites hitting everyone's phones resemble any college party at any campus across the nation. But the truth is, it embraces more Titan Falls lore than a lot of first years are prepared for.

For one, a man in an intimidating mask and a sharpened knife hovers over a cauldron in the center of a small clearing.

A giant, real *cauldron*, I kid you not.

In years past, most people knew who was behind the mask, because way too many females and those of the male persuasion lined up to have their forearm cut and dribbled into the cast-iron pot, asking the accused witches from the Colonial days to provide them with good luck for the year and grant a single wish.

But Professor Morgan is absent this year. Rumor has it he lives in an old manor in the woods now with a gorgeous girl-friend and three other desperately handsome men and no longer has the time or the inclination to entertain giggly co-eds.

I'm not sure of the logistics in that house, but all I know is, when that girl thought of the greatest wish ever, she had the witches on her side. She snatched both Professor Morgan *and* Professor Rossi from the pool of unattainable men at TFU, along with two others who I've only seen glimpses of, but definitely drooled over.

Tonight, the new guy in charge of granting wishes is all I'm hearing about as I weave through the dancing, raucous crowd, holding a sweating cup of vodka punch and pulling my black cloak tighter to combat the abnormal chill in the air. Sasha tossed a heap of silk and lace at me as soon as I walked into our room, demanding I dress in a Victorian-inspired tutu with her or she'd slash my sheets and pillows in a rage.

She meant it, too.

Now, Sasha stops us as soon as we reach the clearing where we join the rest of the curious lookie-loos, while a line for the cauldron snakes through the gnarled trees and trampled grass.

Skull Mask is so intriguing that even upperclassmen are queuing up for another attempt.

"You know what? I think I'm going to make a junior year wish, too."

I snap out of my thoughts and grab Sasha's arm. "Seriously? Sash, *no*."

"Why not?" She pouts at me over her shoulder. "That guy may not be tattooed on all parts of his skin like Morgan, but look at the muscles under that cloak. And how *tall* he is. I bet he smells good, too."

My eyes dart to the empty cup she's holding. "How much have you had?"

"Oh, please. Doesn't the mystery turn you on a little? You can't tell me you've never fantasized about fucking a masked man before."

"Uh, no."

"Huh." She actually looks at me with pity. "Your loss."

Sasha shrugs out of my grip and I'm forced to follow her while pointing toward the cauldron. "That can't possibly be sanitary. Why would you want to go over there and—"

"What? Do it again?" She arches her brow. "Flashback time: our first party of freshman year. We both lined up for

Morgan, and he got to use his knife on us with his buttery, husky voice asking me what my greatest desire was."

My best friend literally shudders with delight at the memory.

I open my mouth to tell her the truth—that when I reached the front of the line, I whisper-begged Morgan not to cut me and just to go through the motions so my friend wouldn't hold it over my head for the rest of my life. He'd angled his head, and I swear he smiled behind his mask, then chuckled like he knew something I didn't. But he gave me the out.

I'm cut off from confessing my lie when a foreboding tingle hits the side of my face.

Sasha and I have walked into the space of the clearing between where the line and the half-circle of spectators are.

And, I'm slow to figure out, we're out in the open.

I don't know why that realization slithers into my mind like a viper, but it coils around my neck, tightening against its base, *warning* me to run.

My attention pulls from Sasha and toward the spiral of steam wafting from the heart of the clearing and the man standing behind it, his mask blurring in and out of focus from the smoke, those two empty black voids and that lipless, plastic smile pointed directly at me.

"*Oh my God*, is he looking at me?" Sasha hisses, then whirls to face me, brushing down her hair with her hands. "How do I look?"

"Totally fuckable," I say absently, unable to tear my gaze from those empty eyes.

I'm so unnerved and confused by the feeling of being

watched that I don't register Sasha dragging us toward the cauldron before it's too late.

I dig my heels in. "Wait, Sash—"

"Relax, El! It's just a silly tradition. A little blood, a wish, and bam—good luck for the year. What could go wrong?"

"You don't actually believe in this stuff, do you? It's all fake. A gross effort for the guys to take stock of the incoming girls and how hot they are. It's a meat market for Meat House!"

I'm desperately clutching at the nickname given to the boys' dorm, Meath House, hoping to break through Sasha's intentional deafness. Anything to stop my gallows walk to the front.

Because that's what it feels like. Like I shouldn't be doing this.

"He's beckoning us with his eyes. We're going, El. If I have to drag you there—oh, shut *up*, Cynthia." Sasha cuts herself off to yell at a trio of girls complaining we're cutting the line. "Consider this a lesson in assertiveness. In life, as in line-ups, it's seize the day, or stay in the background. Class dismissed."

She motions the girls back while yanking me until I smack into her side.

Under normal circumstances, I'm the one who lightens the unfiltered blows Sasha gives out to unsuspecting students, being the nice one, the thoughtful one. But right now…

I can't look up.

My nerves tighten at the masked figure so close. I sense a familiar presence behind it, a feeling that intensifies as I draw closer.

"State your wish and offer your tribute," comes an intonation above my head, the velvet nature of his tone casting an odd shiver down the contours of my back.

I glance up and notice the blade glinting in his hand, freshly cleaned by a sophomore beside him with a table of hospital-grade disinfectants.

Well, that's something at least, I find myself thinking blandly, not that I'm allowing him to slice any part of me.

Movement distracts me from my study, shadows dancing behind the skull man. No—people.

Another cloaked figure appears within the crowd of spectators, much taller than anyone else. His skull mask glares white, the flickers of the candles set up around the cauldron ritual framing the emotionless leer.

I glance away, unsettled, only to clash with another figure on the opposite side, dressed the same way. A cloak and a skull mask.

Blinking rapidly, I whirl to give the cauldron my back, thinking this has to be a nightmare, to find another cloaked skull striding through the clearing toward me.

"Sasha," I croak, my heart falling into my stomach. "I don't have a great feeling about this."

But when I turn back, she's rolled up her sleeve with a flourish. "I wish for the power to never be late to class again, the ability to understand math ... and maybe a date with Mr. Tall, Dark, and Masked," she declares, winking at him. "Not too much to ask from the witches, right?"

He inclines his head, an off-putting angle of study, before grazing her flawless brown skin with the blade, a single line of red curving across her forearm and dripping into the pot.

I don't go faint at the sight of blood, but my stomach

lurches at the thought of my friend giving this ... *thing* ... her life essence.

Blissfully ignorant of more skull figures closing in on us, Sasha spins and gives me the thumbs up before approaching the sophomore assistant for disinfectant and a band-aid.

Probably not something these omniscient witches had in the 1700s, but who am I to correct an ancient ritual?

The Skull lays his blade on the table for cleaning, then lowers his arms, waiting for me to step up.

I don't.

"Ugh, *finally* my turn!" Cynthia says loudly, walking forward.

Until the Skull halts her by quietly lifting his hand without moving his attention from me.

Cynthia abides him without question, even though she frowns with her hands on her hips, sending a cutting glare in my direction.

Then he waits.

"I don't..." I swallow. "I'm just here to support my friend. I'm not interested in—"

He uses his other hand to put a finger to his garish, toothy grin. *Shh.*

I feel more than hear the rustling of cloaks behind me, moving much too close.

"Sash, you ready?" I ask with a high pitch, clenching my hands to my sides.

"Just a sec," she says with her head bent over her arm. "The fucker cut me pretty deep."

"State your wish."

The Skull's voice reverberates through me, striking a deep and controlled chord.

And in that moment...

I'm almost certain it's Cav.

And the three wretched souls at my back are Wilder, Axe, and Kaspian.

But the burning question remains... *why me?*

Cav humiliated me in class. No one's meant to know my history—I've made sure of it and hide it well. What right does he have to taunt me further by dressing up in costume and wanting to cut me?

I've done *nothing* to him.

The top of my ear tickles from a soft breath: "Enjoying the festivities, Miss Wraithwood?"

Whirling, I'm confronted by another mask, another of Cav's loyal beasts.

I regard him coolly. "Immensely. The decor is simply stunning, don't you think?"

He shifts, moonlight raking over toxic green eyes within the dark holes. "My great-great-grandfather helped pass the law to preserve the woods around TFU. He had an exquisite heart." He gestures to the cauldron. "Is this from your family?"

I take a tiny step back in confusion. My family couldn't be more anti-spirit, anti-magic, anti-good luck charms, even if they actually believed in it enough to try.

"The Nightshades held the first ritual of blood sacrifice to witches over two centuries ago," Cav adds.

I spin to face him, heavily aware of the circle of skulls closing in on me. "I don't need any lessons from you."

Cav angles his head. "Why not? We have such ... history together, your family and mine."

"I don't know what you're talking about. Sasha? Do you need help?"

I move toward her, but I'm forced to a stop when another skull cuts in front of me.

"Sasha's fine," this one says, this voice sounding less like velvet and more like gravel under my feet.

Axe.

I struggle to keep my composure, though I'm being treated like a caged animal.

"I have no idea what twisted game you're playing, but I want no part of it," I say, glaring at each mask in turn.

I catch a glimpse of Sasha, still obliviously waiting for her bandage.

One thing about a super social best friend? She assumes the best in everybody and completely ignores danger radar.

"*Sasha,*" I hiss, hoping she has enough sense to turn around and kick Axe between the legs, offering me a getaway.

But no, she's struck up a conversation with the sophomore guy tending to her.

Cav steps around the cauldron, the four of them circling me like wolves. "No need to be scared, butterfly. We're all friends here."

Cav's tone is mocking, almost cruel.

Standing tall, I refuse to show fear. "I don't know what you want from me, but I have nothing to offer."

Another mask, the plastic moving with his grin. Either Kaspian or Wilder say, "Oh, I think you have a great deal to offer. If only you would share."

His hand reaches out, brushing along my arm. I shiver at the unwelcome touch.

The one beside him steps even closer, invading my space. I

recoil, but he catches my wrist in an iron grip. "Don't play coy. You know exactly why we're interested in you. Or should I say, your ancestry."

This close, I'm able to match the throaty voice to Wilder.

I yank against his hold, but he won't let go. He doesn't shift from my struggles. His attention doesn't stray. I'm burning under his stare.

Like a witch.

My pulse races. He can probably feel it under his gloved hand. But I keep my voice steady. "Let go of me."

Wilder tightens his hold painfully.

By process of elimination, the one I dub Kaspian cracks his knuckles next to Wilder. "Time to stop playing nice."

He moves to grab my other arm.

Thinking fast, I stomp my heel down on Wilder's foot. He curses and loosens his grip just enough for me to wrench free. I dart between him and Kaspian, breaking through their predatory circle and past the line of first years and groups of upperclassmen who did nothing but watch these guys' intimidation tactics against me.

I choose the protective shadows of the woods over their entertained bystander approach.

They all love you until they get to see you fall.

Cav, Wilder, Axe and Kaspian are untouchable. Feared and desired, approached warily and wistfully. They hold more power than you ever will.

I grit my teeth, begging my subconscious to shut up, breath sawing in and out as I crash through the underbrush, branches whipping at my face and arms. My stomach plummets when I hear the boys giving chase, their footfalls heavy on the forest floor and the sound-waves of their hollers and taunts crawling along my skin like a trail of fire ants.

I have to get away, have to escape whatever sinister ritual Cav and his beasts have planned. The masks, the talk of my ancestry, the blood cauldron—it all points to something I'd rather not know anything about.

Faster, I have to go faster.

I picture Sasha still dreamily chatting away as these fiends prepare to do God knows what to me. I don't trust them. I don't want to be near them.

A burst of adrenaline pushes me onward even as my lungs burn until the echoing sounds of pursuit fade.

Have I lost them?

I slow, gulping in air. I lean against a towering oak, its bark rough under my palms as I hold myself up. My legs tremble.

What now? I can't go back to the party, not with *them* there. Could I make it back to the dorms undetected? Would Sasha even believe me if I told her what had transpired tonight? Would anyone?

Typical Elara Wraithwood, denying the attention of the most wanted guys on campus. It's so like her to think she's better than them, to run from their attention. Lucky bitch.

I scrunch my eyes shut at the aggressive presence inside my mind that would rather suffocate than free me.

I just want to be liked. I don't want anyone angry with me.

Least of all *them*.

A twig snaps, followed by a low chuckle. I push off the tree and whirl to find a skull looming out of the darkness.

"Thought you could escape, little witch?" he purrs, his voice like claws scraping over cement.

Fuck. *Wilder.*

"Why do you keep calling me that?" I ask hoarsely, my arms splayed out like I want to fight him or surrender to him.

I'm not sure which one is more likely to get me killed.

They're dangerous. No one else at school realizes it, but I do.

Before I can react, he seizes me by the arm, using his other hand to weigh a tendril of my hair while I try to wrench free.

"Red hair and golden eyes," he murmurs close to my face, despite my efforts to angle away from him. "Witch's traits, wouldn't you agree?"

"Let me go!" I hiss, kicking out and connecting with his shin. He grunts but doesn't loosen his grip.

"Fool me once," he says dryly.

I do it again, and he dodges the kick to his groin.

"Stubborn, too," he drawls, moving so fast that my back hits the tree, knocking the air from my lungs.

"What do you want from me?" I pant, glaring while my heart threatens to leap from my mouth.

"Truth is, witches have always fascinated me ... what do you think fucking them was like?"

His honeyed gaze behind the mask flicks down to my mouth, lingering in a way that makes me shudder even as my lips turn hot, my pulse reaching the sensitive skin and throbbing.

His mask rises as his cheeks pull up. "Want to show me some magic?"

CHAPTER 5
WILDER

Elara seethes with her plump, reddened lips, "Magic is bullshit. Just like your pickup line."

I say in a forced, amused tone, "Ah, so you think I'm trying to flirt with you? How flattering."

The way her golden eyes bore through my cheap Halloween mask and burn against mine sends my heart into an irregular rhythm. I'm confused by my reaction until I shove the emotion aside.

Her upper lip twists in an adorable version of a sneer.

"I don't know much about flirting, but I assure you I am quite … unconventional."

My words leave a tingle in their wake, like I have just whispered them into her ear instead of the air between us.

Now that she's getting worked up, she's even more enticing. The scent of her arousal and irritation is all-consuming, making my cock harden in my pants.

Elara's cheeks flush a deeper shade of red as she curses and struggles beneath my firm grip on her arms. "Keep dreaming, big guy."

"Let me guess, Elara," I bare my teeth in an insult of a smile behind my mask, the plastic dragging roughly across the side of her face as she scrunches her eyes shut and whimpers. "Your type is probably those polite mama's boys, right? The kind who say 'please' and 'thank you,' meet your parents on your third date, and take you to church on Sundays?"

I press in closer, anger turning my blood hot, rushing against my ears. "Let me tell you a little secret—it's the assholes who make your heart race and keep you up at night, wondering what it would be like to fuck them."

I raise my head, pulling my mask off so she can see just how much vindictiveness is behind my killer smile. "I'm not the boy you bring home to mom. I'm not even the one you sneak out for at midnight. I'm the monster under your bed, and you've let me corner you."

There's a tension between us, thick and electric as she breathes heavily and holds my stare, her eyes wide with fear but sharp with spite.

I'm not just teasing her; I'm testing her boundaries, pushing her to admit there's more to her than the perfect facade she shows off to everyone else. And for a fleeting moment, I see that shift in her expression, a fracture hinting that she's intrigued and more than a little curious by my words before she staunches it.

Now who's wearing the mask?

I bite my lower lip. This just got exciting.

My fingers graze her warm thighs under her dress, drifting to the middle and up, where she can't close off or clamp down, slipping underneath the silk fabric of her panties, tracing patterns just above her pussy that make her tremble, whimper, and wrench her hips to stay in control. I reach higher with my other hand while she stiffens against the tree until I cup one pale, perfect breast through her bra before pinching the hardened nipple roughly.

She gasps, her head rolling back and knocking against the gnarled bark before she realizes what she's doing.

"Relax, I'm just teasing you, sweet little witch," I promise with a deceptively soft voice. "You're not ready for just how much I require to be sated."

I lower my mouth and nip at her bottom lip until it quivers, then I bite. Her taste is of vanilla and spice, sweet and hot.

I push my body against hers, savoring the feel of her perfect curves against my hard muscles, small, perky breasts with pebble hard nipples that I've always fantasized about tasting in class poking me below my pecs.

It's not long before I bend at the knees and take one of those peaks between my teeth, sucking through the fabric roughly, feeling her shudder and grab my shoulders—pushing at first, then clenching, then pulling me closer while she arches into my mouth.

She groans into the night air, lost to me as I move to the other breast, sucking and biting until she's moaning louder.

The wind around us picks up, rustling the leaves and sending chills down her exposed cleavage. As if someone else is listening in on this forbidden moment, savoring it too.

Let the boys watch.

I'd be happy to show off my skills to my brothers. I *love* public displays.

I trail my gloved fingers down, the leather cold, but my

hand inside pulsing in tandem to the rigid length pressing against my jeans and threatening to pop the zipper.

What did Cav say again? We're supposed to play with her, are we not? Manipulate, dominate, *annihilate* this fabricated princess until she's nothing but a shell of herself, desperate to give us any information we want so we leave her alone?

The Sovereigns didn't order how we should go about retrieving the Heart. Cav didn't leave me with any instruction other than to keep my dick in my pants.

A smile tugs against my lips, her lace trim a welcome friction on my mouth as I tug on it with my teeth to expose her tits.

I can absolutely put a leash on my cock. This time.

I rise despite her protests and lean close to her ear again, my lips able to trace over the shell this time. "You ever had someone bring you to your knees, Elara Wraithwood? Make you beg?"

My hand moves up to pressing against the silk-covered heat between her legs. I brush, testing her moisture with a practiced touch.

She's damp. *So* fucking wet that a groan escapes me, low in my throat.

Jesus fuck, I want her.

"Just … leave. Me alone. Please." Elara's face tips up to the forest canopy, her jaw clenched, her eyes fluttering open and closed.

Aw, like she's fighting against her desire for me. How cute.

"You want me to be the one to fuck you into oblivion, don't you?" I say against her ear once more, my voice a rumble that shakes through both our bodies. "You want the monster to *come out, come out, wherever he is…*"

I chuckle with a devil's laugh.

She looks away when our stares clash. Even as her hips arch against my hand.

"Good girl," I croon and slide a finger underneath the lace of her panties and into her folds, circling slowly and teasingly against her swollen clit. The sound of my gloved finger gliding inside her is almost orgasmic.

I maneuver Elara's leg up high on my hip and impale her on three of my fingers. A poor substitute for my cock, but one must follow the rules.

Her moans spill into the air between us out as we both rock against each other.

As if her body knows what's missing, she mewls ever so faintly, "Please…"

In that moment, I'm certain I have the upper hand with this girl. Not that I ever had any doubts.

I pull my fingers out before she can cum, ripping down my fly and pressing my bared cock against her entrance.

I can't help it. My head tilts up and I groan with need.

She twitches, breathing hard.

"Say it," I demand, my voice rough, "Say you want my cock inside you."

Elara's lids flutter, but she shakes her head slowly, denying even as I feel her trying to burrow my shaft inside her slick pussy.

"Saying no to the bad boy?" I grin, stroking myself, using her pussy juice as lube. "If you're not asking for it, then beg for it."

"I'll never beg for your cock. But I'll beg for you to p-please…" Her voice is soft and breathy. "Just—walk away."

"Louder," I command, but shift my hips up against hers

in a hard move that makes her cry out and spread her legs further.

"Please," she begs now and I can feel her walls clenching around my tip, slurping up my pre-cum, as she comes undone.

"Elara..." I growl, my teeth scraping her neck.

She bucks and moans at the contact.

I lift my face and press my nose into her hair, inhaling deep, catching the scent of spicy vanilla and her need for me.

Damn, I could do this for hours.

But the Court has their own games to play, and I'd best not be caught fucking her before I've gleaned any information to bring back to them—unless I want to end up with carved X's on my back, or worse.

"Fuck," I hiss against her ear, pulling away with enough force, she stumbles away from the tree. "This isn't how I expected our first private conversation."

It's a startling truth. Sweet, innocent, *boring* women rarely interest me. Not in this way. I like them begging and breaking in half underneath me.

Yet, it turns out Elara Wraithwood is anything but boring.

I can't pull my focus away from the sway of her breasts as she tries to catch her breath, to come down from the sudden rush of lust.

Huh. When did I rip open the front of her dress?

I'm pondering the timing while I plunge each shining, gloved finger into my mouth one by one, sucking on them slowly to get all the flavor from her I can.

"Christ, you're delicious," I murmur, more to myself.

Elara flinches, covering herself. "It's not—this isn't..."

I lower my hand from my mouth, saddened to find all of

her pussy juices licked clean. Then I chuckle, meeting her confused gaze with a half-cocked smirk.

"Not to worry, sweetwitch. You're safe now." I lift my chin before turning and walking away, but tossing over my shoulder, "When we claim you, you'll know it."

CHAPTER 6
ELARA

"You completely disappeared last night! Are you sure you're okay?"

Sasha's sitting on her twin bed, studying me with curiosity as I finish brushing my hair in the vanity mirror.

"Yep. Totally."

She's caught me flinching at least three times every time I raise my arm, my shirt brushing against my raw nipples peppered in bite marks. I can't wear a bra and chose my softest, oldest heather gray t-shirt to soothe them, but they've refused to calm down and poke through my the thin fabric like two needy freshmen who want to go back to the senior bad boy for more sexy time.

I glare at them in my reflection. *No, ladies. You did* not *have fun.*

I raced out of the woods so fast last night, there's no way Wilder would've caught me again.

Not that my traitorous tits would've complained.

Still, I couldn't shake off the feeling that I was being

escorted out of the forest and back to the dorms safely by shadows I couldn't see. A snap of a twig there. A brush of leaves steering me back to center.

A soft, meticulous laugh making me recoil to the left.

And it wasn't just one. It was multiple.

Four, to be exact, if my instincts were on point, and they usually are. It also wasn't out of the kindness of their hearts.

They enjoyed my fear at the same time they ushered me home. My chest, lips, and pussy throbbed with terror and remembrance as I clambered through the underbrush, stumbled up the stairs, and unlocked my door just in time to race into the bathroom and finish myself off.

I stared at my reflection while I masturbated. Bared my body so I could see Wilder's marks.

And had the best goddamn orgasm of my life.

Flinching with shame at the memory, I push away from the vanity and grab my hoodie from off my unmade bed.

"Are you *suuuure* you're all right?" Sasha repeats, this time in a tone that tells me she's not convinced by my wellness status at all.

"Course I am. Come on. We've got a psychology class we're going to be late for."

I am fully aware of the irony.

I've done my best to keep it a secret from Sasha that they're the reason behind my insatiable need and hormonal imbalance this morning.

And I have no idea why they've honed in on me. This is after two years of being who I dubbed the Untouchable Four, always lounging in the background on campus with obvious disinterest in college academics and school spirit—a trait which I'm known for. Not because they can't excel. Each of them has a stellar GPA and they're set to take over the world after they graduate.

It's true they're the most gorgeous, emotionless, and oddly fearsome men at TFU, and for that reason, I've avoided them.

A few women in my friend circle have hooked up with one or more of them, and while many make it a goal (or a ceremonial wish to the witches), a lot come out of it withdrawn, untalkative, and with an abject refusal to engage in the gossip they were so willing to take part in *before* they slept with these guys.

Fast-forward to now, when they've decided teasing and torturing me is their new entertainment. I don't like being singled out by them.

Under Sasha's watchful eye, I dig through my closet until I find it—a box filled with jewelry pieces I never wear because they're all gaudy, expensive, and inherited from my grandmother.

I yank the box out and dump it on my bed, knocking a pile of dirty laundry onto the floor. Sasha tuts from her bed.

"So…" She drawls while I pick through the pile looking for a necklace I haven't worn in a while, a simple gold chain belonging to my brother. "You still doing good over there?"

I hear her rise and grab her bag, thankful she's decided to leave. I've never been so thrown off my routine before and I hate that there's a witness.

When I find the necklace, I'm distracted by something tangled with it. I pull the chunky, scratched thing from the pile and hold it up to the light.

A misshapen ruby embedded into a pendant, delicately carved like an old-as-fuck kingdom seal. The metal of the pendant is dark, possibly crafted from blackened silver or gunmetal, the choice complementing the deep red of the ruby.

Gram whispered it was a family heirloom, handed down only to those considered 'worthy.' Subtle engravings decorate the metal, hinting at ancient symbols.

"Hey, what's that?"

I fist the necklace, spinning to Sasha. "Nothing. Just something my grandma gifted me."

"It's … pretty?"

I respond with an amused smirk. "It's evil-looking. You can say it."

"Well, yeah, but you know how I feel about Titan Falls lore and all the witchy stuff that comes with it. Still crossing my fingers that my multiple wishes come true, greedy bitch that I am."

There it is again. The mention of magic curing all ills in life. The desire for some unseen special power that can fix everyone's problem.

I toss the chunk of metal onto my bed. There's no wizardry that can fix tragedy in a person's life. It's an illusion. A con.

"It's bullshit," I mutter.

If it were true, my brother would be alive. My mother could prevail over her crippling paranoia.

"Well, babe, have a good time with that skeptic mentality," she chirps, dimples flashing as she leaves the room.

Alone with my thoughts, I can't shake the sudden desperation to know more about the necklace. The only "witchy-looking" thing I own, to be honest. Why do those boys keep referring to me as a damned witch?

My mother disappeared in grief after Maverick's funeral,

his murder breeding her agoraphobia, but Gram was always ready to help.

I decide to skip psychology and call her, even though we don't talk much anymore.

The phone rings once before she picks up.

"I'm not here," her voice rasps into my ear.

"Hi, Gram," I say, trying to keep my tone light.

Silence. Then a gasp. "Oh! Darling! How are you?"

It's been months since we last spoke, and hearing the concern in her tone sends flashbacks of when we found out about Maverick.

"I'm fine." Swallowing against the lump forming in my throat, I hurry on. "I was wondering if I could ask you about an old necklace you gave me."

"You mean the family heirloom? The ruby necklace?" Her voice trembles and turns husky.

"Yeah," I intone.

Gram knows what I'm talking about without me explaining further, which is … suspicious.

I add, "I never saw you wear it. Why?"

"I don't know, I just … never felt the need," she says carefully. "It's just a trinket from the colonial days, one of our ancestors who settled in Titan Falls."

"Why does it feel so…" I finally give a word to the turmoil in my gut ever since the Untouchable Four approached me. "Dangerous?"

Gram doesn't respond. If it weren't for her devotion to proper etiquette, I would've thought she'd hung up without a goodbye.

"The settlers of Titan Falls," I clarify. "There are other families that are still around, right? What can you tell me about the Nightshades? The Devereauxs or the Valentis?" *Cav. Axe. Kaspian.* I have no idea what Wilder's last name is. "They were in Titan Falls around the same time, and I think they might be interested in—"

Gram's initially warm tone takes a turn.

"Elara, listen. You must never let anyone see it. You're meant to keep it in your jewelry box growing dust." She adds breathlessly, "It's why we don't wear it or share it with anyone else, not that you'd want to. It keeps the family safe."

Safe? Like, magically? Then what about Maverick?

I clench the phone so hard my fingers whiten.

She continues, "It's best not to ask questions, sweetheart."

I ignore her. "What do you know about these families?"

Silence echoes through the line.

"Gram?"

"They're not worth your time, Elara," she whispers. "Look after it, love. Other than me, there's no one else who can," Gram warns before hanging up with a soft *click* of her landline.

CHAPTER 7
AXE

I stand alone on the small bridge leading over a lazy stream winding through campus, my gaze fixed on Elara's distant figure as she exits Camden House, the girls' dorms.

Her pinched expression says she's too caught up in her own thoughts to notice me staring, but I see everything. That's always been my way—watching, understanding, recording information with no need to be at the center.

Elara's fast clip speaks of frustration. On the other hand, she's holding herself with a surprising amount of poise, given the circumstances of what we did to this pretty girl last night.

I've always admired strength, and there's an undeniable toughness to her, a resilience that goes beyond the superficial image she presents to the world.

As she heads into the arts building with a determined set to her shoulders, I can't help but wonder about what secrets she's keeping. She refused to tell us anything about the Heart, even after Cav played his mind games with her, we frightened her, and Wilder seduced her by fingering her against a tree.

Even Wilder didn't glean much, other than a bulge in his pants and an itch for this girl he's now unable to scratch.

All that, and nothing to show for it.

Elara *has* to know something. You're not both on the Sovereign's radar *and* a founding family of Titan Falls if you don't hold your fair share of terrible, blood-soaked secrets in your ancestral vault.

There's more to Elara Wraithwood than meets the eye, and I'm unexpectedly intrigued. It's a rarity for someone to pique my interest, but she's done it.

I wait for the doors to the building to shut behind her before I make my move.

It's easy enough to slip into Camden House in the morning because almost everyone has class and any RAs are in their rooms, enjoying the quiet floor while their demanding tenants are elsewhere.

I slip up the east stairwell to the second floor and peek through the fire escape to ensure no one's loitering in the halls before I unlock Elara's door using a simple maneuver with a credit card.

I gently guide the door closed once I step inside so it doesn't make a sound. Then I stand in front of it, taking stock of a room that smells so much like her.

The scabs on my back itch and I reach over my shoulder and scratch at them absently while I assess the rumpled beds and cluttered surfaces on both sides of the room.

I go to the desk on the left to figure out whose side is Elara's. It doesn't take me long. Propped up in a sterling silver frame is a picture of Elara and another dude, his arm slung casually over her shoulder as they both laugh at the camera.

My eye twitches at the thought of some unknown, no-name male touching her until it occurs to me their features are too much alike. The same brownish-red hair, similar sunburst eyes, and of course, identical joyous, perfect-life smiles as they pose for whomever was behind the camera.

A brother, possibly. I use my phone to input a reminder to ask Kaspian about the brother and what type of nuisance he may be. I forget things if I don't set regular reminders or alarms to go off. It's been a problem for me since I was 4 years old. I'd been in so many foster homes, punted between one too many drunk foster dads, that one doctor once told me I had the brain of an offensive lineman nearing the end of his football career.

I pull out my phone to take pictures of Elara's organized desk drawers with way too many fluffy pens and pink sticky notepads before going to search the closet.

My concentration is interrupted when I find a pair of torn panties on top of her hamper.

I hook her used underwear with a finger, bringing them to eye-level. The soft pink satin holds lingering traces of her scent, and I bring it to my nose to inhale deeply, kissing the material before sliding it over my face.

Why do I feel this way? This ... *doll* is the epitome of dick repellent. She's too put-together, too composed, too pink for the likes of me.

I like women emotionally unavailable and self-destructive, someone with my similar jaded view of this fucked-up world. Elara is so far away from my preference, it's laughable that I'm staring at her dirty laundry with an erection right now.

Fuck if I don't want to see what it's like to have her wet for me, though.

Immediately, jealousy over Wilder being the only one who's tasted her hits me.

I ball her underwear up and shove them into my mouth like a gag, choking, my throat working over time to swallow. I keep them there until my vision sparks with black stars, then drag them out, ensuring I lick clean all that I can. I tongue the remnants of her pleasure in her panties, refusing to allow Wilder to have the sole claim on how delectably she dances over tastebuds.

I shove the damp panties under my pants and against my crotch, cupping my heavy erection with them and groaning while leaning my forehead on the closet's sliding door and giving myself a few rough strokes.

But there's work to be done.

Regrettably, I stuff them in my pocket for later.

I search the closet, running my hands along the shelves, feeling for any clues or hell, the ruby Heart itself. A shoe box in the corner catches my attention: dented, torn, and scratched.

Pulling it out, I lift the lid and reveal a disorganized pile of jewelry, their gold, silver, and other clunky chains tangled together. My fingers brush over the various lockets and gemstones, tracing the sharp edges that could easily cut me but don't. They glint in the soft light from her window.

Other than being fucking annoying to untangle and individually inspect, I find nothing relating to the Heart and put the shoe box away with only the knowledge that, while valuable, this flashy jewelry isn't Elara's style at all.

Look at that. I'm already thinking about her like I know her.

Grunting with amusement, I continue the search on my

knees, lifting her mattress to see if she's shoved anything underneath, feeling the underside to make sure.

Nothing is of interest. Not even a hidden dildo. Of course, a doll wouldn't have a sex toy for her plastic parts.

Yet, that snide thought doesn't ring true. I keep going back to that picture of her on her desk and that smile she shares with the guy beside her.

Elara has a brightness to her. Annoyingly sunny. But I've never seen her smile the way she does in that photo.

It's lower at the corners now, her dimples not as deep. Her eyes aren't nearly as cheerful, either.

The longer I hover near the picture, studying it, the clearer the answer becomes.

Tragedy has a way of showing on the face, and that's exactly what's painted over her smile these days.

I angle my head, murmuring, "Who did you lose, pretty dolly?"

A loud bang in the hallway draws my head up. People coming back from class.

Because of my distraction over the photo, I've lost time in escaping unnoticed.

Straightening, I take a last glance around and give the room a once over to make sure I leave it as I found it.

Elara doesn't know it yet, but as I slip out through her window, I feel a secret bond forming between us.

CHAPTER 8
CAV

I wind through a hidden pathway in the forest, its dense, thorny underbrush making navigation impossible for anyone unfamiliar with the trail, then push apart two particularly angry thorn bushes and step into a small, unmaintained clearing to Thornhaven Estate. The door to the mansion groans as I push it open. I slip inside, closing it swiftly behind me.

After striding through the large foyer, its structure a blend of Gothic revival and Victorian, I head for the stairs. Behind the foyer is the Initiate's Hall, the lower floor serving as initiation and training grounds for new recruits. It's designed with many chambers for education in the Court's history, values, and operations. The area is stark, with minimal decoration.

The upper levels reflect our status within the Court by being significantly more luxurious, reserved for full members. These floors contain private libraries, meeting rooms, and chambers for social gatherings, all decorated with artifacts and symbols significant to the Court.

My bedroom is the last one at the end of the west wing. When I enter, Wilder is poking around the antique desk in the corner, once belonging to the first Nightshade ancestor. Maps, documents, digital tablets, and a state-of-the-art computer system clutter the desk.

"Took you long enough," he intones without turning around.

I resist the urge to put him in his place. The others are also here—Kaspian lounging in one of the plush sofa chairs by the hearth and thumbing through his phone while Axe paces the perimeter of the four-poster bed dominating the room.

The room is spacious, with high ceilings and large, arched French doors opening to a balcony. My color scheme is predominantly dark—deep blues and grays offset by the warm browns of polished mahogany.

All I can think of as I scan over my home for the last two years is: *I can't lose this.*

"Any updates?" I ask, keeping my tone neutral as I take a seat in the chair opposite Kaspian.

Axe shakes his head. "I tried, but…" He takes out his phone and confirms his answer with a furrowed brow. "No. I didn't find anything."

"So, that's two failures." I send a pointed look Wilder's way, including him in our current fuck-up. "If I have this right, Wilder couldn't finger it out of her and you, Axe, can't sniff it out of her bedroom, either."

"We'll get her," Wilder says softly as he turns and leans against my desk with folded arms. "I've only just gotten started tearing her to pieces."

I suppress a scoff. His new obsession makes him careless.

Reckless. But I won't rein him in. For now, his tenacity has its uses.

Elara is indeed a problem. Intelligent enough to prevent us from instant success, resilient enough to endure Wilder's unfiltered assault, cautious enough not to leave clues in her room. Even I, the last Nightshade in the Court, can't unravel the secrets locked away behind those tawny eyes.

What are you hiding, butterfly?

I'm convinced she's aware of what we want but unable to understand why. She'd rather keep any idea from us than solve all our problems, including her recent predicament of four violent men refusing to leave her alone.

I shake away thoughts of her, ignoring the inexplicable melody her name plays in my head. "The Sovereigns grow impatient. Have *any* of you uncovered anything we can use as leverage?"

Kaspian leans forward, eyes on his screen. "I may have something. Elara's parents divorced when she was young— Dad's not in the picture, died in a plane crash when she was a baby. The brother, Maverick, helped raise Elara. He was five years older. Mother has turned into a recluse."

I bury my face in my hands and sigh. "I truly don't care about her broken home. Half of the population can empha-size with her instead."

"I wasn't done. Mom's a recluse because Elara's brother was murdered six years ago."

I lose my agitation. "Oh?"

"You wouldn't fucking know it with the way she prances around campus," Wilder mutters.

"It was violent, too," Kaspian continues. "He was twenty-one when he died, found in the greenhouse on their family estate. A groundskeeper discovered the body early in the morning and the greenhouse was immediately ruled a crime scene: broken pots, upturned soil, and rare plants destroyed by a clear struggle." Kaspian taps his screen before continuing, "I went through a few back doors to access the autopsy report—"

"Can I see the pictures?" Wilder asks eagerly.

I cut him a warning look, then gesture for Kaspian to keep going. "Cause of death is a deep laceration on his neck, caused by a piece of broken glass from one of the greenhouse windows. The police initially suspected a burglary gone wrong."

Wilder makes a face. "Who would break into a multi-million dollar estate for plants?"

"Pollen and other extracts can function as poison or hallucinatory drugs," Axe answers quietly.

I arch an appreciative brow. "Axe is right. Creative weaponry always interests criminal enterprises. Was anything taken?"

"The mother, Caroline Wraithwood, was a rare botany collector before she stopped altogether after Maverick's death," Kaspian answers. "The mess made it impossible to determine if any plants were stolen."

Wilder asks dubiously, "How can you even tell if someone took a leaf?"

I ponder, "The police would notice and become concerned if there were any toxic plants on private property. Wolfsbane, hemlock and the like."

Kaspian shrugs. "Growing poisonous plants is perfectly legal. And their report mentioned nothing related to dangerous toxins."

"How very unfortunate," I say, steepling my fingers. "And the killer was never found?"

Kaspian shakes his head. "The case remains unsolved to this day. Left the family quite traumatized, from what I gather."

What a tragic end to the Wraithwood family's golden days. I imagine Elara gasping at the news of her beloved brother's death, her haunted eyes filling with despair ... and my desire to have her look at me like that.

It makes me hard.

I share a kindred look with Wilder. He's alert, on edge, hungry for Elara's continued hunt.

"Then we have our opening," I say. "If the police failed to find the culprit, perhaps we can succeed where they could not."

Wilder stops his stewing. "We solve the case, clear up this 'tragedy'—"

"—and Elara will be in our debt," Kaspian finishes with a sly grin.

I nod. Of course, we'll dredge up no actual evidence. We don't have time to solve a cold case while saving our own asses. But the mere offer could persuade Elara to cooperate.

Although she tries to hide it, we've found Elara's vulnerability. My cock twitches, demanding attention again.

I *love* finding people's shortcomings.

I turn back to the others, resuming our plotting, but Elara lingers at the edges of my awareness. A distraction. A puzzle I can't seem to solve.

I tell myself it's only frustration at this additional obstacle. But underneath, I feel the stirrings of something else. Fascination? Curiosity?

Whatever this unwanted attraction and intrigue toward Elara, I can't forget who we are and what brought us here. What divides us from the Sovereigns and curses our family names from ever regaining elite status in the Court. Hell, the Nightshades fucking *created* the Cimmerian Court, and look at me now.

No matter how alluring the temptation is, I must not falter from my mission. Too much depends on it.

I instruct Kaspian, "See what else you can find out about this dead brother of hers. Where he went to school, who he was friends with, what could've motivated him to enter the greenhouse at night, that sort of thing. Find what we can use to convince Elara there was more to this crime than a break-in gone wrong."

Wilder curves a smirk at me. "You think you can manipulate her like that, Cav?"

"I don't think," I retort. "I know."

I find power in being the one who pulls the strings, the one who can orchestrate someone's undoing with a whisper and a well-placed hint.

These are my brothers, my loyal comrades. But I don't trust anyone completely.

There's only one companion I can rely on without fault.

Myself.

CHAPTER 9
ELARA

K *eep it safe.*

Gram's words swarm like a gnat cloud in my head.

What does that even mean? If the Wraithwoods were supposed to keep the necklace safe, why isn't in a bank vault?

The necklace in my bag feels heavier now that I know what it represents. I didn't feel comfortable leaving it in my shoe box, because I've realized it's not just an heirloom. It's a key, a shackle, a riddle as haunting as Titan Falls history.

The ruby is jagged, like it broke off from something. It's shaped like a fat lightning bolt. If I actually wore it, one of its sharp tips would point directly to my heart.

Gram might've tried to explain the controversy around this amulet when she gave it to me. I was so devastated by Maverick's death, I didn't want to hear it.

So instead, I'm carrying around this cursed necklace in the front pocket of my backpack, pretending like it's just another school day and that four incredibly nebulous men haven't suddenly cornered me.

My frustration must show on my face. I'm not pulled into conversations or asked to get involved in the upcoming activities like I usually am between classes. Lots of people say hello and I stop and chat to a few of my closer friends, but they're short-lived. I'm too distracted to contribute anything.

Despite my misgivings, I make it to all my classes without running into any of the guys. It's a relief not to have Ancient History today so I can embrace the time off from their silent judgment. They've only recently decided to pay attention to me, but it's fucking effective.

What do they think about when they look at me? Why do I care?

I'm tempted to just avoid them and complete my assignments behind the gates of the Wraithwood estate until they get bored, but my heavy curiosity prevents such a thing from happening. No, I'd much rather figure out what's so important that they're chasing me down.

Calculus is my last class of the day. I'm filing in with everyone else, my daily routine settling comfortably around my shoulders, when I spot Darcy O'Neill taking her seat in the one directly behind mine. She's pulled back her raven hair in a tight bun, with tendrils falling on her face while she studies something intently on her phone.

Darcy has the privilege any kid who isn't already stupid-rich dreams about. Her parents pay for her to attend TFU, but like a lot of children of the elite, she doesn't have to work hard to achieve perfect grades. She goes to enough classes to keep her attendance acceptable but otherwise parties, experiments, and goes through boys like her daily pack of cigarettes.

I'm not judging. To me, it simply shows that she's connected on campus and has potentially damaging information on anyone at this school.

"Hey, Darcy," I greet while dropping my bag on the empty seat next to me.

"Hey, girl." She doesn't look up from her tiny screen. "Did you have fun last night?"

I pause in pulling out my laptop. This is the thing about Darcy. You never know what *she* knows.

"Sure," I say with feigned nonchalance. "Wasn't much different earlier this year. Or the year before that."

"You don't think a new ritual leader was different?" She looks up from her phone, and there's a gleam in her eye that's vaguely wicked. "I saw you get cornered by all the skull masks, then make a fast exit. Not that they had to wear masks." She leans back and laughs softly. "Everyone knew who they were. What mystified me is why they wanted to play with you."

I keep my expression placid. I expected this from her. What's more important is that I get the information *I* want while she amuses herself. "Believe me, I'm just as confused. Until yesterday, I thought they didn't know who I was."

Darcy just smiles. "I witnessed every single one of them go after you."

"That's what I'm hoping you could help me with." I glance over my shoulder at the professor readying his materials to begin, hoping there's still enough time. "What do you know about them? Cav, Axe, Kaspian and Wilder?"

Darcy's smile grows wider. "I know they're more than just rich guys who like to chase pretty girls."

She glances forward at the professor, then narrows her

eyes conspiratorially at me. "They're in the Cimmerian Court."

"The—what?" The name sounds familiar, but I ignore the chill spreading over the nape of my neck and focus on her words.

Darcy doesn't answer immediately. I wait, letting her take another drag off her vape while my knee bounces with frenetic energy.

Darcy eventually answers, "Secret society."

Like that explains everything.

"I need more than that," I press, furrowing my brows.

She nods with a self-important air that suggests she's about to drop some bombshell gossip. "It's old as shit, started at the end of the 17th century and super exclusive. Supposedly, they have this legacy to uphold in order to maintain their status as the most powerful families on campus. And beyond. There's also this whole myth about them being cursed and involving themselves in the occult." Darcy rolls her eyes while twirling her vape. "Cav believes it. Wilder's obsessed with proving it wrong while Kaspian is on the tech side of things and has kept his family's dirty past from unraveling publicly. And Axe, always thought to be the dumbest one, thinks of it more like a gift to his family, if he can prove he deserves it."

I cling onto her every word. I *knew* there was more to them than their money, looks, and power on campus.

But why do they want me?

"Thanks, Darcy," I smile at her, trying to keep my voice light and dismissive.

But she's not done.

Darcy looks around before whispering again. "It's said

that they're pretty ruthless in their dealings. This college stuff they do, that's like counting to five on one hand. They have connections everywhere—in the university, D.C., even further than that. It's like they're part of this old, powerful network. Some say their influence can make or break careers, reputations ... lives."

I frown, skepticism mixed with concern. "That sounds a bit excessive."

Darcy leans back, a knowing look in her eyes. "Maybe, but if the rumor mill is right, people who've gotten on their bad side suddenly face 'unfortunate' incidents. Accidents, scandals, academic downfalls. The Court never gets their hands dirty, but somehow, things just happen."

Just as Professor Salazar begins his lesson, Darcy eyes me with a mixture of pity and intrigue. "And now they're interested in you. I'd be careful if I were you. The Court isn't just dangerous because they're powerful; they're dangerous because they're smart, covert, and always a few steps ahead. These boys may look house-trained, but they'll always be feral. They're actually very charming when they show no mercy."

Darcy's words should instill fear, but they miss their mark. I'm too wrapped up in this Court's interest in me and how easily I submitted to Wilder yesterday.

And how I want more of him.

I clear my throat and ask, "Wait, if they're super secretive and only talked about in rumors, how do you have all this info?"

Darcy gives a casual shrug. "Because if I had a dick, I'd be in it."

I can't argue with her on that.

"Thank you," I say again, a small smile on my lips despite my racing heart. "Really."

Darcy waves it off, eyes back on her phone as the professor scribbles on the board. I shift away and immerse myself in the lesson, but I can't shake the Court from my thoughts.

Now I know more, but how do I use this information?

Darcy has no reason to lie to me. I've entered a realm where secrets, shady dealings, and power conflicts prevail. Never mind that I'm just looking for a little stability and security for what remains of my family.

My pulse gallops as the class drags on. I want to know why they want me. And what they'll do to anyone who gets in their way.

A small part of me is afraid that finding out will be dangerous, even deadly. But the rest?

I'm finding it hard to resist.

CHAPTER 10
ELARA

After my last class, I plan to pick up groceries for Mom, who only trusts me to not poison her food. I'll spend the evening with her, making sure she takes her medicine and comforting her until she falls asleep, promising that no one will hurt her.

It breaks my heart every time. I hate how quickly my world changes as soon as I leave campus.

Old, wrought iron street lanterns light the pathway to the student parking lot and I pass the time by allowing my mind to drift to the night before, how Wilder's touch unsettled my fears even as he provoked them. Axe's rough hands on my shoulders while he held me in place in front of the cauldron, Cav's subtle control of the situation, and Kaspian's persistent, hollow stare.

A shadow casts into one of the lantern's arcs of light. My steps slow. The air turns from the smell of fresh spring leaves to a hit of cologne and an earthy smell of moss. When someone clears their throat, my mouth goes dry, the taste of the coffee I had earlier turning bitter on my tastebuds.

I raise my head, finding Cav standing under the streetlight with a smirk on his face.

Oh, *fuck him*, he scares me with that smile alone.

"Can I help you?" I ask.

He takes his time answering, his eyes, blue as a ghoul's, roving over my face and body before settling on mine. His gaze burns through my skull and tries to melt my brain.

"Actually, I believe I can, Miss Wraithwood."

He advances, lips curving. My nostrils flare at the scent of his tobacco cologne, mixed with something darker, more sinister. Like … soil on a grave.

"Leave me alone." I spit out, blinking away my fear. "I'm not interested in any of you. How many times do I have to say it?"

I fist my key ring in my hand, the jagged ends of my keys poking out between my fingers like homemade brass knuckles. It brings me comfort when I turn my back on him and continue the walk to my car.

"Wilder tells me differently," he says.

Cav follows me, swooping around and placing a hand on my car door when I try to open it. I yank at the handle again, then push at his arm, but neither budges.

I snarl, "Get away from me before I screa—"

Cav flips me around until my back slams against the car and his arms frame me on both sides.

He leans down and whispers in my ear. "Scream all you want. That's what I like."

My cry dies in my throat.

It hurts to breathe, even when he pushes off the car and steps back, putting space between our bodies.

Cav draws out the moment, his focus moving from my eyes to my mouth when he says, "You've been asking about the Court. What a brave little soul you are."

My heart deafens my hearing.

I'm not sure if Darcy told him about our chat, or if he knows enough rats around the university to alert him whenever his name's brought up. Both could be true. But I look at him with a straight face.

"Not exactly. I wanted to know about you and your friends. It never occurred to me you were part of a secret boys' only club. But I'm curious, do you meet in a treehouse in your backyard?"

Cav's amused smile drops. For a convincing second, I think he's about to kill me until a low, deathly chuckle escapes his lips. "Your kindergarten insult tells me all I need to know about your ignorance."

He's all corners and edges under the dim glow of the streetlights. Cav Nightshade is not someone you forget; his name is as unique as his attractiveness. Pale, but with so many angles, he carries shadows on him at all times.

I can't allow him to get under my skin, no matter how much of a dangerous heartthrob with an agenda he is.

If Sasha could see me now…

"I'm not the one who sought you out to insult you," I say. "So if you don't mind, I'd like to get into my car and leave you in my rearview mirror."

I turn to the driver's side door, but he follows with ease, cutting me off. We stand there, a breath between us. My skin responds with heat I can't understand, so I retreat, but he keeps up, maintaining our heated proximity.

Cav inclines his head, then lifts his hand, running his fingers through my hair.

I want to flinch, but don't. I'm too focused on his face and how mesmerized he is by my strands flowing through his long fingers.

"Tell me about your brother," he murmurs.

My muscles spasm at the word *brother*.

Cav senses my unease because his smile widens. Wrapping an arm around my waist, he pins me to his body while his other hand strokes my cheekbone gently.

"Your brother's death has haunted you for far too long, hasn't it?"

It's not a question. His voice resonates against my skin like living darkness as he leans in closer.

I struggle, try to lean my face away as much as I can, but it's useless.

I nod stiffly, unable to speak past the lump forming in my throat. Cav is cruel in his pain, knowing full well how raw this wound still is after all six years of living with Maverick's unsolved murder.

"Why do you want to know?" I ask hoarsely. "I thought you were all about trying to bang me like Wilder."

He stills. If I thought his smile dropped before, it now disappears like his lips have never been weightless with happiness.

Cav's cold thumb strokes my cheekbone. "Don't talk about things you don't understand, butterfly. You might get hurt."

"Stop playing games with me." I force myself to meet his eyes. "And do *not* mention my brother ever again."

He hums and kisses my jaw gently, just below my ear. "You're so stubborn."

"You're pathetic," I spit out, fighting the shivers racking my frame. Fighting *him*. "You think that's the only way to make me weak? Through his memory?"

Cav pulls back just enough to look at me, his eyes sparkling like he's hiding evidence.

"No, I think you could use our help to solve his murder."

If Cav wasn't holding me up, I would've collapsed. My bones have liquefied.

"W-what did you just say?"

"Think about what you've learned about us. Power. Manipulation. Control. We pop those traits like pills. And since you're so prickly about answering our simple questions, I've decided that perhaps we can work together."

"That's not teamwork—that's using my trauma for your personal gain."

My voice cracks under the weight of my rage and the desire to slap him away.

He leans in, his breath teasing my lips. "Truer words have never been spoken. I'll be honest with you, butterfly: Give us what we want, or we make your life hell. If I decide I like you, I may solve your brother's murder while you're mine, just because I can."

I shove at his chest. Uselessly, but I need *something* to showcase my horror. "Are you out of your *mind?* I'm not fucking property, asshole."

Cav continues as if he doesn't have a furious woman

locked in his arms. "We have more connections than Titan Falls's hick-ass police force, and you've intrigued me enough to offer our services. But if you want us to offer you a deal you, ask nicely."

"And like I've told you before, *I'm not for fucking sale*," I rage-whisper.

But the thought of finding out who killed my brother, why they needed to take him from this world … it's too agonizing to put to words. "And don't you dare talk about my brother like he's nothing but a bonus-round in your *Dungeons & Dragons* game."

An almost-smile crosses his lips.

"You're more difficult to convince than I expected. That will make this more interesting."

I stare, bewildered by how much I hate and desire him at the same time. It makes me push him away only for me to inch closer, needing to fist his shirt and feel the heat of his chest under my hand before I let go. To prove he's human.

And when I look away, embarrassment replaces the lust.

He croons above my head, "I'll get what I want."

I push him away roughly with both hands. He allows the shove, taking one step back while fumble for the handle, slide into the driver's seat and slam the door, clutching the steering wheel once the engine starts. Cav smugly stands aside, but not before his eyes narrow with a warning glance.

My mind reels as I put the car in drive and leave him behind.

My driving is chaotic, blurred. I take deep breaths to calm myself, reasoning that crashing into a pole is no way to get back at Cav.

I blink away enough tears to see Wilder leaning against his motorcycle near the university gates, watching me leave. His jaw tenses as if he could chew through the metal of my car and get to me, his hands digging into his leather jacket pockets.

I spin my tires, narrowly avoiding plowing into him.

He slams my car's hood with the flat of his hand, his eyes an umber storm as he stares through the glass and forces me to screech to a stop.

"Roll down the window, Elara."

His voice is muffled, yet the lash of his tone could crack the very barrier that quiets him.

I cover my mouth to stifle the scream of frustration ripping from my throat, my tears coating my hand.

Any mention of Maverick is upsetting, but to use his death as a *weapon*, to demand ownership over me as payment for getting his killer's name…

Wilder rounds the car, his fist bashes against the driver's side window. "*Elara.*"

I crack the window just enough to hear him better, my engine idling, the heat from my car billowing in the chilled air around him.

He doesn't hesitate. "Why are you crying? What did Cav say to you back there?"

"Just—get out of the way. So I can leave."

"Answer my question or I'll get on my bike and run you off the road until I have your red tin can wrapped around a tree."

I glare, but my defiance gets me nowhere.

He lifts his foot, ready to kick the driver's side door in a rage.

"I—I hate you," I mumble through my quivering lip, my heart threatening to jump into my throat.

Wilder grins and lowers his leg. "You hate everyone who doesn't worship the ground you walk on."

I shake my head but don't bother explaining that being friendly and involved in university activities doesn't make me expect worship. Besides, Wilder and his kind don't understand my world—they think violence equals respect.

My pounding pulse stutters at the thought. Wilder may threaten violence against me, but I'm convinced he wouldn't let others do the same, not even Cav. At least, not without punishment.

Because the obsession is clear in his eyes.

I swallow. "Cav said you would help solve Maverick's murder—for a price."

Wilder nodded along as if this wasn't news until I mentioned an ultimatum. His chin lowers, his brows shading his eyes.

Though he doesn't cover the calculation in his tone. "What do you mean, a price?"

"That I have to accept your ownership over me."

Wilder's stunned enough not to have an immediate response, but I notice anger streaking over his russet eyes before he blinks it away.

I fill the silence. "What does that even mean? What would you own, for God's sake? I'm a person, not a—"

"It's very simple, actually."

The more opportunity Wilder gets to think about it, the more his lips stretch wide.

Oh God. I shouldn't have cracked my window open even a little for this man.

"We own your body, you obey our orders, and if you're a good girl, you get a reward."

At each of his points, my jaw drops a little lower.

"Does that about clear it up, sweetwitch?"

My answer is to rev my engine and peel away, hoping I've spat up enough gravel to permanently blind him.

CHAPTER II
ELARA

"Mom? Where are you?"

I hesitate to open the door to my childhood home.

I've learned that, when I get caught up in studies and campus life and leave her too long, she sets up booby-traps around the house. Even when I tell her to expect me, she forgets to deactivate them.

The stale air pricks at my nose, and I inhale sharply as I step inside. It's an odd mix of neglect and lavender. Her favorite herbal scent is one I never adapted to, either before or after Maverick.

The Calcutta floors echo under my heels as I walk toward the cobwebbed halls leading to her bedroom.

I flick on the switch to the nearest hallway, my lungs filling with relief once I see she hasn't set up any traps. She's done everything from pressure-activated floor tiles (triggering a screeching alarm when stepped on) to tripwire alarms, to hiding non-lethal chemistry sprays near entry points, easily accessible to her if someone pushes her to the ground and attacks her.

I feel especially sorry for the staff who touched her electrocuted doorknobs. She uses a low-voltage current running through metal door handles, not enough to cause serious harm, but sufficient to give a startling zap to discourage further exploration.

When I reach her room at the end, I pause outside to listen for any signs of movement before pushing open the door, calling her name once more. The closed curtains create a cool darkness in the room that makes me shiver.

She's sitting in front of a window in her favorite armchair, knitting slowly, eyes distant as she stares out the window into nothingness.

Her luscious auburn hair has thinned and grayed significantly since my brother died; it's now tied up in a messy bun on top of her head. Her once vital body seems smaller and frailer when she doesn't turn around.

She startles when I close the door behind me.

"Oh!" Surprise pulls at her features and she drops her knitting needles with a small clatter. "Sweetie, you scared me."

"Sorry, Mom." I smile softly and sit beside her on the chair, my fingertips tracing the soft wool blanket before I pull at it to cover both of us. Despite everything, it feels good to be beside her; it's like coming home even if it's haunted by memories better left buried.

"Did you bring the groceries?" she whispers before looking back out toward the greenhouse.

"I ordered them on my phone," I answer, my fingers clenching against the blanket.

Being railroaded by two villain incarnates at the university did little to motivate me into completing errands. As soon as I found a safe, well-lit place to park in downtown Titan Falls, I submitted a delivery to be here within the hour before heading straight to Mom's.

"Let's go to your bed." I push to my feet and lead her by the hand gently, feeling like an adult more than a daughter sometimes, and guide her there.

"Are you feeling alright today?" she asks, settling against the wooden headboard.

She doesn't sleep with pillows. She's too convinced someone will suffocate her if she does.

Her amber eyes search mine as she pats the bed beside her, and I oblige by perching at the edge of the bed. My fingers massage my eyelids to relieve the tension of the day.

"Just, you know… school stuff," I lie weakly, knowing she won't pry.

"You're a smart girl. You'll get through it. I wish…" Her voice drifts off as if she cannot bring herself to finish the thought.

It could be anything: I wish Maverick were still alive, I wish you still lived here with me, I wish I could move away from here but it's the only place I know, I wish we could lock ourselves away from the world forever.

The room holds the same antiquated decorations from when we first moved into this house. Dark wooden furniture with velvety fabrics that retain dirt, heavy curtains that block out any natural light. Jewelry boxes and figurines fill the room, many of them gifts from my father before he died.

I lower my hands from my face. "Mom, have you ever seen the Wraithwood family jewels? Or Gram's collection?"

She pauses in her fidgeting before she looks up at me, uncertainty clouding her expression. "Why do you ask?"

I bite my lower lip and lean forward to take her hands in mine. They feel cold against my skin. My mom's bloodless touch always sends shivers down my spine, even if it's just accidental.

"I think they might have something to do with a family story I've been trying to figure out."

Tales of Wraithwood history are precious to me, since she rarely speaks of the past, other than how she met Dad or how they married young because of an arranged marriage between two families with immense sway in Titan Falls. The Wraithwoods and the Farrows. Gram is Dad's mother, a Wraithwood blue blood who was always warm and sweet to Maverick and me, but cool and distant toward my mother.

"Did your grandmother mention it?" she asks after what feels like an eternity.

"Sort of. At—" I almost say *Maverick's funeral*, but stop myself. "She gave me some family heirlooms a while ago, which I only just started looking at. I found a strange-looking necklace."

Slowly, as if turning her head through molasses, she centers her attention on me. "Strange-looking how?"

Rather than describe it, I reach for my bag and pull out the necklace from the front-zip pocket.

The jagged ruby glints in the soft light of the room, the necklace creepy in its intricacy. The blackened metal setting is even more detailed up close, resembling vines twisting around each other, but the pieces seem like they should form a complete circle instead of a ruby lightning bolt.

Her eyes widen.

"This is ... old. Why did your grandmother give it to you?" she whispers, her voice trembling.

My heart races as I realize she may know something, but not in the way I imagined. Mom is always fearful, but this is the first time I've seen her keep a steady eye on the thing that terrifies her.

"She said it was hers when she was younger and that it was time for another Wraithwood female to keep it safe."

Mom swallows hard and looks away, her knuckles turning white as she clutches both her hands together.

"Your grandmother never told me about that," she murmurs, her voice barely audible over the ticking grandfather clock down the hall.

She doesn't ask why she didn't inherit it first. Mom isn't exactly close with her mother-in-law, who cut her off after Dad died. We all know why, but no one talks about it: Gram blamed Mom for his death. I've never understood how someone could hate so much when they lost a child, too, but it seems the Wraithwood family only knows how to be cruel when at their lowest.

"Do you recognize it?" I ask softly.

She reluctantly untangles her fingers and takes the necklace from me to inspect it under the dusty lamp by her nightstand.

"I do..." she trails off, carefully cleaning off the dirt and grime before studying it again. Her fingers trace the strange design etched into the metalwork that holds the ruby in its setting.

She pauses and looks up at me, her eyes wide with recognition this time. "This is Anderton work."

"Anderton?" My mind splays out the information with

the speed of falling cards. "Like Sarah Anderton? The accused witch of Titan Falls?"

The Anderton witch legend is the source of Titan Falls's booming economy. It's responsible for all party themes, tourism, and the heavy superstition flowing through town. Initially known as the town healer, Sarah achieved notoriety when people unearthed she assisted nobles in poisoning their enemies, including their husbands and wives. Once discovered, the nobles were so concerned Sarah would publicly name her clients that they branded her a witch. People assume they included her young, disfigured teenage daughter in the torture and death, even though no one ever found the daughter's body, and there are no records that mention her.

"It's only rumors, Elara," Mom says, reading my thoughts on my face and sharing in my lack of enthusiasm for real-life magic. "Your great-great-great-grandmother was killed for being a witch, but really, she's just a tragic figure who died too soon."

The truth-bomb takes a second to blow my head wide open. "Wait—what?"

Learning about a secret, ruthless society operating beneath Titan Falls University is one thing. But my recluse mother casually mentioning my blood relation to a famous witch makes me want to become an expert in crafting her booby-traps.

Is this why the guys are calling me a witch? Something to do with the... "Oh, fuck."

"Language, sweetie," Mom says, but there's no force behind it.

"The treasure," I breathe out. "There were reports that

Sarah Anderton had left a hidden treasure of gold and jewels from her pay-offs. It's never been found. "

"Allegedly."

Mom shrugs as if the treasure is the myth many people think it is.

"Is this part of it? This giant, weirdly shaped ruby? How much is something like this worth?"

"Millions, at least," Mom casually answers as if she hasn't just upended my entire knowledge of my entire family and told me I've been carrying a multi-million dollar necklace in my backpack.

"And Gram has just held onto it? Why? And who am I a descendant of? The daughter that has no name? The one that disappeared from all records?"

My stomach drops like I've been pushed off a cliff. Does the Cimmerian Court want Sarah's hidden treasure? Was Gram protecting it? Fuck, am I?

And why did no one decide that it was important to tell me the Wraithwoods are part of Sarah Anderton's ancestors?

My head's close to exploding again.

"I don't know anything more," she says quietly. "Gram is tight-lipped about anything connected to Sarah, so I stopped asking."

A knock at my mother's bedroom door jolts me. We both freeze.

Nerves etch into my mother's features before I turn—but it's just a maid with food trays, one of the two employees left on the estate.

The scent of rich soup and warm bread fills the room, making me realize how hungry I am despite feeling so nauseous from talking about witches, curses, and courts.

After the maid leaves, I question mom further. She vaguely discusses Sarah's beauty, power, and charm, information I could easily look up online, but reminds me I shouldn't delve into history too much when I should focus on schoolwork and friends at this "sensitive time".

She means Maverick's death that happened six years ago, but doesn't say it aloud.

Her lips are the color of ash despite the hearty soup. The room seems colder now that I know my family's legacy is loaded with more murder and violence. The ticking of the clock sounds like a warning bell.

Suddenly, I want out of this place.

"Thanks for telling me." I stand up abruptly, my hand rubbing my aching stomach. "I should go back. I have a study group later."

She doesn't stop me as I gather my bag and jacket, not because she wants me to leave, but because she knows something bigger has come between us.

"Okay, sweetie. I'll see you next time. I love you."

"I love you too, Mom."

She hands me back the necklace, the metal still cool despite being held in her hands for so long.

The moonlight paints the property in a chilling white as I walk away from the Wraithwood estate, and I think about the answers I've been given. Why I've become of such interest to the Cimmerian Court.

I'm part of the dark, bloodstained history of this town.

Just like them.

CHAPTER 12
KASPIAN

My contact leans casually against the wall, flicking their dagger open and closed. This part of Titan Falls has seen better days, all crumbling bricks and boarded windows.

"You're late," he hisses under his hood.

"Fashionably so."

He pushes off the wall, shoving his hands—and the dagger—into the pockets of his long coat.

I get straight to the point. "What do you know?"

"Payment first," he grumbles.

I sigh and pull out the crisp bills I've brought. The sound of cash crinkling fills the empty alleyway as he takes it from me.

"There. You're bought," I say. "Now tell me about the ruby Heart. I hear it's quite the commodity."

A shaft of moonlight highlights his profile. He squints, studying me for a moment before leading me further down the alleyway. "It is. But I don't think you can handle it."

"Why not?" I ask, feigning nonchalance.

He stops abruptly, turning to face me with a closed-mouth smile and obscured eyes.

"Because you're soft," he says quietly, gesturing towards my tailored suit and designer watch glinting in the dim light. "You wouldn't survive where it comes from."

I grin in response, walking closer to him.

That's when I allow my mask to fall.

My smile disappears. The careful amusement I hold in my eyes dissolves under the poison of hatred that spews into my stare, souring my mouth and paralyzing my victim.

He falters, stumbles back, at the sheer force of venom centered at him.

And just as quickly, I pull the switch and my expression brightens. "You were saying?"

My contact pulls down his hood, staring with a mixture of disbelief and revulsion. "Fair enough. I can see you have some ... hidden depths."

I tolerate staying behind him while he takes us on a path behind the small buildings downtown, my family being one of the original lawmakers mandating that no structure be over three stories tall. On Main Street, that is. Any manors can be as tall as they fucking like.

He turns and continues down the narrow alley, the tap of his boots echoing off dingy brick walls tagged with graffiti.

I follow silently, hands in my pockets, senses alert. This neighborhood has a reputation for being unsafe after dark. Not that I'm concerned. My older brother trained me well in the art of self defense at a young age.

The man who refers to himself as The Broker stops beside

a rusty door and pounds twice. It creaks open, a sliver of light slicing across the alley.

He tilts his head, indicating for me to enter.. "After you."

I roll my eyes at the location. Next thing you know, he'll have a store of illegal apothecary goods under a bright purple light with a smoke machine going, but I can't be picky. Not when it took me weeks to track down a broker dealing specifically in black market antiques and documents.

So many illicit brokers have turned to selling Fentanyl mixtures instead for a quick profit. It's annoying, really.

The room is dim but surprisingly tidy, filled with shelves upon shelves of leather-bound books and curios. My contact slides behind a heavy wooden desk and opens a drawer, removing a parcel wrapped in worn velvet. He sets it down between us.

"This is what you're looking for."

"Surely, you haven't found the Heart for me," I jest.

He doesn't return the smile. He eyes me warily instead.

My fault, I suppose.

I reach for the parcel, hesitation flickering only briefly, and untie the golden cord. The velvet falls away, revealing an ancient journal, leather cracked and pages yellowed. My heart pounds as I open it delicately. The handwriting in the journal is faded but still legible, with ink splotches as if someone hastily dried it.

As I scan the contents, the broker leans back in his chair, regarding me through hooded eyes. "Well? Are you a satisfied customer?"

His not-so-subtle way of getting me the fuck off his property.

When I don't look up, he feels the need to fill the silence.

"The ruby," he says, clearing his throat. "It originally belonged to a witch. Sarah Anderton. Burned at the stake or hanged—not sure which—centuries ago for crimes against the town. That's her only journal in existence."

Liar, liar, cock on fire. "Is that so?"

"You're holding a priceless artifact right there. No one knows it exists."

I wait silently for him to continue, letting his discomfort build.

"Anderton cursed the necklace before she died," he says. "Said it would bring ruin to whoever possessed it. It's all written in there."

I incline my head, my attention on him unblinking. "You've read it, then?"

"I—sure, yeah. Have to authenticate my goods."

"Superstitious nonsense," I reply dismissively, going back to the journal and turning the page.

Inside, my mind races. My Valenti ancestors obsessively believed in this curse. Died for it. Killed over it.

Defiled themselves because of it.

"Maybe it's bull, but misfortune seems to follow that ruby." The Broker watches me with veiled eyes. "First, it corrupted the noble family who prosecuted Anderton. Then it passed through generations of fallen dynasties. Vanished from history. Until..."

"Until?" I prompt in a light, endearing voice.

The Broker steps closer. "Until it came into the hands of a respected state leader a hundred years ago. A man at the peak of power. What's his name? It's on the tip of my tongue. Valentine? Veroni? Oh, I got it. Valenti—"

He never noticed my hand move into his pocket. Take the dagger.

And slit his own throat with it.

"Sad," I muse while he shambles back, clutching his gushing throat and gurgling, "being brought down by your own weapon. Surely you saw that coming. I gave you enough hints to have you running out of here and into the street, cartwheeling your arms and screeching for help."

I hold the journal out of reach while he grabs for me, deftly moving out of the splash zone while he crumples into his own bloody shit and urine-stained filth.

A vibration in my pocket interrupts my thoughts. I pull out my phone to see Wilder's name flash across the screen.

Of course he would call at this exact moment.

I silence the call before slipping the phone back into my pocket.

The broker's eyes are wide, filled with terror as he gurgles his last breaths. "You're a Valenti—"

"Shh." I crouch down, pressing a hand to his mouth to muffle the rest of my name.

"Thank you," I say softly into his ear, "for your cooperation. And for your silence."

I move to the desk and re-wrap the journal in the velvet cloth, tuck it into my inside pocket, then leave, carefully locking the door behind me.

I spot Elara in the quad the next day, perched on the rim of the massive gargoyle fountain in the center, her hair catching the rising sun.

Elara doesn't see me yet, too focused on the open book in her lap. I approach slowly, taking in the sight of her and draping the reality of her image with the fantasy of tying her one of the humanoid statues spurting water from their gaping mouths while gagging hers. Tying her legs to their clawed ones, spreading them so wide her cunt stays split open for me.

Alas, I cannot.

Not that she knows who I am, what I represent, and how willing I am to maim, torture, and kill to get what I want from her.

I sit down on the fountain's edge, my back to her. The cool stone is soothing against my pants-clad ass, but not enough to soothe the raging hard-on that's been my constant companion since watching Wilder go at her in the woods during the solstice party.

Sneaking glances at her exquisite form in her skin-hugging jeans and scoop-neck top isn't helping either. Neither is the knowledge of what she's hiding under that shirt, and from me—from all of us.

I smirk to myself, and I know it bodes me no good.

It's going to be so sweet, using her to get to the ruby.

Lord knows I need it to stop the Sovereigns from punishing me for my father's sins. My father's reputation took a nosedive into the dirt after he took his own life. Especially when the entire city saw him leap from Valenti Tower, screaming his guilt about his shady dealings and how he was framed.

After he burned all evidence linking him to the tobacco trade and his darker side deals that cost my family everything. My future. My legacy.

Cav's failure in acquiring the Heart last year may have given us a hiccup, but I'll be damned if I suffer long for it.

"What are you reading, Elara?" I ask, the question a ghost whispering in her ear.

She jumps out of her skin before twisting.

Elara stiffens, the surprise fleeting before she composes herself. "Just some required reading for class."

Her voice is steady, but there's an edge to it, a defensiveness born of our unfamiliarity.

"Ah, the life of a diligent student." I lean back slightly, feigning a casual interest. "But we both know the campus and this town offer more intriguing subjects than trust-fund elites and what's found in 'required reading.'"

Her eyes narrow, suspicion clouding the clear depths. "And what would you know about it, Kaspian?"

I smile, a slow, deliberate curve of my lips. "More than you might think."

I pause, letting the words hang between us, charged with unspoken meaning. "There are legacies and secrets at Titan Falls that textbooks won't tell you about."

She looks away, a flicker of vulnerability crossing her features before she masks it with indifference.

"I'm sure there are," she says, turning back to her book, but her fingers have stilled, betraying her pretense of reading.

Seizing the opportunity, I edge closer, lowering my voice. "A legacy that might interest you, given your ancestry."

Elara's hand tightens around the book, her knuckles whitening. "I don't know what you're talking about."

She's lying. Her voice betrays a hint of curiosity, a crack in her facade.

"I think you do," I press, watching her closely. Wilder was

right—Elara has at least some idea who she's descended from. Whether she's figured it out after our hints at the solstice party or she's always known makes no difference to me.

I test her further. "Sarah Anderton's journal speaks of a ruby Heart—a cursed one, at that. Sound familiar?"

Her eyes flick up to mine, sharp and assessing. "Why are you telling me this? None of the other guys have found it necessary to explain anything while they scared the shit out of me."

She says it with a murmur, tinged with a mix of fear and fascination.

"They have their ways. I have mine, preferring to deal in information. But our goals are the same. We're all entangled. Your ancestors, mine, theirs, we're all at the heart of this curse. Pun intended."

Her book shuts with a firm *thwack*. "I don't believe in curses."

Fuck, I've lost her.

But how? Every woman around here loves the idea of witches and hauntings and gloomy, foggy nights filled with obscure sex. It's why more than a third of the world's most powerful graduate from TFU. Few consequences, lots of fun, tons of dark corners to get away with murder in.

True, women have a higher attrition rate than men around here, the official statement being they've dropped out and couldn't hack it. The more superstitious of the bunch say the dead witches have claimed them in the woods.

Obviously, both views are a load of horseshit.

The women are dead. Clearly.

Elara rises, drawing me further into my wonder. It never

occurred to me that she shared my view of black magic being nonsense.

I can't let her leave.

"Wait." I reach out to grab her wrist.

Her head whips around, anger and resentment blazing in her eyes. "Get your hand off me."

"I just want to talk—"

"Then take your fucking hand off me and talk," she hisses, yanking her wrist free from my grip. "Never put your hands on me again, understood? You all may be members of the Cimmerian Court, but that doesn't give you or any other assholes the right to treat me like I'm yours for the taking!"

Her words freeze me in my thoughts, but I don't let it show. "Touché. I apologize if I overstepped."

It's a lie, but it buys me time to debate how to proceed.

Elara knows about the Court.

Cav and Wilder may enjoy cornering her, but I'm of the mind that scaring her off won't do either of us any good, especially not when we need her cooperation.

But that doesn't mean she isn't still hiding something. After all, Sarah took my family jewel before she was hanged, and it's been playing hard to get with my family ever since.

I may be the only one to be aware of that, but it's still true.

Elara crosses her arms protectively. "Apology accepted, since you're the first to actually give me one. Now, if you don't mind—"

"I mind," I retort sharply, striding around to block her path. "Are you going to keep pretending to be naïve or can we get down to the real reason we're all here? Where is it? The ruby?" I ask, unable to help myself.

Her spine stiffens like a rod, but she doesn't meet my demanding stare. Her fingers grip the strap of her bag, knuckles white. She looks ready to bolt at any moment.

"Don't play games with me," I snarl, leaning in close.

Elara flinches but stands her ground.

"That ruby belonged to the Valentis. That fucking witch stole it generations ago."

Elara shakes her head slowly. "You're insane. I don't have any antique necklace."

I latch onto the word. "Necklace?"

Elara's top lip curls up in a silent hiss. She knows she fucked up.

"Your family has been hiding the jewel for centuries," I sneer. "Don't deny it."

I can almost hear Elara's heart pounding in her chest. She glances around the empty quad. Everyone's gone to class. And, a lot of them like to avoid me. We're alone.

"Okay, fine." Elara sighs. "Say I do know something about it. Nobles paid Sarah to assassinate their rivals. Male, female, children, she did it all, so the story goes. That means your family gave it to her as payment for murder."

I purse my lips in thought. "Good girl. You've figured out we're both descendants of vile people."

"I'm not pretending to be dumb. Maybe I just don't want to *know* these kinds of things. I'm happy working toward a positive future and leaving the past alone. I want to be *left alone*."

I give her a crooked smile, which is answer enough: I'm not planning on letting her go. Ever.

She shakes her head in frustration, hair falling across her

face. Her continued denial frustrates me. We're so close, yet she's still holding back.

Time for a new tactic.

I step closer, backing her against the lip of the fountain. She inhales sharply, bunching her fists in my coat's lapels to stop from toppling backward.

I savor her surprise, the spike of fear in her eyes.

"What are you doing?" she cries.

I lean in, lips grazing her ear. "Getting answers."

My hand slides up her side and under her shirt, feeling her tense under that supple skin. She shudders out a breath, eyes squeezing shut. I trail a finger along her jaw with my other hand, tipping up her chin.

"Tell me about the necklace, Elara."

She shakes her head weakly. "I don't know anything."

My touch trails down her throat. Her pulse flutters under my fingertips.

"You do."

I sweep her hair back, baring the slender column of her neck.

She swallows hard. I press closer, my body caging hers. Alarm and something else wars in her eyes, hot amber melting to molten gold.

A spark ignites in my blood. I want this infuriating, secretive girl. I want those full lips parted and gasping. I want her secrets spilled along with her screams.

"Tell me," I repeat, voice low.

She shudders, clutching my coat tighter. "Kaspian, please..."

The plea in her voice thrills me. I lean closer, my nose a mere inch from hers.

"Playing dumb isn't going to work anymore. You know what I want. I hear Cav even offered you something in return. Your brother's killer."

Her breath hitches, her pupils dilating. Good. Nervousness and something else—desire?

That *is* interesting.

My lips quirk at the truth in her eyes. "Where is it?"

"I—" she starts, chest heaving with each sliver of breath. "I can't tell you."

I lean in further, my lips the barest inch from hers. "You don't have to. I'll take it."

And I will.

I find her mouth, devouring her softness with a brutal, punishing kiss. She tries to push me away, but I'm stronger. My other hand tangles in her hair, holding her still as I claim her, thrusting my tongue into her mouth. Tasting her sweetness, feeling the thud of her heart beneath my palm.

Finally, she goes slack against the hard fountain edge. I tilt my head to deepen the kiss, drinking from her lips as my cock hardens.

She doesn't want to do this the easy way? Fine.

Her fingers dig into my shoulders when I pull away, her eyes glazed over.

"Please ... don't..."

"Your pleas are wasted on me," I warn huskily. "And I'm the nice one."

I school my expression into patience as I watch the war behind her eyes. Lies versus truth. It's never a tough decision for me, but this one's innocence is very kind and pure.

She submits under my touch. Truth wins. "I promised Gram I wouldn't—"

A stiff wind hits us. Before she can finish, Wilder comes strolling out of nowhere. His face twists when he sees us.

"Taking it slow, Kaspian?" Wilder says, sounding *very* unamused.

I don't move from Elara. He's not here on my or Cav's orders.

Elara shoves me away angrily, not meeting either of our eyes. She grabs her bag, ignoring us completely.

Wilder *tsks*, wandering closer. "Leaving so soon, sweet-witch? Playing hard to get?"

I narrow my eyes at him while moving aside, letting her go but watching Wilder warily. He's always been a gamble.

"Fuck off, Wilder," Elara says sharply.

"Or what? You'll scream?" he taunts.

I scowl. "Before you came along, I was making her see sense."

Wilder scoffs. "You call that sense?"

He turns to me, eyes burning with something that makes my skin crawl. "Cav's hoping you haven't undermined the deal by claiming her as your own."

"Deal?" Elara halts her step and frowns. "I didn't agree to any *deal*."

I watch her.

There it is: that concoction of confusion and fear. Good.

"She's ours now," Wilder says darkly to me. "Not yours alone. Any touching has to be approved by us all."

I scoff, then snarl, "You're one to talk—"

He stalks off without allowing me to finish—the only man who can and not gain a lasting scar from doing so.

He leaves Elara standing there, stunned. She fumbles with her bag strap.

"You're welcome for the interruption," he says to her mockingly over his shoulder.

As Wilder's contemptuous words fade into the distance, Elara's gaze finally lifts to meet mine, a storm of emotions swirling in those depths.

For a fleeting moment, there's an unspoken question, a plea for answers as to *why her*.

I don't give her the relief of an answer, but I find myself bound to her, our fates intertwined in the search for redemption, for truth.

She's afraid of our touch. Elara doesn't like the rules involved in our claiming of her and didn't agree to any of our attentions.

And yet, I'm clinging to something far more dangerous than she is—*her* touch.

I liked it far too much.

CHAPTER 13
ELARA

I click through endless search results on my laptop, my eyes glazing over the endless strings of text and images on the screen.

Nothing.

Hours of searching, and still not a shred of evidence linking my family to Sarah Anderton.

Only my mentally fragile mother's word, and Gram isn't answering her phone.

Sasha isn't in our shared room tonight, choosing to go to a party at Meath House. She pulled out every magic trick she had trying to convince me to come, but my unexpected heritage kept my butt firmly planted in my desk chair.

First Wilder, then Cav, now Kaspian. All three possess toxic and addictive pheromones that my sex-deprived body refuses to ignore. Luckily, my brain is doing much better against them and keeping focus, which is to figure out why a necklace could be so important to them and how it relates to a long-dead accused witch from the 1700s and her possible hidden treasure.

Not difficult at all, right?

And where the hell I fit in to all of it.

I rub my temples, exhaustion and frustration mounting. There must be *something*, some breadcrumb I'm missing in this digital haystack.

Because I'm desperate for another avenue other than relentlessly searching the online TFU library and the internet for information on Sarah, I move to clicking around for details about her daughter. Although they never found her body, people presume she was killed at the same time as her mother, even though official records never proved it.

As I expected, there's nothing online about her other than what I already know. Not her name, nothing about her involvement in the witch trial against her mother.

In an online historical mystery forum, one user theorized that she may have been buried with the jewels Sarah received as payment for murder. If found, it would be worth millions. *Billions* on the black market.

I read, then dismiss. I have enough thoughts and opinions. I need *facts*.

I'm about to give up for the night when a post further down, almost buried from all the down-votes it received, catches my eye. It reads:

Do people really believe the Anderton line died with Sarah and this alleged deformed daughter? Historians have just decided this girl is dead because they have no fucking clue what happened to her. Like, why isn't it questioned that

the daughter was deleted from trial records because she was being hidden somewhere *alive*? Think about it guys. Daughter is what, 16? That's like middle-age in the 1700s. And I don't think she was deformed. I think that's only mentioned to turn people off of the idea that a girl like that could ever get pregnant. I bet you the daughter was knocked up and Sarah used her connections with the nobles that hired her to get her kid out of there when they were caught. So she could continue her lineage. Do you agree? Discuss.

My heart quickens. I may not have solid evidence, but if my mother is right, I'm proof the Anderton lineage existed well after Sarah's death.

And proof there are jewels.

NO. I shake out of that thought. This amulet could've come from anywhere. I only have Mom's word and Gram's cryptic warnings. The chances of me stumbling on a piece of treasure from two hundred years ago are below zero.

But then … why are the boys involving themselves with me? It's not just to bully me.

I'm not shy about my looks. I know I'm pretty. But I'm not *that* pretty.

Behind their cruel veneer lies an intensity that borders on desperation.

I look at the handle of the person who wrote the post to see if they made any other posts.

Nothing. This was their only one, written three years ago.

I fall back in my seat with a sigh. Is this theory possible? It's not hard to believe Sarah was protecting more than her fabled lost jewels. She was a smart woman who evaded detection for over a decade. A murderer, yes. Cold-blooded, for sure. But never stupid.

What secrets did she take to her grave?

A muffled thud against my door interrupts my thoughts.

Sasha's slurred voice filters through the wood. "You in there? My keys ran away."

I take a sip of my now-tepid coffee and push the laptop to the side, smoothing my frazzled hair with one hand.

"Coming, dear," I call back.

The door squeaks open, and Sasha stumbles in with an armful of bags from Meath House's infamous snack room, her eyes heavy-lidded and makeup smudged.

Sasha drops the bags on the floor and then pouts at the pile. "My keys went on an adventure without me."

I eye her stash at my feet, impressed she carried so much. "Doesn't look like it."

Swaying, Sasha deadpans, "Truly awe-inspiring comeback, you nerd. I can already see the comedy specials in your future."

"I'm paid handsomely to hide my talent."

Sasha stifles a giggle that turns into a hiccup. "What's got you so squirreled away and serious, anyway?"

"Just some old gossip about the Anderton Witch Trials." I shrug as if it's not a big deal. "Might do a paper on it for history class."

She rolls her eyes, used to my focus on academics as she takes out a bag of chips and tosses them over my head.

"Oops. Missed. If you're looking for new dirt on the Anderton witches, stop wasting your time. They were all confi —consip—*conspiracy* theories made up by bitter old men who didn't get the women they wanted and killed them for it. Besides, I think we have more important things to focus on."

I return to my seat, frustrated enough with my research to take time off and entertain her. "Like what?"

"The subben—*sudden* attentions of Kaspian, duh!" she huffs, popping a chip in her mouth as she lays back on her bed, looking at the ceiling like it has answers. "You think I wouldn't hear about your make-out session by the fountain? Everyone was talking about it at the party. How Kaspian, one of the Untouchable Four, touched you."

It wasn't just Kaspian, I think with a blush.

The heat in my cheeks deepens when she uses my nickname for them. It has a whole other meaning now. By "untouchable," maybe I meant that I wanted the opposite. That I wanted to feel what it's like to brush up against each one of them.

Even if they terrorize the shit out of me while I do it.

Her head lolls to the side, and she stares at me with an off-kilter squint. "Let's put aside for one sec the fact you didn't tell your best friend you got to kiss a god. Why the sudden interest in you? No offense, but he doesn't publicly get with anyone."

I nod along, because she's right. There's only one reason he kissed me.

"Maybe it's because I'm considered an attractive and valuable pawn," I joke, but it's met with silence.

Sasha sits up abruptly, sending a chip tumbling out of her mouth. "Have you thought about what they could want with you? Those four guys, they're always together. I don't think I've seen any of them single out a girl. They are *not* nice." She wrinkles her nose like she smells something off.

Her voice lowers into the seriousness that only comes when she truly cares about something, even while drunk. It reminds me of our talks about boys, our dreams, our fears during freshmen year and my eventual confession about losing my brother so violently. She's the only one on campus aware of Maverick and fully supported my need to be someone other than the little sister of a dead brother. She hasn't questioned me since.

"Nothing they do is an accident, either," she adds.

"No," I agree, hiding my worry.

It's too soon to tell her about the necklace, too soon to admit how close they're already succeeding at getting what they want out of me.

She nods once and reaches for another chip with a small smile on her face as if she's made a decision while in dreamland. "Curiosity may have killed the cat, but if I were nailed by Kaspian, I'd be one happy pussy."

I snort, thrown out of my thoughts of doom, and toss an unopened bag of chips at her. "You *just* said they weren't nice and I should probably leave them alone."

"Why are you listening to what I'm saying? I'm drunk as shit."

"Good night, Drunk-Face," I say to her.

"Mm. Good night, Sober Nun."

Sasha doesn't bother getting undressed. After kicking off her shoes, she slides under her covers and is asleep within minutes amidst crumbs, empty chip bags, and her phone half-gripped in her hand.

Once I hear her soft snores, I stand and swipe my keys off my desk.

Sasha's warnings haven't deterred me. If anything, I'm

more motivated to discover what's drawing Kaspian, Wilder, and the others to me.

Is it my connection to the Andertons? Wilder keeps calling me *sweetwitch*.

Or is it that I might know the location of a supposed treasure? If so, Kaspian wants it badly.

And then there's the Cimmerian Court's involvement. What did Darcy say? Oh yeah, Darcy mentioned they created it at the end of the 17th century. Right around the time Sarah was alive and in business.

This necklace I have … If my thinking is right, it means a lot to some powerful families. Kaspian, Wilder, Cav and Axe can't be the only members of the Cimmerian Court. If such a society really exists on campus, my necklace just became way more valuable.

And it starts with Sarah Anderton.

After grabbing my coat, I text Sasha that I'll be spending the night at Gram's, and head for my car.

An idea hits me as I pass the library to the student parking lot, veering inside to unload the heavy burden in my backpack and put it somewhere safe where the Court won't find.

I drive through the TFU gates, determined to unravel the mystery of Sarah Anderton and her—*my*—connection to this necklace the Court so covets.

CHAPTER 14
ELARA

I pull up to the Wraithwood mansion, the fog rolling in, thickening the air like a blanket.

When I get out, I can see my breath in front of me, the front steps slick with dew. It occurs to me it would've been easy for someone to follow my car without being noticed.

I assure myself that a skulking, watchful form isn't melting out of the fog before heading toward Gram's home.

No, the boys use brute force in cornering me, making it clear what they want. They wouldn't slink around the outskirts, waiting for me to make a mistake. Wilder chased me during a party, Cav cornered me in the parking lot, and Kaspian grabbed me at the fountain.

All in plain view.

The only one I'm unsure about is Axe, asocial and often appearing lost in thought, but who I'm convinced is eerily analytical. It's the way he tracks with his eyes, his lips in a neutral line. You can learn a lot when everyone else does the talking.

The grandiose building looks more daunting and fore-boding on a misty night like this. Steeples jut out like black talons, shadows dancing around me from the wind as I make my way up the stone steps.

Mom and Dad stayed at Farrow Manor, an estate willed to Mom through her parents who died before Maverick was born and where Mom stays now. Part of it was because Gram refused to move out of Wraithwood Manor, but compro-mised, saying my parents could live with her. I'm convinced Mom's decision to move to Farrow Manor rather than live with her mother-in-law caused the bitterness in the air.

I enter through a side door with a key I keep on my school lanyard, the inside just as cold and musty as it was during our yearly visits. Old portraits of previous Wraith-woods hang on the walls, their eyes seeming to follow me as I flick on a single lamp near the staircase. I stop midway up the stairs at the portrait of my father, Darian Wraithwood, painted when he was in his early thirties. He sits in a red high-backed chair, almost throne-like, the background of what's now Gram's study giving it a traditional, serious vibe. The painting hangs in the middle of the double staircase's mezzanine, just where Gram wanted it. A memorial to her dead, only son at the heart of the manor.

Maverick died before one could be painted of him.

I give a small-voiced, "Hi, Dad," before my gaze slides away.

Even though I never knew him, it hurts too much to stare for long. It's painful imagining what it would be like if he were here, helping me, helping Mom, get through our grief.

The place smells of old books, must and leather. Gram gets her home cleaned once a week, but in centuries-old houses like this, you can never get out that aged smell, no matter how much incense Gram lights.

Gripping my phone, I shake away the tragic memories of my family and resume my mission.

You've got this. Time to discover what makes this ruby so damned special.

Wraithwood Manor feels more like a museum than a home, each room a testament to the family's long and storied past. I quickly check on Gram, ensuring she's safe in bed and therefore willfully ignoring my calls rather than because something bad happened to her.

While Gram's sound asleep, I start my search in the obvious places: the library, with its towering shelves of dusty tomes; the drawing room, where portraits of stern ancestors gaze down with silent judgment. But they yield nothing, no hint of a ruby necklace or the secrets it supposedly holds.

Not unless I want to pore over upwards of 1,000 books.

Part of me wants to hire the guys to help me, but that would mean working with them toward their unknown goal —and I can't *stand* the unknown.

My stomach flips when I picture Kaspian in one corner with a sly glint in his roguish green eyes, silently ordering for me to press myself up against the bookcase so he can trap me.

Then Wilder storming in and hooking my arm, his whiskey stare on fire as he yanks me against his mouth.

I don't know what Cav would do to me yet. Circle me until he sees the right time to bite, probably. And Axe … would he watch? Or would he step in and whisper what he wants to do to me in my ear?

"*Omigod,*" I say in a rush of breath and dart out of the library, away from that unexpected, *unwanted* fantasy.

What am I thinking, toying with those boys, even in my thoughts?

My frustration mounts as I wander through the dining hall, running my fingers over the cold, carved mahogany of the buffet, hoping for some hidden drawer, some overlooked clue. Nothing. The silence of the house presses in on me, a tangible reminder of the distance between the past and my understanding of it.

Dad passed away before I was an age where I cared about ancestors. Maverick might have known something, but whatever he found out, he took with him when he died.

In a place like Titan Falls, the founding families of the town are always intriguing, since the town itself was created through violence, blood, and fractured skulls.

I was 16 when Maverick died, and all I cared about was the right shade of blue to wear to my junior prom, afraid of what would clash with my hair.

If *only* I could go back to that girl and ask Maverick what I should have done to keep him safe, keep him *inside*.

Great, now I'm sounding like Mom.

I deliberately avoid the greenhouse, trudging up the grand staircase again to the bedrooms, methodically searching through the guest room. Gram leaves her jewelry boxes there, considering she has no guests and has turned it into another closet, but they contain nothing more unusual than strands of pearls and clip-on earrings from the 1920s to now.

My own room offers no secrets. It's just as I left it, a stark contrast to the rest of the house with its modern conveniences and lack of history.

Sliding my bag off my shoulders, I plop onto the cream

queen-sized bed with a huff, its draped canopy fluttering with my movement.

The weight of failure sits heavy on my shoulders. How can I uncover the truth about Sarah Anderton and the ruby necklace if I can't even figure out where to start?

That's when I notice the grandfather clock, standing alone in the long, dimly lit corridor, its pendulum swinging with a steady, unwavering rhythm that always lulled me to sleep, whereas it drove Maverick insane.

It's an heirloom that Gram has always meticulously maintained, its twin making its home at Farrow manor on Gram's insistence, its chimes a constant backdrop to my childhood memories.

Yet now, its hands are frozen, marking neither the hour nor the minute accurately. It's unlike Gram to neglect it. A pang of worry for her well-being tightens my chest.

I approach the clock, intending to right what feels like a minor oversight.

"Gram's probably too preoccupied lately," I mutter to myself, justifying the anomaly as I reach out to adjust the clock's hands. It's a small act, but one that feels significant, a way to care for Gram. She's always alone in this too-big house.

As the hands align to midnight, I barely register the soft click that follows, too caught up in thoughts of Gram's health and the strangeness of our last conversation.

But when the wall beside the clock shifts, a surge of surprise eclipses my worries.

The click that follows is the sweetest sound I've heard all day, a whisper of possibility in the deafening silence of my search.

The wall slides open enough to be a doorway, revealing a stone corridor that quickly turns black.

"What the…?"

Curiosity propels me forward, my phone's flashlight navigating through the narrow passageway, the ceiling nearly brushing against the top of my head. The darkness seems to swallow me whole, but my stubbornness is stronger than my fear.

The passageway stops when I reach a small, cracked wooden door with iron hinges. It creaks open under my touch, and I step into a room that feels like a portal to another era. Dust motes dance in the sliver of light from my phone.

I take a moment to bark out a laugh.

I've rummaged through every inch of Gram's mansion, expecting dust and maybe a few moth-eaten letters. What I didn't expect was to stumble into a hidden room straight out of a movie, all because I decided the old grandfather clock looked too forlorn with its hands stuck at the wrong time.

It's a discovery that makes you question if you've accidentally wandered into a parallel universe where your life is suddenly way more interesting.

The room is about the size of a home office, crammed with shelves of leather-bound books, maps strewn across a large oak desk, and yellowed papers with faded ink filled with a code I don't recognize. An eroded brass plaque on the desk catches my eye, engraved with the name *William Jonquil.*

The name means nothing to me, yet I lift it up anyway, inspecting the letters for answers.

It's then I notice the plaque was resting on top of a

cracked, plain leather-bound book. Placing the plaque aside, I carefully flip the book open.

I half-expect to find mundane entries about daily life centuries ago. Instead, the name *Sarah Anderton* leaps off the page, written in a tight, careful script that feels oddly personal.

My heart skips.

But it's the miniature portrait tucked between the diary's pages that truly stuns me.

The painting is small, but the likeness is unmistakable. William Jonquil's face, with sharp eyes and a half-smirk, is almost a carbon copy of Maverick's. With the same intense gaze that could either warm your heart or freeze you out, depending on the day.

The realization hits me like a physical blow.

This isn't just finding an ancestor in the family tree; it's seeing my brother's face looking back at me from the past. It's eerie, comforting, and utterly bewildering all at once.

My hands tremble as I hold the portrait, tracing the lines of William's face. Tears fill my eyes. I've avoided looking at pictures of Maverick, save for the single photo on my desk at the dorms. It's all I can take.

How is it possible that he and Maverick could share such a striking resemblance across centuries? This room, his belongings, they're not just relics. They're a bridge to the past, to a man who now feels as familiar as if he'd walked out of my own memories.

I force myself to put down the portrait and recenter my priorities. I'm here for information on Sarah or the ruby.

Nothing else.

With a hard sniff to lock my emotions down, I turn the

journal's pages, filled with rows of meticulous code. As I turn the journal's pages, I struggle to understand the entries because of the old-school encryption. Yet, the repetition of certain symbols and numbers hints at a structured method to the madness. It's clear William Jonquil wasn't just keeping a diary. He was maintaining a ledger, a detailed record of activities too risky to write plainly.

The name *Sarah Anderton* appears again and again.

Doings is a word that crops up frequently, too, a vague term that could encompass anything from daily chores to grand schemes. But context is key. Entries mentioning *doings* are often followed by lists of names, locations, and dates, all encoded.

My mind races—could these "doings" be operations, missions of some sort? The notion of smuggling leaps out at me, an act of moving something—or someone—secretly and safely.

But that wouldn't make sense. Sarah didn't deal in rescues or benevolent acts, rather the clandestine movement of secrets, potentially dangerous substances, or even individuals marked by her lethal skill set.

Poisons.

Uh-oh.

Was my brother's doppelgänger ancestor a murderer for hire, too?

But nothing prepares me for the jolt I feel when I stumble upon the mention of the ruby Heart, a name Kaspian specifically mentioned before he swallowed my breath and infused me with his heat.

I need more time to decode, but I've figured out enough to know the ruby Heart here isn't just an artifact. It's entwined with words like "curse" and "doom," just like Kaspian said. And Cav.

Was it an instrument of her alleged witchcraft, a tool in her assassinations, or something even more sinister?

My shock deepens as I realize this journal implicates Wraithwood estate not just in Sarah Anderton's shadowy world but in a legacy considered cursed.

I need to know more, understand how deep this goes, and what it means for me. The mention of the ruby in this context, surrounded by talk of misfortune and bad acts, isn't something I can just pass on to the Untouchable Four and then forget all about it.

The last entry is a hand-drawn map with several locations marked—none of which are named.

"Of course not," I mutter. "Why would you make it easy on me, my how-many-greats-grandad?"

My fingers trace the markings on the map, finally settling on one location. It's the closest to where I am now, and I can't help but wonder how many more hidden chambers I can uncover before I go to bed.

"Maybe it's time to take a little field trip," I tell myself, excitement bubbling inside me, mixed with trepidation.

I snap a photo of the map with my phone, then carefully tuck the journal against my chest, deciding to stash it in my bag as soon as I get back to it.

As I step out of the secret study, I find myself daydreaming about what else I might uncover. Will it lead me to the truth about my family and Sarah Anderton? Or will it only raise more questions?

Whatever awaits me, I vow to figure it out before the Untouchable Four do.

CHAPTER 15
ELARA

The winding mountain road carries me deeper into the fog-shrouded Appalachians. My hands grip the steering wheel as I scan the tree line for any signs of life.

I expected solitude, but the prickling on my neck whispers I'm not alone.

A flash of movement.

I slam the brakes, heart hammering.

"Dammit," I breathe out with a hiss as the figure bounds away.

Just a deer leaping out of the deathtrap of my headlights and into the thicket.

Get it together, Elara.

But my senses remain on high alert, certain someone is out here and they know what I'm up to.

I park at the base of a craggy outcropping marked on William's map and step out of the car with the tentativeness of stepping into another world—one where every whisper of wind is a voice and every crackle of dry leaves is a footstep.

I'm here because of a faded map and a family legend that suddenly feels too real, too close.

My heart is a steady drum of excitement and fear, a rhythm I've tried to ignore since I left the safety of my car. The silence presses in as I follow a nearly invisible trail into the woods.

"Alright, Mr. William Jonquil. What were you doing for Sarah?"

I scan the area for any sign of what I'm supposed to find.

There.

Some kind of hole in the stone that grows larger the closer I get to it. By the time I'm at its mouth, the top of the opening is well above my head.

It gapes like a gateway to hell.

My shoes scuff against the dirt ground as I slowly back away.

I'm not curious enough to wander in.

After double-checking Jonquil's journal, I confirm this is the spot. According to his notes, it used to be a mine.

Using my phone's camera, I document the area; the flash outlining the surrounding brush and jagged stone like lightning.

I'm so lost in thought, tracing the path my great-however-many-times-grandfather might have walked, that I don't hear anyone approach.

Not until it's too late.

A hand on my shoulder, firm and unexpected, spins me around.

I choke on my breath, my heart becoming a sentient being who wants to rip open my chest and escape, as I come face to face with a man who seems to embody the very essence of the legends I'm chasing.

Black hair, sea-green eyes that pierce through the night, tall and imposing with a paleness that speaks of moonlight, not sunlight.

"You're a long way from anywhere safe," he says, his tone amused, yet somehow chilling.

I jerk away, not from fear, but from the shock of being surprised.

"Who are you?" I demand, more out of reflex than any real expectation of an honest answer. "Were you following me?"

He studies me for a moment, and I can tell he's weighing his answer.

Then he releases a low chuckle, though there's no humor in it. "I'm someone who knows the dangers of digging up the past. Especially a past as complex as Sarah Anderton's."

He doesn't answer my second question and I sense it's deliberate.

But his casual mention of Sarah makes me lurch. How does he know who I'm researching?

I'm about to voice my confusion when he continues, "You're looking for answers about her, aren't you? About her hidden 'treasure'?"

The way he says "treasure," like he's mocking the very idea, piques my curiosity even more.

Despite the alarm bells ringing in my head, I press on. "Maybe I am. What's it to you?"

He steps closer, and the moonlight catches in his eyes, giving them a predatory gleam. "Because, Elara Wraithwood, that 'treasure'... let's just say not all that glitters is gold. And

Sarah's legacy? It's more curse than blessing. Many people have died trying to look for it."

I'm taken aback by his use of my full name, a reminder of how little I know about him, and yet he seems familiar with me.

"You're trying to scare me off," I accuse.

"Consider it a friendly warning," he counters, his gaze never wavering. "The treasure, if that's what you're after, it's not what you think. It's not shiny baubles. And people like you?" He gestures between us, a wry smile playing on his lips. "You're better off leaving it closed."

The connection clicks, and I remember where I've seen him—linked to that girl, the one who lives in a mansion with four other guys. But not him. He's...

Her brother. Tempest. And he has a gorgeous blonde girlfriend who's in her senior year at TFU. I see her in some of my advanced credit classes.

My heart pounds harder, the fear leeching in. The last thing I want is *more* men involved in the search for my family heirloom.

I decide to test him.

"I'm not looking for a fortune, Tempest. Not in the way you think, at least," I say.

His eyes flare at the use of his name.

I knew it. It's him.

Surely, a guy so devoted to his sister and his girlfriend wouldn't want to harm another woman. Me.

"I'm researching her," I say, which isn't entirely a lie. "Her ... murders, and what she might've left behind, like her daughter, and the Heart."

Tempest's reaction is subtle, but unmistakable. A brief tightening around his eyes, a momentary stillness.

"The Heart," he repeats.

I nod, emboldened by his reaction. "Yes, the ruby. You know about it?"

"The Heart," he says slowly, "is not what you think it is. Sarah Anderton's story is far more complicated than any history book or online forums will tell you."

I tense at his pointed use of forums. Am I being tracked online? Followed by him in person? *Why?*

Then it hits me. "You're—you're part of the Cimmerian Court, aren't you? Jesus, how many hot, scary men are in your club? And how many are they going to send my way before they get the hint that I don't have anything and wouldn't give it to you if I did?"

Unnervingly, his lips curve into a genuine, amused smile. "I'm not with the Court. I'd rather juggle live grenades in a thunderstorm than play in Cav's little kingdom of rhymes and riddles. That man has a way of turning allies into adversaries without even trying."

For a second, I agree with him, offering a small smile of my own.

Then I get smart again, my expression falling closed.

Tempest's amusement also fades, a more contemplative shadow crossing his features.

"But it's curious, isn't it?" he muses, more to himself than to me. "The Court still chases after a myth, looking for a Heart that, for all intents and purposes, doesn't beat outside of a fairy-tale."

"Wait a minute, you don't think the Heart exists as a jewel?"

But as he talks, all I can think about is the piece of that "myth" snug in the TFU library. His words clash big time with the solid, very real piece of ruby I've been carting around lately.

Part of me wants to pull it out and show him, giving myself the upper hand and all these alphaholes the shock of their lives. But the better, smarter version of myself scolds me into keeping my lips sealed. That there's more to this than jewelry and showmanship.

Even though I *love* being right.

Tempest's brows arch in one of resigned surprise. "I suppose you also believe there's a hidden ruby, the largest in the world, that Sarah expertly hid before being killed."

Want to bet? Because, dude, I've literally touched it.

I stay quiet, my expression giving no answer.

It hits me that maybe Tempest's just messing with me, trying to throw me off because, for all his talk, he doesn't know I have a big-ass ruby. Or maybe he does know, and this is all some game to see what I'll do.

My head's spinning with the possibilities, and not in a good way.

Tempest's smile is thin, almost rueful. "Cav looks for a beacon in a storm he doesn't understand. The Heart is more than a simple treasure or talisman. If it were as easy as digging up a chest or prying open a vault, it wouldn't have eluded so many for so long."

I'm standing in front of him, feeling the weight of the hidden necklace like it's suddenly ten times heavier.

"You're hedging." I cross my arms against my chest. "If you have proof the Heart doesn't exist, just say it to me plain."

Tempest continues, his tone turning serious again, "I may

not be with the Court. But that doesn't mean I'm any less informed. Or any less dangerous."

I cut through the bullshit. "Then who *are* you with?"

"The Vultures," he says, as simply as I asked him to answer.

It sends me back a step.

"We've been watching you ever since your brother's funeral," he says. "And trust me, Elara, you're not the first to go looking, and you won't be the last. But you should be the wisest."

A shard of ice cuts into my chest. "Why are you mentioning Maverick? Did you know him? What were you doing at his funeral? *How* did you know him?"

My questions come out in a cold rush, my heart frantically cracking through the deep-freeze of my soul.

Too many strangers are mentioning my brother's name. Too many enjoy dangling his death in front of me like a fucking *carrot*.

Tempest withdraws, his expression hardening. "Not everyone gets a warning. Consider yourself lucky. I'd hate to see history repeat itself."

"What are you talking about?" My cry is close to scream as Tempest slinks into the forest.

I give chase, my vision blurred with hot tears. *"Answer me!"*

The only response is nature telling me to go home with a biting wind and a burst of purple martins leaving their shelter for the night.

"I don't scare that easily!" I yell.

But I'm alone, with only the echo of his warning whispering through the trees.

CHAPTER 16
AXE

I hate crowds. Each shout from the quad or pack of students trampling by causes a wince before I shuffle deeper into the crevices of TFU.

Away.

Usually, I take my classes via video streaming in my room. The dean allowed me to listen to lectures via video streaming as soon as I was accepted into the Court. One of many powerful benefits given to us as members, almost as mighty as the punishments administered.

This morning, I'm strictly prohibited from attending through my computer camera. It's less embarrassing when I'm able to pause and transcribe the lecture, then repeat a sentence out loud three times before it finally fits into my head.

I've been assured multiple times that I don't have to take exams, attend classes, or even lunch hall. My graduation with top marks is a guarantee by the Court. But nothing in my life is granted so easily, and I refuse to let my inability to concentrate be a crutch. I will graduate under my own rules and earn those top grades. Others may see me as a liability, but I know that I am not.

Take today, for example. I share two classes with Elara: one with Cav, Wilder and Kaspian, and one where it's just me.

Guess which one I've been ordered to personally attend?

I'm not the only one skulking around her, either. As soon as I step onto the path to the Media Building, two sets of mismatched eyes track me from the other side of the quad. Wilder and Kaspian both give me measured stares as they lounge on a bench, one with an arm slung over the backrest, one with his legs stretched out in front of him. They look like they don't have a care in the world.

I know better.

It takes every ounce of self-restraint to keep my stride casual as I walk past them. Not that it matters. Wilder can smell weakness a mile away, and he's practically salivating at the idea of making my life difficult.

I just have to get through this semester without him deciding he hates me enough to go higher than me on the Court's food chain. Cav can be... persuasive, but even he has his limits where Wilder is concerned. And I don't want to find out what happens when he exceeds them.

As for Kaspian, he's his own person. One that a demon uses for a host.

I slip inside the classroom right on the bell and pretend to search for a seat while I scope out Elara.

When I finally spot her, I'm not disappointed. Her mane of hair cascades in waves down her back, the tips brushing against the richly colored leather of the chair below her. Her posture is perfect, back straight, shoulders pulled back, as she listens intently to the eloquent ramblings of our TA about the upcoming lecture.

The sight of her so absorbed makes something warm unravel in my chest. I want a thousand reasons to stay away from her, but my body has another idea.

Just as I slide into the vacant seat beside hers, she glances over at me. The surprise in her gaze is brief, but there, before it's hidden under suspicion and mulish defiance.

Amusement tugs at my lips.

I understand Cav, Wilder, and Kaspian's complaints about her stubborn refusal to let them intimidate or frighten her into doing what they want—their favorite tactic. Probably because it's used on us all the time.

I can't even feign an interest in the professor as he begins with Elara in the room, her gold-soaked eyes flickering to me every once in a while before she returns her attention to the front.

"No use in staring," I murmur low, so only she can hear me over the professor. "You know you don't have a chance with us."

"Oh?" she drawls back, voice dripping with disdain. "Didn't realize I wanted one."

Her comment stings, and I grip my pen tighter.

She has no idea how much I wish it were that simple.

Of course she wants nothing to do with me. I'm Axton Devereaux, the family's only son and bound for the decrepit basement of the empires Cav, Wilder, and Kaspian will eventually own. Even with my mother being who she is—*was*—I'm still nothing more than a consolation prize, destined to live out my days as a part of the Court, but never a full member.

Unless I can find that damned ruby.

Despite everything—losing my mother young, the foster care system that broke more than it fixed, and battling every day with the fog in my brain—I've clung to one truth: the ruby Heart is my chance to rewrite my story.

I swear under my breath as Elara's heel bumps mine under the desk, effectively ruining my attempt at focusing on anything other than her and her too-soft eyes.

Repeating the sentence in my head, I remind myself I'll be a true Devereaux, someone whose very name will inspire respect and obedience.

The thought sits heavily on my mind as the professor drones on about media studies and their impact on society. As if any of that matters when the Court is still fighting over a gemstone about which we know so little.

I've barely paid attention to the last twenty minutes of the lecture when Elara rises from her desk, slides her notebook into her bag, and strides towards the door.

Escaping me so soon?

I have to act now, before I lose my nerve. Before Cav or Wilder or even Kaspian gets wind of me hesitating where it comes to the, in their words, "*fucking* Wraithwood girl."

My heart thuds in my chest as I quickly pack my things and follow her out.

The second we're out of earshot, she whirls on me with her hands on her hips.

"What do you want, Axe?" she spits out. "You and your little friends have been following me for days—"

"—I just want to talk," I interject smoothly, hands raised in surrender. "I'm not here to push you around or bully you or any of that. Swear."

She side-eyes me like I've just offered her a road trip around the rings of Saturn.

"Your recent experience tells you otherwise, I know," I say. "But if you want my opinion—"

"—I don't."

"Hear me out. If you want my opinion," I repeat, "I think the boys got it wrong. I'd rather approach you with reason. We want something from you, yes, but you should also get something from us in return."

She doesn't immediately walk away. It's a small victory, and I'll take it.

I lead her to a secluded alcove lined with textbooks no longer in print but displayed like trophies, the stacks tall enough that no one should overhear us.

The first time I saw her here huddled in the corner with a book in hand, admiring these dusty tomes, Elara was a freshman and oblivious to her surroundings—and me spying on her.

When I took in the sight of her, all silky reddish waves and hearth-soaked eyes, I'd felt a stab of longing so fierce it physically hurt.

What is it like to carry beauty instead of the slash of scars?

How was it possible that she could find solace here when all I've ever known is an expensive cage?

"I know you're looking for information on the Cimmerian Court," I say bluntly, startling her.

Her eyes, which had been a liquid topaz before, harden.

"The what?" she drawls out, oozing boredom I'm positive she doesn't feel.

I can practically hear the gears turning in that pretty head of hers as she weighs her options on whether ignorance or cleverness works best with me.

"You're aware I don't talk much," I say. "And a sincere girl like you would realize I make up for it with what I observe. What people do when they think they're not being watched. I know what you've been up to. Who you've spoken to, like Darcy and her envious theories about a secret society on campus."

She blinks, righting herself after hearing what she likely did not expect me to say, then glares at my pants' side pocket where the rectangular shape of my phone juts out.

And there it is. Elara is well aware I *record* and document everything I see.

For my memory's sake. Not for blackmail. Usually.

"I've been where you are," I continue. "Not knowing who your family is, wondering what kind of sordid history they hid from you and the worry of figuring it out when it's too late."

Elara works her lower jaw, her stare cutting to the side.

"I'm offering you a partnership," I say. "We both want the same thing. The truth. I know the Heart's provenance not only affects me, but your family as well. It's a cursed thing, isn't it? Taints everything it touches, right? Condemning us to live out generations of misery? Your brother's death, my..." I trail off, glancing down and scrunching my brows, trying to remember the Devereaux legacy. I'd check my notes on my phone as a prompt, but I refuse to embarrass myself in front of her or endure the horror of her pity.

Her eyes widen with the realization that I'm having trouble recalling something, but she quickly schools her expression into that unreadable mask again.

I internally thank her for it. God knows I despise the questions that usually follow my internal struggle.

I get to the point with a heavy sigh. "I need to find it, too. It's ... personal."

She's silent for a beat too long, and I internally panic.

"And why would I trust you?" she asks finally, her voice hard as the marble and stone around us, but there's a spark in those beautiful eyes.

There it is—the chink in her armor that I've been waiting for.

I rake a hand through my hair. "You're so suspicious of us, but what's your endgame, Elara? Why go through so much trouble for a dusty old necklace? Yes, Kaspian told me," I add when her lips curl at the word *necklace*. "You let that slip, probably because you have no idea what the fuck is going on. My brothers are blunt force trauma rather than subtle finesse. But you're smarter than that."

Her eyes darken, warning me to tread carefully.

"Think about it," I say, sensing if I push any further, she'll bolt. "I'll give you tonight to consider my offer. After that..." I shrug. "There's no telling what Cav will do. Force you live with us until they get the answers they want, probably. And you don't want to be trapped in our basement. Believe me."

Elara physically recoils like she can't believe I've so calmly threatened her.

"Fine, Axe." She hisses my name like a curse. "Then prove it by giving *me* an answer right now."

I expected as much. I incline my head, waiting.

"Who are the Vultures?"

The name reverberates my bones, though offhand, I don't

know why. When someone mentions the Vultures, is it fear, respect, or hatred that pricks me?

I'd have to defer to my notes.

I clench my jaw at doing that in front of her.

She seems to read it in my face.

Her full, glossy mouth twists ever so slightly. "Consult your 'brothers' about it, then give me your answer. I'm sure they'll have their opinions on it, too."

Elara doesn't sneer and call me stupid at my vacant expression. I stare at her, befuddled not in my usual way, but in complete and utter shock that she wouldn't take the window to shame me and storm away.

It immediately makes me suspicious. Nobody with a brain takes the less effective option in an argument without considering the benefit. No one is actually *kind* deep inside.

"Oh, and tell Cav I met Tempest. That should give him something to chew on before he barks at the rest of his dogs to drag me back to your lair."

With that, she saunters off, her hips swaying just enough for me to admire her ass.

Fucking Wraithwood girl.

CHAPTER 17
ELARA

I'm still shaking when I return to my dorm and drop my bag on my bed.

It isn't easy being under Axe Devereaux's exhaustive scope. Those smokey gray eyes and ash blonde hair warn of a fire, yet his soft voice assures safety.

He's the only one who's approached me like a human being, and yet my instinct warns me to be the most wary of him.

Would they really tie me up in a basement?

Axe said it like he was asking me for my notes on the lecture. So offhand and *expected*.

That can't be an actual threat, though. They may be members of a secret society, but that doesn't give them free reign over campus to ... kidnap people, does it?

But what do I really know about them?

I pace my room, my thoughts swirling as images of the week's events replay themselves in my mind—Tempest and the Vultures, Kaspian and Cav's dark warnings, Axe's sudden appearance, and then Wilder's glib attitude.

"Aargh!"

I scream into a pillow, frustrated at the vile web wrapping me tighter with each passing second.

The Cimmerian Court shrouds itself in secrecy, and I only know about them through hushed whispers and urban legends.

All I know for certain is that they took a vague, then intense interest in me, but it's good to know my suspicions about the Vultures possibly being enemies of the Court were correct. Axe's pause, then long stare, told me all I needed to know, especially after noting Tempest's inability to say "the Court" without disgust twisting his lips.

I pick up my phone and text Darcy.

Hey, do you know anything about the Cimmerian Court kidnapping people?

Sorry, but the time for subtlety is over. If anyone can allay or heighten my fears, it's her.

I lay back on my bed, staring at the ceiling. The fan turns above me, casting shadows on the wall from the setting sun outside. It does nothing to cool me down or ease my growing paranoia.

No, I'm just shaken up by this entire ordeal, that's all.

I've been through worse.

After an hour of self-care in the shower, then in front of the mirror like the Elara from last week used to do, Darcy still hasn't texted back. But I saunter down to the dining hall for dinner, wearing my make-up like a piece of armor, more confident and cleaner than I've felt all day.

Let them see how little they affect me.

Sasha—who has ironically become my only compass of sanity in this place—sits at our usual table. She glances up from her phone, eyebrows arching at my newfound poise as I scan the entire hall.

"What has gotten into you?" she asks as I set my tray down and sit.

"Oh, you know, just had a friendly chat with Axe Devereaux," I say casually, as if it were the norm to be counseled by the resident phantom.

Her fork freezes mid-air.

"You mean *Axton*, Axe? As in the one who's more likely to become a serial killer than graduate? The man that can make a grown frat boy cry with just a look?"

I felt my cheeks heat, but I shrug her off. "He's not so bad."

I may have left out the part where he threatened to kidnap me in an alcove, but that's neither here nor there.

"You sure about that?" Sasha asked skeptically, her brown eyes narrowing. "He's one of the shadiest guys at school. No one really knows his family background or how they made their wealth."

Shady?

That much is true. Even my Google searches provided little information about him and his family, except for his mother's suspicious disappearance years ago, which investigators had deemed voluntary. But that was it.

No pictures of his father or any extended relatives

surfaced either. It seems like Axton Devereaux III appeared out of thin air when he enrolled at Titan Falls University two years ago, and no one ever questioned him about it.

Sasha doesn't buy my nonchalance, but thankfully doesn't insist any further. "Well, I'm glad I caught you, because you're coming tonight."

"Tonight?" I ask, startled.

"The Titan's Brew event," she reminds me. "You promised you'd come and support me, right?"

Right. I'd forgotten about her open mic night at the town's most popular bar.

"Of course!" I smile wide and wave my fork for emphasis. "I wouldn't miss it for the world."

Sasha rolls her eyes but smiles. "Cool, see you then."

I wave her off as she leaves with her tray and turn back to my food. I tell myself it isn't dread that's clenching my stomach. The Titan's Brew would be a delightful break from all this Court and ruby business.

And as if on cue, my phone buzzes.

Hey there, dollface, sorry for the late reply. The CC doesn't need to kidnap people. They're more into blackmail and coercion. Why do you ask?

I exhale with relief and type out a quick response. **Just curious.**

I hit send just as my phone vibrates again.

. . .

Careful. They don't like nosy people in their affairs.

I shiver, despite myself, as chills numb my arms.

I power off my phone before any more dread could settle in my bones, promising myself I'd have a normal night out.

A few more people I know take seats around me, and I laugh and catch up with them, pretending that I haven't been ensnared in an ancient conspiracy the past week.

After finishing dinner and waving goodbye, I finish an overdue paper in my room, then take the time to dress in a tight pleather cocktail dress and shiny black heels. Sasha left a while ago, so I order a car and head downtown.

The Titan's Brew is just as packed as I imagined it would be, with students spilling onto the sidewalk and music drifting into the cooling air. Couples walk past arm-in-arm, laughing, and drunken giddiness wafts all around me.

A cluster of sophomore women stumble by, jostling me out of the way as they double over in belly laughs reserved for their inside joke. One of them calls, "Sorry, Elara!" over her shoulder before her friends' arms snake around her and she surrenders to more laughter.

That used to be me.

Rarely was I without a circle of friends, all of us linking arms and tripping onto the street after a full night at Titan's Brew. Sasha was always the first to fall, and I'd be hiking her up by her armpits before she topples me like a giant because I'm laughing too hard to help her.

God, I miss that. A lot of it was an act, sure, a way to protect my past by appearing carefree and joyous, but the belonging wasn't fake. The hysterical glee was absolutely real.

Tonight, I'll join them. I'll forget about the Cimmerian Court and their dark secrets. I'll aim for normal and focus on Sasha and how we used to be, and of course, her dreams of being the next Taylor Swift.

I internally recite this mantra as I elbow my way through the crowd, my eyes scanning for her familiar head of black curls before spotting her near the stage.

"Hey! Over here!" she shouts, waving me over to an empty seat at her table.

"Incoming!" I yell over people's shoulders, weaving through the crowd with two drinks in hand.

The heat from their bodies and dim lighting reminds me of high school parties. My chest constricts at the memories of the ones Maverick used to have at our house that he kept having to shoo me out of before I shove them down. Tonight is about Sasha.

"Thank you," she sighs gratefully, sipping from her drink. "I really appreciate you coming."

"Of course," I smile genuinely, clinking our glasses together before downing half of mine in one go. "You deserve a night of pure admiration."

"Cheers to that." She clinks back before downing hers as well. "And speaking of what we deserve—"

"No," I cut her off, my hand up in protest. "No matchmaking or meddling tonight. I'm here for one reason only, and it's not to be a pawn in your dating schemes."

Sasha grins, unrepentant, but the emcee takes the stage and her attention shifts.

"Ladies and gentlemen, welcome to open mic! First up, we have Sasha Sterling!"

The room claps as Sasha stands, her natural stage presence

in full display as she waltzes on stage, strumming her glittery pink guitar once before looking out at the crowd. Her eyes meet mine with a single twitch of nerves before she relaxes her shoulders and begins.

Soon, her sweetened voice fills the speakers, singing her own acoustic renditions of popular tracks.

Closing my eyes, I surrender to the beautiful rhythm. The sound becomes my tether to reality as Sasha's voice dances above the ambient noise of the crowd. Resisting the pull of my own turmoil, I lean back in my chair, letting her words of almost-love and heartbreak wash over me.

Then, an intrusive shadow eclipses the warm light of the overhead lights. The sudden shift in brightness yanks me from the solace I'm chasing.

My eyes snap open. A tall figure obstructs the warm yellow glow of the overhead fairy lights stapled into the wooden rafters, casting an almost ethereal halo around his sharp features.

My heart freezes for a fraction of a second as a familiar face descends moves and ruins the halo.

Axe, his ash-blond hair stark against the dull glow of the bar, looms over me.

He regards me with his smokey eyes that hold a hint of a ruse beneath their icy veneer. He doesn't speak, but simply angles his head in a silent greeting.

In an instant, my battle-worn resolve to be normal again crumbles with him so close and all-too-real against the back-drop of a loud, crowded bar.

I swallow hard and set down my glass on the table with a clink that I seem to hear above all else. Searching for words, my gaze shifts from his face to his tense hands, resting deceptively casually on the back of an empty chair across my table.

"I didn't expect to see you here," I manage to say. "This doesn't seem your vibe."

His lips curve into a small grin that doesn't reach his eyes. His gaze remains locked with mine, unblinking.

"Can I join you?" he finally asks, breaking our silent duel.

A myriad of warnings blast through my mind, from Darcy's cryptic texts to my earlier conversation with him.

But despite it all, I gesture toward the unoccupied chair with feigned nonchalance. "It's open."

His mouth widens to a full-fledged grin that makes me wince. His face seems unsuited for smiles.

I shift uncomfortably in my chair. His attention never wavers off me as the latest chorus of Sasha's break-up revenge song bounces cheerily around us.

My breath hitches when he reaches over the table, stretching his hand toward mine. Before I can react, he clasps my wrist, ostensibly to get my attention.

His palm is ice cold. Shivers blast from the area like a dropped nuke, but I don't complain when they reach my core, cooling the heat that's been pooling there since he put me in his shadow.

"You look like you could do with a refill," Axe says, lifting my empty glass with his other hand.

Confusion flickers through me at his unexpected offer.

I blink at him once, then twice, before nodding. "Yes. Sure."

I watch him push off the table and stride away towards the bar, wondering what the hell he's up to now.

Despite myself, nervous anticipation chokes me like a vise

and I hold my breath until he disappears into the throng of students lining up for their drinks.

The weight of his absence hangs heavy in the space between us, and I keep shivering despite the heat radiating from the bodies dancing nearby.

Just as Sasha strums the last note on her guitar and the crowd erupts into hoots and applause, I feel another cold swipe against my arm. I glance down to see droplets of condensation splattered on my skin and look up in surprise.

Cav, standing sentry beside me like he's my protector.

Or enforcer.

He sets down two glasses filled with an amber liquid that sparkles in the low light. But just as my survival skills finally kick in and I'm about to stand and leave, his hand grips my shoulder firmly, causing me to plop back in the chair, gasp in surprise, and look up. His eyes lock onto mine—predatory, exhilarating, dangerous.

"Drink," he orders.

His grip on my shoulder tightens, not painfully, but enough to convey the message that he's in charge.

"Why? Are you trying to get me drunk?"

My voice is surprisingly steady as I gesture towards the two glasses.

There's a cloying scent wafting from them. Whiskey, by the smell of it.

My nostrils flare slightly and my stomach churns. "Or have you spiked it in order to get me out of here and lock me up the easy way?" I shift until I'm angled toward him. "Which is interesting, because you strike me as a guy who likes a girl who puts up a fight."

Cav's stare narrows, his gaze as sharp as a blade under the moonlight.

His lips stretch into a half-smirk, half-snarl. "You've proven you're not one to shy away from danger. And I'm not here as a servant." He jerks his chin towards the glasses he's set before me. "So, drink."

I take a moment to cast a glance around the room. It's filled with college students, all intoxicated by the music, alcohol and each other. None of their attention falls upon Cav and me. I don't know where Axe went, not that he'd provide any buffer.

This was probably all part of the plan: unnerve me, then rattle me.

How long they'll commit to that before outright snatching me is anyone's guess.

All I know is, they're loving the game.

Cav's hand remains on my shoulder, reminding me I am still very much under his scope.

A part of me wants to bolt from this situation. A larger part of me knows that it's futile to resist him here in a public place with hundreds of witnesses. Cav's revered on campus.

As if to provide evidence, my usual group of friends for fun nights out, also here to support Sasha, arrive and spot me almost immediately. Ariel makes her way to me first, but halts the other four the instant her gaze moves infinitesimally to the right and spots Cav. After saying something that barely moves her lips, they all retreat into the crowd.

"So distrusting," Cav's smooth voice says above my head.

He takes both glasses and swigs from each of them before setting them back down. "There. If you're drugged, then so am I."

"How chivalrous," I murmur.

I reach for one of the glasses before quickly downing half of it.

Cav watches me for a moment longer before abruptly pulling his hand back.

His lack of touch should leave me feeling relieved, lighter. Instead, I feel ... empty where there once was a powerful pressure.

He picks up the other whiskey. The overhead lights cast long shadows over Cav's features, turning him into a daunting fiend in a raucous bar, which seems to have taken a turn for the oppressive.

The crowd of students has become merely a blurred backdrop to Cav's unyielding stature.

Heat spreads through my veins as I put down my glass. The whiskey burns my throat, but it also brings about a flush spreading where goosebumps once did.

Cav leans in close, his breath warm on my cheek and his voice deep, silky, and mocking. "Do you need a moment to catch your breath?"

My heart hammers in my chest. The adrenaline rush is intoxicating, stronger than any drink.

"Yeah," I admit, my voice barely above a whisper.

If I turn, I'd catch his lips after scraping my cheek on that stubble of his.

How would he taste? As frosty as a mint? Or would the heat of his mouth be more of a spice, a burning cinnamon?

Cav nods, his mouth brushing against my cheek before he straightens, offering a brief, knowing smile.

He raises his glass towards me, as if in toast, and tips back his head to take a long sip.

The seconds stretch into minutes as I watch him finish his drink. His gaze remains on me the entire time, pinning me in place with its lethal precision, daring me to look away or flee.

But I don't. Instead, I lift my glass once more and meet Cav's chilling stare as I down the rest of my whiskey in one gulp.

Cav leans a hand on the top of a chair, studying me for a moment longer.

He finally speaks, each word deliberate and precise. "You know why I'm here."

My stomach knots at his declaration. The Cimmerian Court's machinations hang heavy over me—their plans for me as clear as they are terrifying.

But during my less turbulent moments in my dorm room tonight, staring at my fan spinning and spinning, I'd come to a conclusion. One that works for both of us. They want the necklace, and I want answers. One can't be had without the other.

Dread pools in my stomach. I wish I had more whiskey to gulp so I could set it on fire and burn it to ashes.

Sasha's next song starts up, a slower number this time, and the crowd quiets down to listen. I use this distraction to compose myself and finish my drink.

Cav mistakes my expression for something else. His arm shoots out, and he grabs hold of my wrist.

"You're not leaving," he states with cold certainty.

"I'm not going anywhere, Cav," I reply, almost daring him to tighten his grip.

He doesn't, but his hold remains firm. "What are you playing at, butterfly?"

My lips twitch in a bitter imitation of a smile. "*The crows crooked the maid, and the maid crooked the crow, and they all lived together in the tulip tree so.*"

Cav blinks, momentarily taken aback, before returning to his usual sleety expression. "And what is that lovely poem, exactly?"

I shrug nonchalantly, giving him a look that says I know more than I am letting on. "Just an old nursery rhyme, nothing that would interest you boys."

He narrows his eyes and releases my wrist as if it's set on fire. I rub it discreetly, trying to appear like his eyes aren't as scathing as his grip.

"I believe the lady has had enough of you, Cav."

A tanned, sinuous arm reaches over my shoulder, plucks the empty glass from my hand and sets it on the table with a thud.

Wilder slips into view, taking the chair neighboring me on the other side. After sending Cav a snarky smile, he winks at me.

"She's a big girl," Cav says coolly. "She can make her own decisions."

Ironic, considering he was just commanding me like a general.

Wilder's hazel eyes twinkle under his mass of unruly chestnut waves. "Can she? What do you say sweetwitch, do you want me to kick his ass on out of here?"

He leans forward until his hand rests on my bare knee. His sheer, dry heat seeps into me like the hottest desert. "Tell me what I want to hear and I'll kick him in the balls so hard, he'll be choking on testicles."

I roll my eyes, but I don't pull away. Instead, I sit frozen as a statue, caught between two equally dangerous men.

Cav on one side, his eyes as cold as an arctic tundra and Wilder on the other, grinning like he just committed the perfect murder.

Not one of these men makes the Cimmerian Court look weak. Not even when they're joking.

Yet, part of me is tempted to say yes, just to see if Cav's smug expression will falter—even if it's only for a second.

But it's Kaspian's voice that finally snaps me out of my daze.

"Gentlemen," he drawls as he comes up behind Cav, his voice a sensual purr. "You're both so uncouth. Can't we have one civilized night out without resorting to threats?"

Kaspian's attention burns through my polished veneer, affecting me in ways I don't want to think too hard about.

His gaze slides across to Cav and Wilder before returning to me. His green eyes glint with amusement and something else. "Surely, if you two can't share, Elara will choose me instead."

I force my discomfort into a glare. I hiss, "What makes you think I'd choose any of you? This isn't *The Bachelor*."

Kaspian chuckles, as if he hasn't just suggested what I think he did. "*The Bachelor* is so outdated, Elara. If anything, I'd at least upgrade us to *Survivor*. Much more our style. Think of the drama."

Before I can rebut, Axe appears like a vapor behind Wilder.

"Here's your drink, Elara," he murmurs, sliding a glass of ruby-red wine across the table towards me.

When his eyes meet mine, I feel like I'm drowning in the ocean—an endless gray sea where my fear and yearning drown in each other.

He doesn't touch me, but his gaze caresses my skin, scorching me alive.

Axe's fingers brush against the delicate stem of the wineglass before he takes a spot next to Cav. And I instantly realize he's not just standing there, he's taking up a position.

I'm surrounded.

Every part of me is alert as their excitement builds around me, like some savage pack circling its prey.

They've blocked me from Sasha's view, their tall, broad bodies blocking me from *everyone*.

How is that even possible in a packed bar?

Nerves frayed but my resolve ever present, I take a sip of the wine. It tastes like sin on my tongue. Rich and full-bodied, with hints of smoke and spice that linger on my palate.

Wilder continues to grin at me as if he's won some sort of invisible game between us, while Cav's gaze hardens. "You should know better than to cross us and go to the Vultures for help."

I pause, my wine glass halfway to the table.

"I didn't go to them for help," I say. "They came to me."

"Why."

Most people would phrase it as a question. Not Cav.

The four of them circle me, their eyes feasting on mine as if daring me to deny them the chase.

They're all so different yet so similar—dark, hungry creatures who seem to know exactly what I was up to but want me to say it anyway so it gives them the excuse to bite.

"I was..." I have to think fast. "...looking into my heritage."

"And you ended up at the mines on the outskirts of

town?" Kaspian inclines his head, his green eyes shifting from charming and inviting to calculating in an instant.

"Yes, we track you," he says to my surprised expression. "Nothing you have is off-limits to us. Your room. Your belongings. Your car."

I inwardly curse. Of course they'd have access to all the creepy electronics this fucked up world has invented and get to use them for their own twisted pleasure.

"How about my bathroom?" I retort with a rush of defiance. "You like seeing that, too?"

Kaspian doesn't flinch. "Parts of it."

Frustration, the sheer feeling of ineptitude when battling them, makes me want to vomit.

Wilder's fingers trail down my arm slowly. "You're as intriguing as you are frustrating, sweetwitch. There aren't a lot of people who'd continue sparring with us at this point."

"None alive," Axe murmurs, but I catch it.

"What's that supposed to mean?" I ask. "You're going to kill me?"

I mean, these guys clearly aren't just rich boys enjoying power-plays in their secret club. But killers? Murderers?

My throat nearly closes up. I turn to Cav. "Did you have something to do with Maverick's death?"

Cav's eyes crinkle with a soulless smile. "No, sweetheart. We wouldn't be playing with you so much if we had."

I shrink into my seat, unsure if that was an answer or not.

I feel Wilder's hot breath against the side of my neck, his lips trailing up to nip at my earlobe, sending another thrall of shivers through me.

Damn him. Damn *them*.

"Such a tease," he whispers, his voice rough with desire. "Probably should've warned us you were going out tonight."

His hand slides on my knee and starts tracing slow circles just above the hem of my skirt. "I would have prepared myself for how fucking irresistible you look tonight."

I bat him away, but his fingers curl like spider-legs, claiming their spot and daring me to test his fangs.

My body doesn't hate it. Heat, slick and wet, practically coats my inner thighs even as my mind screams at me to end this.

The scent of alcohol and sex fills the surrounding air, making it thick and heady as if we're all drowning in it.

As if in sync, they all press closer.

Kaspian's fingers dance across the back of my neck before trailing to untie the clasp of Maverick's simple gold necklace, pulling it off over my head with a wink. "Not the one we're looking for, but pretty and warm from your skin. I think I'll keep it."

"Give that *back*," I snarl.

Axton bites his lip as he watches me intently, seemingly aroused by their playful assault.

Cav doesn't touch me, either, but his watchfulness is pure, mind-fuck intimidation. "You've pushed enough of my buttons. Getting the Vultures involved in what is purely *our* territory, *our* find, was too much. You're coming with us. Now."

"I'm not going anywhere—"

And just like that, Wilder's large hand clamps down on my thigh, digging into the muscle. Kaspian re-winds the necklace around my neck.

"What a pretty garrote it makes, too," he muses with enough nonchalance that I whimper.

"You wouldn't," I stutter. "You wouldn't do anything to me in public. I'll scream."

Cav chuckles at the same time Kaspian tightens his improvised noose. Wilder digs in and I wince.

"Do you really believe I don't have the power to pay off every single one of these people?" Cav says. "Or get the TFPD to turn a blind eye? I have all their resources and more, butterfly."

"And if that doesn't do it," Axe says quietly. "We can always go after your friend. Do you think she sings so beautifully when she's in pain?"

I cut him a long, hard glare.

I knew it. I *knew* he was the worst one.

The ambient music changes to something darker, more brooding, as if playing along with the mood.

Through the small cracks between their bodies, I see people grinding against each other, writhing on the dance floor.

I no longer have an eye on Sasha, but I have no doubt Axe does.

Wilder releases his painful clamp, his palm sliding under my dress and fingers pressing into my exposed panty line. His pupils dilate when he finds me wet.

"You really think I can't fuck you right here and now?" he asks in a whisper, his voice rumbling like thunder from his chest. "With all these eyes on you?"

Wilder bites my earlobe, then licks it as if to taste me. He knows I'm already turned on. Knows how much he affects me and uses it against me so well.

Cav smirks at Kaspian before I feel Kaspian pull down the zipper at my back a few inches. His touch is feather-light, but it sends a shudder through me as he exposes more skin to the cool air-conditioning of the bar.

Kaspian's hand slides over my shoulder and slides into the front of my dress, cupping one breast as if to test the weight while his thumb rubs over my nipple.

Though I try to choke it down, the moan comes out anyway.

Wilder gives me a lopsided grin as he retreats, then takes my hand and pulls me to a stand. Kaspian zips me back up with a quick yank, his expression when I glance over my shoulder schooled into apathy.

I struggle against the others, pushing against them, but they don't budge, their grips iron clamps on my skin.

Sasha's clueless about what's going on. Is that a good or a bad thing? Probably great for her, but it's not looking so good for me.

They all escort me out of the bar, never breaking stride. The chilly night air dissolves the sweat beading on my brow, my back. The smell of cigarette smoke and late-night greasy food fills the air.

There's an unmarked car waiting for us at the curb.

Wilder grabs my ass in a tight grip. "Get in, or I'll have to show everyone on the street what happens to little girls who play hard to get."

I get in the car, trying to keep up a straight-faced front, but inside, I'm quaking.

The drive is long and silent except for the low hum of the engine and roads flying by outside of the window.

I keep my eyes on Axe's arm resting behind me on the

backseat. It's heavily muscled and tense, anticipation rolling off him in waves.

Wilder growls at me on the other side when I try to move away from them even though I'm in the middle, possessiveness stretched thin over all their faces, including Kaspian and Cav in the front.

Oh, Mavvy, I plea silently to my dead brother. *I know I put on a brave front. I know I said I could handle them. But I really wish you could help. Because I think I've gotten myself into a world of trouble.*

CHAPTER 18

AXE

Breath rattles in Elara's lungs as we haul her across the threshold of Thornhaven Estate.

The interior grandeur of the manor looms like the mouth of Hell, its ornate windows wide and staring, the walls gilded with fading portraits, the floors made from the rarest marble.

But it's the basement that will swallow her whole.

Elara pushes against Kaspian and Wilder's hold, eyes wide open, revealing metallic pools of fear.

"Where are you taking me?" she whispers.

I steel myself against the tremor in her voice. She is nothing but a heartless mission. Just like the other ones before it.

I tried to warn you.

I keep silent.

We descend the staircase to the basement, a sunless underworld where even the air feels like a frigid caress. Flickering candlelight can't penetrate the depths of the corners, casting slivers of light seeking escape to the outside.

It's a place designed for one purpose: to isolate and intimidate.

A dungeon.

"Please," she whispers, but the plea only feeds the anticipation coiling inside me.

The basement is an icy sepulcher, the chill seeping through the stone walls. I feel more than see Elara's shiver, but the way her nipples press against her dress's fabric is a telltale sign of her body's involuntary reactions.

There's no warmth here, no comfort.

"Stand here," I instruct, my voice echoing slightly as I motion to a stone slab in the center of the room.

Kaspian and Wilder release her, letting Elara be the one to walk forward of her own damning volition.

This could have been avoided, I almost tell her, then remember she's more aware than our usual victims. We gave her so many openings, tireless options to avoid this—

I'm pretty sure we did.

One eye twitches as I work on recall rather than reach for my crutch—my phone full of reminders.

I redirect my focus on the space around her beautiful form. We will force Elara to bend to our will, but there is no way she should be here.

Elara stands in the center of the room, her fiery hair cascading over her shoulders, a stark contrast against the icy pulse of the underground chamber. Her dress clings to her like a second skin, an unintentional provocation that stirs the beast within me.

My men flank me, our dead calm a shared language of intent.

The wide basement contains sparse furnishings except for

a few pieces that hint at the unspeakable. Chains dangle from the ceiling, their purpose as clear as the fear in her eyes. Old, brown stains decorate certain corners and dig into cracks we couldn't fully remove the blood from.

Elara stands in front of the slab, folding her arms around herself and shivering while Kaspian winds around the rectangular room lighting the torches on the wall.

"I've changed my mind. Let me go, Axe." Elara's gaze meets mine, a flicker of desperation shining through.

Muscles shift behind my expression. The kind I'm not used to, the ones that want to be sympathetic. But it's not enough to change the course she's on.

"By the time we're done with you," I say, moving closer until I can feel the heat leeching from her body, "you'll be begging to give up all your secrets."

My words are an embrace and a curse, wrapping around her like the very shadows creeping around the room.

The others hang back, observing me at what I do best.

Elara's eyes, wide and calculating, flick between us, trying to read our expressions as if they hold the key to her escape. But there's no leaving—for any of us. Not until we get what we came for.

I step closer, and my hand reaches out, hovering just above her collarbone.

With one swift motion, I grip the front of her dress between her breasts and jerk her forward. Her breath catches, the sound echoing.

Kaspian comes up behind her and drags her zipper all the way down while I pull at her front, loosening the dress, revealing inch by tantalizing inch of her freckled, porcelain skin.

The heavy dress plops at her feet.

"Please..." she whispers, her trembles almost becoming a full-on seizure.

Elara's pupils are blown, that ethereal amber non-existent, pitch darkness taking its place. Her nipples are small and piercingly hard, making it unclear whether she's pleading for mercy or challenging us to proceed.

"Shh," I say, fingers grazing her lower lip. "Words won't save you here."

She's trembling, yes, but there's a defiance as she remains standing, a refusal to be broken so easily. I respect that even as I plan to test it.

"Turn around," I command softly.

Obediently, yet with a spark of rebellion still alight in her blackened gaze, Elara turns.

She's a vision of vulnerability, her back exposed to Cav and Wilder.

Kaspian draws in a sharp breath once he gets the full frontal of her. His eyes turn nearly as pitch as hers.

Taking her baby blue thong between my fingers, I pull it down with deliberate slowness, allowing the tension to build. It falls, joining her dress, and I can't help but admire the view down here.

Her pussy ... a small racing stripe of pubic hair glistens in the firelight.

I blink, my vision complete with a full, pert ass. My tongue darts out, readying to part it and lick, until Cav clears his throat in warning.

Right. We're not here for sex. I'm to do the mission. To break her, not bend her over and—

"Axe," Cav snaps.

I blink again. My hand twitches toward my phone so I can recall Cav's instructions exactly, but I clench my fingers before I can.

This is what I do. It'll be fine.

"Beautiful," I say to her gruffly, because even in this plot of terror, truth has its place.

Elara's bare skin glows as if lit by fire underneath her skin, her nakedness a stark display of our control versus her lack thereof.

Yet, there's power in her exposure, too—a silent assertion that while we may have her body, her spirit isn't so easily conquered.

"Take a good look, gentlemen, and remind yourselves why we can never rebel," Cav says, seeming to read my mind. "Because this is what defiance looks like. Stripped bare and alone."

"I'm truly sorry, Elara," Kaspian says, his expression the most sorrowful I've ever seen it. Who knows if he actually means it. "Every secret has its price, and yours is no exception."

"Lie down," Cav orders in a deceptively soft voice, then purrs, "Or would you prefer one of us force you to?"

Elara breaths hard through her nose, brows crashing together like she's weighing her options, but ultimately, she cedes. The numbers are not in her favor.

Her flesh pebbles against the chilled stone as she submits and lengthens her body along the slab, the air in the basement clinging to her skin like an unwelcome suitor.

I reach under the stone and find the restraints with practiced ease, the leather straps firm against her delicate skin. The sound of the buckles clicking into place is a symphony to my ears.

Elara's exposed now, her breaths coming in quick gasps that do nothing to warm her environment.

Securing the belts against her wrists, I then loop more around her delicate ankles, spreading her legs to each corner.

Each fastening is a promise of restraint, a statement of our control over her willful spirit. The straps are an extension of my grip, binding her not just to the cold marble slab beneath her, but to *us*.

"Comfortable?" I murmur, though we both know comfort is far from what's intended here.

She shifts ever so slightly, the restraints allowing only a tease of movement, enough to feel the bite of her bindings.

"Remember," I say, voice low as I lean closer, ensuring every syllable drips with clarity. "Obedience is your path to freedom. Resistance..." I let the word hang, a heavy weight in the charged atmosphere, "...will only sink you deeper into depths you can't imagine."

From the corner of my eye, I see Wilder nodding, his expression undeniably ravenous. Cav's lips curve into a smile that doesn't quite reach his eyes, while Kaspian stands stoic, clasping his hands in front of him, his gaze never leaving Elara's form.

They're readying to take their leave, to let tonight play out as planned.

And I remember it. The plan.

"Each of us will return, one by one," I say, my hand trailing over the contours of Elara's ribs under her breasts, a gossamer touch that promises more. "And each encounter will test your resolve, your ability to hold on to the information you clutch so tightly."

With a final glance that must sear terror into her skin, I signal the others. They exit the basement without a word, allowing me to be the first.

It's my usual benefit, the promise they make, every time I submit to the Sovereigns' punishment and receive another scar.

It hurts them to have me endure it more than it does me. I don't mind the scars so much. Each one is a reminder of what I've done.

However, I don't have to think of that right now, or try to remember anything further. It's just me and Elara now, our breaths the only sound.

"Choose wisely, Elara," I say, stepping back to admire the restraints' craftsmanship—and the beautiful canvas they secure. "Because every next word you utter has a consequence."

"Tell me where the ruby necklace is," I demand.

I keep my attention locked on her face, fighting the urge to indulge in her body, searching for any flicker of surrender. But she remains silent, her lips pressed together in a stubborn line that only fuels my commitment to break her.

"Wrong answer," I say as I reach into my pocket, pulling out the pink satin underwear I'd taken from her room—the one she'd worn the night I watched her from a distance, our plans for her taking shape.

Her scent still lingers on the fabric, a sweet, intoxicating blend that has plagued my thoughts since the moment I broke into her sanctuary and claimed this prize.

With deliberate slowness, I bunch her panties up, keeping my eyes fixed on hers. The air between us crackles with such ice, I'm surprised we're not creating snowflakes.

Then, without breaking eye contact, I push the cloth past her resistant lips, filling her mouth with the taste of her own hidden desires. Her muffled protest vibrates against my palm, a sound that sends a dark thrill through me.

"Next time, don't make me ask twice," I growl, baring my teeth close to her face.

I step back, watching as conflicted emotions dance across Elara's features—trepidation mingling with an undeniable glint of arousal. It's there, beneath the surface, a heat that belies her cool exterior, pooling against the hard stone under her pussy.

It twists something deep within me—a carnal desire for domination wrestling with an unexpected respect for her resilience against us.

"Every time you deny me, every time you resist," I continue, the rough timbre of my voice betraying my rising arousal, "it will only escalate pain over pleasure."

At least, I hope so. This girl is nothing but conundrums against my already over-worked mind.

"I'm coming to realize," I muse, almost to myself, "this isn't just about the ruby Heart, is it? It's about dominance. And whether you admit it, part of you craves to submit."

Her eyes flash with indignation even as her body betrays her, responding to the raw authority in my voice, the terrifying presence I exude.

It's a heady power to know that, despite her predicament, I affect her.

A shocking revelation, considering I send most women running.

Elara shifts against her bonds, the leather straps creaking softly. The sight of her restrained and gagged form makes my hard-on throb painfully.

Yet, amidst the embers of lust, I sense a kinship forming, a recognition of the kindred spirit that exists within her.

And it's because of that crucial observation that I change tactics.

"Give up the location of the necklace, and I promise you the rewards will surpass any fleeting pleasure you've known," I tempt her. The allure of surrender against the instinct to fight. "Would you like me to eat you out, right here and now? Fuck you in your pussy while you're locked down and splayed out, then cum in your ass?"

I really get into it. "Or would you like the others to join? Cav would want to replace your gag with his dick, of course. Wilder will take any hole promised to him, but Kasp ... well. He doesn't skew toward traditional methods, if you understand what I'm saying."

The last woman Kaspian had under him checked herself into a mental institution directly after. But I leave that detail out, mostly because I can't remember all the details.

"Or, continue to defy me," I reason, "and discover depths of sensation that will leave you gasping, writhing... begging, and not in a good way."

A shudder courses through her, and I can't help but wonder if it's born of anticipation or apprehension. Likely both. In our Court's underworld, the lines between horror and passion blur to nothingness. We get what we want. Literally anything.

And this pretty doll is our new obsession.

I pull the underwear out of her mouth, requiring more dexterity than I expected when I try to avoid her snapping teeth.

"Never," she hisses through a sneer, the word a venomous promise.

Her refusal should infuriate me. It doesn't. Her strength is an aphrodisiac, her willfulness fueling my need to conquer. Despite her precarious position, bound and naked on the marble slab, there's an inferno in her that refuses to be quenched.

"Such determination," I murmur, tracing a finger down her flushed cheek, watching her struggle to maintain composure while trying to chomp my fingers off. "It will make your eventual surrender all the sweeter."

Elara jerks her head away from my hand and scrunches her eyes shut with frustration, but her rapid breath betrays the conflict raging inside her.

I sigh. "Well. I tried to be gentle."

Then I retreat, nodding permission to the cloaked figure entering the room.

CHAPTER 19
ELARA

The chill of the basement bites into my skin, the marble slab beneath me sucking out every ounce of warmth my adrenaline hung on to when surrounded by all four of them.

I'd clung to it while Axe stuffed my underwear down my throat and looked at my pussy like a meal, licking his lips like a barely tamed beast.

He stalked around me, waited patiently for me to break from the fear of being naked, restrained, and spread out enough for him to climb on top of me and do what he wanted.

But he didn't. He … he admired me from a distance, like he was painting each part of me into his memory.

I wonder if, even now, he's typing on that phone of his, desperate to retain the image of my crucifixion.

This cavernous hollow reeks of despair, much like my own heart.

Vulnerable in my nakedness, I can feel each droplet of remaining sweat that trails over my skin.

Because it's not just the cold stone that has me trembling.

A sound disrupts the silence, footsteps echoing off the walls, heralding another one of them. My breath hitches as a figure materializes out of the curved stone archway, evil outlined by flickering torchlight. The hooded robe he wears appears black at first, until the small flames around the room reflect the deep, malicious purple the closer he comes. The cloak sways gently, as if caressed by the stale air of this forsaken place.

He steps closer.

Against my mind's orders, my pulse races. A porcelain mask with endless black holes for eyes comes into view. It's a blank canvas of eerie perfection, hiding any hint of emotion or identity.

It makes me have no fucking clue which one of them it is.

"Where is the ruby necklace?"

His voice is a distorted melody. Altered.

But there's an allure within the menace, an undercurrent that vibrates against my senses, sending an involuntary tremble through me unrelated to the atmosphere.

I bite back a whimper, meeting where I imagine his gaze lies behind the mask.

"I don't know," I reply, my voice a mix of feigned ignorance and genuine confusion. "I only learned about it when you demanded it from me the first time."

The ruby necklace, a gem as red as my bloody family history, a symbol of mysteries I'm entwined with yet still unraveling.

An ominous chuckle escapes him. He reaches out, his

fingers dancing across the skin of my thigh, light as a feather but laden with threat.

"We'll see about that," he murmurs, and I know whoever it is smiles behind that mask.

He bends toward me.

"You may not know much about it, but you know where it is," he hisses. "So *where is it?*"

His voice is like a slithering serpent's tongue, dripping with the promise of toxins.

But there's something else beneath it all, a tightness I can't quite place. Desperation? Need? What is it about this jewelry that sends these guys into a frenzy?

I shake my head, trying to deny him the answer he seeks. "Tell me why you want it."

He makes an indistinct sound in his throat.

He trails his hand up to my stomach, fingers dancing over my sensitive flesh. A tingle courses through me at his touch. It makes no sense, but feels so wrong at the same time.

Then he moves lower still, grazing my breasts with gentle fingertips before circling my nipple, then going in for a sudden pinch that twists sharply.

Pain shoots through me and I cry out, but also... something else. Arousal?

I cut off my cry despite the mix of emotions assailing me. His hand continues to wander lower still, brushing against my pussy teasingly before squeezing between my legs roughly enough to make me gasp.

His hot breath fanning across my cheek sends shivers cascading into my breasts as growls out the same question: "Where is it?"

Despite myself, I squirm under his touch. The contrast

between the cold stone and his probing hands sends mixed signals to my brain, creating a maelstrom of need and denial. Each caress is a question, each probe a demand for answers I refuse to give.

"Tell me why you want it," I whisper stubbornly.

I won't let him see how his twisted ministrations fracture my resolve, how they peel away at the layers I've built around myself.

His index finger pauses against my cleft. He huffs out an impatient breath, then answers, "Its existence has cursed my family for hundreds of years. My ancestor wronged yours, and now *I* am the wronged one. I need this necklace, butterfly, to maintain my place in the Court. And believe me when I say I will do so much more to you than simple misfortune if you don't give me what I want tonight."

His action belies his nasty threat. His finger slides down, curves, and enters easily. My voice betrays me with its traitorous response, a choked moan.

I close my eyes tightly, trying to anchor myself in the storm he conjures, but I am adrift in a sea of sensation, caught between the need to escape and the urge to sink deeper into the abyss he offers.

His thumb circles my clit, presses down, pinches.

"Now that I've given you want you want, answer my question."

Something wrenches inside of me, a mix of confusion and yearning that leaves my insides feeling like molten lava flowing too quickly in my veins. I don't want this darkness. I don't crave it. But damn, he knows how to make me feel things... confusing things...

The porcelain mask glints in the flickering light, an

emotionless visage that fingers me and conceals the man I know is Cav.

Butterfly.

His other hand, cool but unsteady, as if he too fights an inner battle, glides down the valley of my breasts.

I should feel repulsed and terrified by this carnal interrogation, yet there is something about the way he worships my body that stirs a dangerous longing within me. Is it the artistry in his touch or the enigma of his cloak and mask that draws such forbidden pleasure from this unknown layer of myself?

What did Sasha say? *Have you ever slept with a guy in a mask?*

I get it now. I *so* get it.

"You want me to stretch out our time together, don't you?" he says, almost musically with his altered voice.

"Tell me about the Vultures, then," he demands, pressing down on my clit while pinching hard on one nipple with a possessiveness that sets every nerve ending alight. "What did they want with you? And why would you consort with them over us?"

I gasp, arching as much as I can. "I don't—I don't know them," I stammer, the truth pouring from my lips like liquid metal. "Tempest approached me first."

"Tempest," he repeats, the name rolling off his tongue like a curse.

There is a history there, a storm beneath the calm of his voice that speaks volumes of the Court's enmity toward the Vultures.

Yet, even as his hands map my skin, painting my territory with my own juices, I am acutely aware of the power he wields—not just over my body, but over the secrets that pulse beneath my flesh, waiting to be unlocked by someone as skilled as Cavanaugh Nightshade.

I'm helpless to stop the whimpers that follow. The heat between us crackles like a roaring fire, consuming all reason and restraint. The dungeon's chill is a distant memory now.

"Elara," his voice is a dark melody, distorted by the mask and whatever he's using to disguise his voice, yet it vibrates with an unmistakable authority that resonates deep within my core. "The ruby Heart—what do you know of it?"

My mind races, but the pleasure he invokes muddies my thoughts. "Sarah Anderton, it's related to her. It's related to Sarah Anderton," I pant out, the truth serving as a fragile defense against his sensual onslaught, as my mind races and the pleasure he evokes muddles my thoughts.

"Good girl," he soothes, even as he re-situates himself between my legs, bends down, and presses the mouth of his mask against my pussy.

I can feel the moisture between my legs coating the cool, hard planes. Feel his exhale against my sensitive clit.

He moves his head up and down, creating friction between me and his mask.

The way he's rubbing me—so rough yet so restrained—makes me want to beg him for more even as I try to hold on to my defenses.

"Where is it?" he demands against my pussy, those two black holes staring at me over my pubic bone.

I whimper in response, unable to form any coherent words as he thrusts his fingers inside of me, stretching me wider than I thought possible, hitting that spot that has me crying out in pure bliss.

He grunts low in his throat, taking pleasure from my reaction even as he manipulates my body for his needs.

The sound of my leather restraints creaking reverberates against my cries. I'm helpless to stop both.

And then, I hear it—the sharp intake of breath, the rustle of fabric against skin.

Cav, the unyielding Court member, pleases himself, driven to the brink by the sight of me laid bare before him.

It's obscene, the sound of his self-indulgence mingling with my moans, and yet it is achingly erotic.

"I don't want to tell you," I whisper in stutters, my voice breaking on the word, a plea for mercy or perhaps for more. It's hard to tell where one ends and the other begins.

"If not us, then who?" he presses, his movements relentless. "Who tempts you away from me, butterfly?"

"Nobody," I breathe, lost in the labyrinth of sensation he creates. "There's only you here, only this."

A growl rumbles from behind the porcelain façade, a sound of animalistic satisfaction that makes me respond in kind.

I hear him cum, throaty with release, his upper body sagging as he spills all over the floor.

Then a vicious, resounding, "*Fuck*," before he pulls his fingers out of me and storms out.

Cav's abrupt departure leaves me shaking, vulnerable even in the aftermath of our encounter.

The sconces cast long shadows across the dungeon, and

within moments, they morph into the shape of my next tormentor.

Another cloak steps forward, his presence filling the void left by Cav. There's a glint in this one's black holes, a gaze that speaks of violent intentions and the greed to dominate completely.

"Which one are you?" I ask hoarsely. "Wilder or Kaspian?"

He ignores my question.

"Let's see if you're as resilient with me," he murmurs, and I steel myself for the firestorm that's about to come.

As he looms over my head, I catch sight of his hand moving down to cup my breasts, squeezing both of them roughly with a single grip. It stings and hurts, pulling at the flesh like they're not mine anymore.

"You've got quite a mouth on you," he drawls with a voice like whiskey and smoke.

He doesn't alter his voice. Maybe because Cav tried and failed as soon as he said too much.

The masked face comes close to my chest. He adjusts it, exposing his mouth so his tongue can flick out and taste the droplets of sweat beading on my neck before trailing over my collarbone.

His hand finds its way between my legs again, roughly rubbing at the swollen heat between them.

"Tell me where the fucking necklace is," he says.

His rough fingers probe deeper into my folds, as if searching for the answer hidden within my wetness. I'm growing wetter still under his touch and I wriggle, both with temper and craving.

"Am I going to have to fuck you for the answer?" he asks, more to himself.

His free hand grips the opposite side of my waist harshly, pulling my hip against his hard cock as he continues to probe my folds with unforgiving fingers.

My body responds to the touch, clenching.

The smell of him—smoke and sin, musk and sweat—envelops me, turning the air heady and sweet.

His hooded head lowers towards my breast. I can hear the steady rhythm of his breathing against my skin...

I try to push away from him, but our bondage holds me tight, unable to escape even an inch.

Wilder—it must be Wilder—groans slightly against my flesh as if savoring every moment of this power trip over me. His tongue circles my nipple before flicking it between his teeth, extracting a moan from somewhere deep within me.

I twitch under his attentions, instinctively pulling away from the overwhelming sensations, only to feel his other hand clamp down on my hip, holding me still.

I buck against him helplessly, feeling the unyielding stone beneath me grow damp from our combined needs.

"Tell me where it is," he demands through gritted teeth, "or I fuck you right here and now."

Part of me wants to tell him and stop this. Another half is tortuously curious about how far I want to push him.

I'm so swollen, so tied down and desperate, and I can't even touch myself to relieve the ache.

"It's just a necklace!" I sob out, my voice cracking. "Why is it so important? Why do you want to torture me for it?"

Wilder laughs under his breath.

"Just a necklace," he mocks. "Was Maverick 'just a death'?"

He climbs onto the slab, then kneels until his legs are on either side of me. His mask and hood make his weight even more threatening.

I say in a tight voice, "That's not the same—"

"It's up to you how far I step over the line," he says, exposing his dick through the folds of his robe, hard, thick, and lined with veins.

He presses his tip to my pussy, seeking entry where Cav left off. I hiss at the unexpected intrusion but also crave it; the feeling of being owned by these men is unlike anything I've ever experienced before.

I wince at the pain that twinges through my abused flesh, but also feel a dark famine in my chest, prowling, seeking, *growing*.

I could stop this. Give him the answer. Maybe he'd back off as soon as he had it. Possibly he wouldn't and fuck me, anyway.

He grabs my hair roughly, pulling my head back to expose my neck as he chuckles menacingly.

"I see it in your face," he says. "Wondering whether you'll cry for mercy or beg for more."

He doesn't wait for my reply.

Wilder pushes past my resistance, stretching me wider until he's fully sheathed inside me with one powerful stroke that takes what little air I had left in my lungs. He moves with a starved rhythm, pounding into me in short, sharp thrusts.

Despite myself, I arch into Wilder's ungracious pounds.

Wilder growls low in his throat and bites down on my shoulder, displacing his mask.

It stings, but also awakens something primal within me.

I wonder if the others are watching.

His teeth marks seer into my skin as he pounds into me harder still—an aggressive claim on my bound body that I'm stunned to discover writhes for more of his punishing touch.

"You're ours now," he grits against my swollen skin. "Every inch."

My heart races as Wilder's hard length slams into me, claiming me with each ragged thrust. His teeth graze my shoulder again as he bites down harder this time. I gasp at the sting that shoots through my skin and down my spine.

Right to my pussy.

He makes a growl of satisfaction that sends tremors cascading over my body. Wilder's hand finds its way between us, rubbing against my clit in a steady rhythm that only serves to heighten the ache between my legs.

He doesn't ask for anything more—he demands it.

As if reading my thoughts, he pulls out of me suddenly, leaving me aching and empty.

"Where is it?" he whispers, his hot breath sending chills up my neck despite the heat coursing through the rest of me.

I shudder under his lack of touch and try not to betray how much I crave him, how much I crave this darkness he weaves around us both.

"Please," I whisper, knowing full well they'll never hear me beg like this again once they get what they want from me.

Wilder releases a frayed sigh. His eyes burn with an intense heat that has been building for far too long.

"Your choice, sweetwitch. Because we left the worst for last."

CHAPTER 20
ELARA

In the too-quiet dungeon, where the scent of rot and rusted chains intermingle, I wait with bated breath for the inevitable.

The flickering torchlights dance along the walls, casting long, ominous arcs of light that seem to sway in anticipation while the air grows dense, a palpable change that whispers his name before my ears catch the sound of his steps.

Kaspian.

My body betrays me, nipples tightening with a blend of cold and a fear-tinged arousal. Wilder is the flame that always promises heat, but Kaspian … he's the ice to extinguish that fire.

Footsteps, soft but sure, approach. I crane my neck, straining against the ties binding my wrists above my head.

Kaspian emerges from the archway. He hasn't bothered with a mask, but the hood over his head shrouds his face.

"Elara," he says, and his calm voice is a melody that resonates through my bones.

The mere sound of it should send shivers of dread through me, but instead, there's a perverse thrill that spikes through my core.

"Kaspian," I greet with a tremor in my voice that I can't control.

Attraction? Panic? They're so entwined now, I can't separate one from the other.

His hands emerge from the folds of his robe, and even in the meager light of the chamber, I can see they're steady, unyielding—the hands of a man who shapes the world to his will. His fingers are long, capable, tipped with the promise of both pleasure and agony.

"Are you ready for me?" he asks, and there's no mistaking the challenge in his words. He has the worst of their fetishes, Axe said. "You made it through three of us, but I promise you, not me."

"Am I ever truly ready for you, Kaspian?"

My question hangs between us.

He steps closer and I can't help but arch toward him, drawn to his particular shade of black.

There's starvation in his silence, with a predator's patience that tells me he relishes this moment just as much as I dread and crave it.

Heat pools at the base of my spine, a cruel reminder of the denied release Axe, Cav and Wilder refused me. Wilder's taste for control has left me swollen, each pulse between my thighs a silent scream for completion.

Kaspian circles me, his steps measured. I feel his gaze like a physical touch, inspecting the marks of possession that litter my body—bite marks that sing with a dull ache, nipples tender from relentless pinching and biting. He's savoring the sight, feasting on the evidence of my torment with an appreciation that borders on reverence.

"Exquisite," he murmurs, and there's a murky pleasure in his voice.

I'm positive it's not just the sight he enjoys. It's the state I'm in—raw, exposed, teetering on the brink of madness from the need to climax.

"Help me," I whisper, my voice hoarse.

But my plea dissolves into a gasp as Kaspian leans down, his breath cool against the heated welts on my skin. His lips graze a particularly sensitive bite mark, and I moan, caught in his merciless grip.

"Patience," he chides softly, straightening. "I know better than to rush the experience."

I swallow hard, bracing myself for what comes next. I can't see his face, but I sense the shift in him, the air stilled by a hunter's intent.

He retrieves something from the folds of his robe, and my breath catches. A set of gleaming clamps. My heart pounds, forceful beats that jump against my skin.

"Stay still," he instructs, his voice low and commanding.

I bite back the retort that I have no choice, barely suppressing a whimper as he attaches the first clamp on my nipple, a bolt of lightning shooting through me, followed by a surge of unwanted arousal.

When he affixes the second, I can't hold back a cry, the intensity of sensation skirting the edge of unbearable when he pulls wires from under the slab and attaches them.

"Perfect," Kaspian breathes out, satisfaction lacing his tone.

He stands back, admiring his handiwork, the clamps a glinting testament to his unique brand of cruelty.

"Kaspian..."

My voice breaks, a mix of entreaty and accusation.

But there's no room for reproach, not when every movement tugs at the clamps, sending endless waves of sensation coursing through me.

"Shh," he soothes, his fingertips playing over my abdomen in a mockery of comfort. "You'll thank me later."

The words are a promise, a vow that despite the torment, he will guide me. And as much as I loathe to admit it, a part of me believes him—craves the twisted fulfillment only he can provide.

And as he watches me squirm, a deity presiding over his supplicant, I realize that, in this moment, I am utterly and irrevocably his.

"Look at you," Kaspian murmurs, his voice low and husky, dripping with sinful promise.

He stops just out of my line of sight, his presence a phantom's stroke against my heated skin.

A click sounds in the silence, and then the soft hum of machinery fills the room. The stone slab tilts, slowly raising my hips upward, presenting me to him almost upside-down in an obscene offering.

"You are a portrait," he breathes as boots stop just short of my nose, his hooded figure both menacing and magnetic.

The clamps attached to my nipples ache with a sweet torment, each subtle movement amplifying the sensation until it's all I can feel—all I am.

Kaspian's eyes, piercing and endless, lower to mine.

He doesn't touch me, not yet, and the absence of contact is its own form of torture.

"I'm not going to ask you where the necklace is," he says, his words wrapping around me like silk laced with steel. "Because I honestly don't want you to answer yet."

I gasp at a new, sharp bolt running through my nipples, the machine guiding electricity through the wires and into the clamps.

My sharp inhale is laden with unspoken pleas. I need release, a reprieve from this edge that he's brought me to and left me teetering on.

Then he moves, a shadow come to life, and his hands are suddenly everywhere—exploring, claiming, igniting.

"Time for me to paint."

His fingers find the tender spots left by Wilder's teeth, pressing just enough to elicit quick intakes of breath that don't provide any oxygen.

But it's when he adjusts the clamps, twisting them infinitesimally until the electric current is constant, that my world narrows to a pinpoint of blinding pleasure-pain.

"Kaspian!" I cry out, the name torn from my lips.

"Shh, Elara," he whispers, his voice a velvet darkness coaxing me closer to oblivion. "I'm here."

His breath tickles my inner thighs. I'm throbbing, *pulsing* for him, the ache building to such unbearable levels that I sob.

Kaspian presses his lips on the inside of one thigh, so close to my pussy, but not close enough.

That's when the tears come, blinding me as they run up my face.

"K—Kaspian, *please.*"

I'm on the precipice, so close to the abyss of insanity, when his mouth descends on my pussy.

His kiss is a paradox—both punishing and tender—and as his lips move in a dance as old as time, he ups the electricity running into my breasts.

Kaspian gorges on my nectar like it's his last meal.

A groan escapes him as he savors the taste. His tongue does the work of a cock with its own mind, diving, curling, flicking.

I'm so blacked out from sensation, my eyes are rolling into the back of my head, but not so much that I don't notice his dick spearing out from his cloak and headed for my slack-jawed mouth.

"All of you belongs to me," he growls against my soaked pussy.

Kaspian thrusts his erection into my mouth, forcing it past my teeth and ramming the back of my throat until we're locked in a brutal 69 position, contorted and twisted like some monstrous creation. Even Frankenstein himself couldn't have imagined such depravity.

I gag, fresh tears running over old ones. I have no way to defend other than to bite down—

"Don't you fucking dare," he rips his lips off my pussy and snarls. "I'll turn the current up if you so much as graze me with a molar. You do as I say. And I say, deep throat me until you're choking on my cum."

Kaspian grips my jaw and yanks it wider, burrowing his dick deeper inside.

The smell of his musk fills my nostrils, an intoxicating mix of power and domination that makes me dizzy.

I gag on his cock as he thrusts it deeper into my throat,

feeling it scrape along my tongue, and all I can think about is how much I crave more.

His hips pump in rhythm with his own perverse tune. The electric current from the clamps on my nipples zaps through me with every thrust that sends shock-waves of pleasure throughout my body.

I'm strangled by his cock, desperately trying to take as much of him as I can, to breathe, as he moves against me.

Every nerve ending is on fire as he devours me from both ends, leaving me unable to think or do anything except surrender, endure, survive, *and fucking have multiple orgasms.*

The head of his cock presses against the back of my throat again. I want to hold him there, to keep feeling that burning sensation, but I also need air.

Kaspian controls the pace, plundering my mouth while teasing my clit with his tongue.

My hips buck against nothing but air as he pumps into my throat harder, faster. My hands are tied above my head, rendering me helpless against wave after wave of rapture washes over me.

The room is stifling hot now, and Kaspian's dark presence looms over me like an ominous bird of prey.

He seems to know just how to work my body, pushing me to multiple brinks without mercy. My pussy clenches around his probing tongue and I try hard to come *right now.*

What happens after this sweet torture, what will be next, I can't predict, but I'm sure it will be even worse.

"Where is it?" he murmurs against my pussy, halting his assault.

The clamps immediately stop their buzzing.

I moan in disappointment so hard I almost cry. And not the sweet, sorrowful wails of loss. No, I'm going to ugly cry.

I was so close.

"Kaspian ... please..."

"You know exactly what to say to make me continue, darling." He brushes sticky, wet tendrils of hair from my face, his cock glistening, dripping with unspent cum. "Tell me what we want to hear, and I'll give you your release. I'll fucking make you *convulse.*"

"Hidden... in the library," I sigh between ragged breaths, the secret spilling forth amidst the crescendo of my surrender. "Behind the portrait... of Lysandra Wraithwood."

"Good girl," he praises.

The pride in his tone is nearly my undoing.

Kaspian doesn't take a moment to savor his triumph. He doesn't hold his breath in shock or even smile.

It's like he knew he was going to get it out of me. It was only a matter of time.

Kaspian steps back, savoring his power over me.

Then he pulls a small remote from his robe pocket and presses a button. The slab returns to its horizontal position and the clamps release, their hum filling the room as they retract.

I howl at the sudden lack of sensation, my body aching for more.

Was it a lie? Will I never find release? Am I about to be dropped off at my dorm, naked and wailing and begging for cock?

That is what they've reduced me to. I should feel shame, but all I want to do is mourn.

Kaspian moves behind my head, unbuckling the bindings on my wrists.

It takes all of my willpower not to plead with him for more as he frees me, my arms heavy and aching from their restraints.

In one swift motion, he slips off his hood. The carved planes of his face are striking in the light—harsh angles and a sardonic half-lift of his lips that guarantees more torment than Wilder or Cav's teeth-baring grins.

My heart won't stop pounding as I clench and unclench my fists, feeling the blood rush back into them.

Kaspian runs his fingers down my arm, tracing goosebumps left on my skin by his touch.

"Are you sad, sweetheart?"

His words are like a knife twisting in my gut, digging deeper into the raw wound of my emotions. I refuse to answer, gritting my teeth and clenching my trembling lips as they struggle not to give in to his manipulation. Tears prick at the corners of my eyes, threatening to spill over and betray the humiliation I'm trying to hide.

The question hovers like a dark cloud, taunting me with its simplicity, daring me to admit defeat.

But I refuse. I will not let him see me crumble, even as my heart feels like it's being crushed in a vise.

But a choked sob escapes my throat.

"My sweet, sweet girl," he says, toxic promise dripping from each syllable. "Only the women I've shattered may ride my cock."

Before I can even process his words, Kaspian grabs me roughly by the hair and bends me over, forcing my upper body onto the slab where I had been confined moments ago.

In one brutal thrust, he sheaths himself deep inside me. The stretch is both torturous and divine, filling me up as if he were made for this spot.

My pussy clings to him, my lips parted in a silent gasp at the intrusion that feels both violent and right.

He sets a punishing pace, pistoning into me, the slapping sound of skin on skin filling the room. His hand finds my hip, the other still knotted in my hair, gripping me possessively as he plunges in and out with a vengeance.

I still have his taste on my tongue. I meet his thrusts with desperation, unwilling to let go until he gives me release.

My thighs quake under him; sweat beads on my skin as he increases speed.

"*Yessss...*" I moan into the moment, unable to hide my wanton need.

A growl rumbles from Kaspian's chest as he slams into me faster still, ramming my hips into the stone's edges, which will surely leave angry bruises.

I bite down on my bottom lip to stifle my cries, wanting nothing more than to beg for more, but knowing better than to challenge him now.

With a sharp tug on my hair, Kaspian pulls my head back to until it feels like he's trying to tear it off.

And at last, finally…

Sharp pain and pleasure explode in a cacophony of impacts that has me shrieking his name.

But as the echoes of our shared ecstasy begin to fade, a heavy stone settles in the pit of my stomach.

The necklace, a mere trinket with the power to shift destinies, pulses to the forefront of my mind with malevolent intent.

In that moment of vulnerability, I'm forced to realize the gravity of my predicament. I steel myself against the rising tide of uncertainty.

I don't know if revealing the whereabouts of the necklace will lead to salvation or ruin—for Kaspian, for me, for everyone entangled in the twisted spires of the Cimmerian Court.

CHAPTER 21
ELARA

A sudden wind howls through the archways of the dungeon like a coming storm, the kind that I'm positive sweeps through this entire manor with wild abandon.

Kaspian left me. Alone, panting and bent over cold, gray stone like a broken doll. Time blurs as I try to catch my breath and command my trembling legs to steady again.

I don't know how long I had to compose myself until Axe strides back in, carrying a navy cashmere blanket over his shoulder and a damp cloth in his hand.

Without a word, he uses the cloth to clean me, the warmth soothing against my back, the jagged impression of teeth marks, my chapped, burned nipples.

When he reaches between my legs, I yelp—shock twining with pain.

Softly, carefully, Axe continues until he eases the ache and I go quiet.

When he's done, he swoops the blanket over my shoulders, the incoming billow of fabric sending a fresh wave of trembles through my over-used body. He catches me as I buckle, wrapping me in a soft cocoon, and lifts me into his arms and carries me out of the basement.

His touch doesn't feel like duty. It carries an unspoken assurance of comfort, my first human connection after being led down here like a lamb to slaughter.

And yet I dragged the torture out as much as I could, reveling in the various ways they wanted to sexually torment me, curious about who would do what.

What does that make me? A masochist? A child with a secret trauma she never dealt with? Fucked up? Or is it just that I'm more sexually free than I ever realized?

Once Axe climbs three sets of stairs, his arms a constant, secure pressure under my body, he passes me on to Wilder, whom I side-eye the entire time Axe sets me down and gently pushes me forward.

I'm almost certain Wilder's going to take me into his bedroom and use me as his personal plaything for the rest of the night.

Turns out, I'm right about him guiding me into his room, which is almost as raw and untamed as himself.

Rugged, yet strangely welcoming, with the large wrought-iron bed that seems too small to contain the chaos within its rumpled sheets.

There's no headboard. Instead, the bed is positioned to face the room openly.

Large, curtainless windows offer a view of the estate's untended areas, thorns growing so tangled, they press against some of the panes. In one corner, there's a custom-built, heavy-duty punching bag, well-used, hanging from a metal chain.

That's all I manage to document before he rips the soft protection of the blanket from my body and pulls scented cotton over my head.

My head pops out, cutting short my muffled scream, and I realize it's just a shirt—an oversized, plain black one that smells like cut grass and pine. He settles it over me with a teasing tug at the hem and then drapes the blanket back over my shoulders.

"Damn, sweetwitch, you look good in my clothes."

With a firm hand on the small of my back, he takes me out of his room and into a common area on the same floor, complete with a professional kitchen.

"Sit." He jerks his chin to the long table at the center. "Our chef is making you some tea."

I'm unable to hide my quizzical expression. "Tea?"

"Yeah." Wilder reclines in the chair across the table, threading his hands behind his head. "Your throat must be parched."

My lips purse to the side. In any other situation, I'd think of a proper retort, but my mind is too addled by the past few hours—and what I've given up to these men.

I told them where the necklace is.

I can't believe I did. Their torture was relentless, but couldn't I have held out? What more could they have done to me?

As if in answer, Cav appears in the doorway, his hands nonchalantly tucked away in his pockets, though experience has taught me that there is much more to those hands than just muscles, tendons, and bones.

With Wilder and Cav now so close, the space around me

pulses with an energy that makes my skin tingle and my breath catch.

Wilder's shirt caresses my frame, both as an oath and a reminder.

You are not in control here.

"Elara," Cav's voice is a low thrum. My posture goes rigid.

I think I liked it better in their sex dungeon.

His dark presence fills the room, snuffing out Wilder and Axe's previous gestures of kindness.

The soft glow of the kitchen lights casts deep hollows across his angular face, his eyes reflecting a duty that both frightens and beckons me. There's a barely restrained ferocity about him, tempered by an elegance that belies his capability for ruthlessness.

A lock of my hair falls across my cheek at my head turn, and Cav steps toward me. His proximity is overwhelming, the heat of his body like a matchstick striking against my body.

"Your hair," he murmurs, lifting the strand away from my face with a gentleness that contradicts the coolness in his gaze. "It glows in this place like a single candle in an arctic storm."

His fingertips graze my neck, a touch feather-light.

The scent of him—cedar and mint—fills my senses.

"You don't have to be afraid anymore," he whispers near my temple, though whether it's a reassurance or a warning, I can't tell.

"Don't I?"

The question slips out. His nearness is intoxicating, dizzying, and for a moment, I lose myself in the turbulence of his attention.

He searches my face as if looking for a sign, a confirmation that I've given all I had to give. "You gave us what we wanted. There's no more to be done."

The light wind his body emits as he takes a seat beside me is like a velvet caress that seems to stroke the very air between us.

Wilder's hawkish scrutiny never strays from Cav and me, as if he's etching every detail into his memory.

His gaze, sharp and rapacious, slices through our conversation.

"Now, was that so difficult to do?" Wilder says to me.

He discreetly shifts, adjusting himself under the table.

In the back of my mind, the ghostly sensation of Wilder's touch haunts me—a map of teeth marks etched onto my skin beneath the grip of cold stone and unyielding straps.

And then Kaspian enters, sauntering through the doorway freshly showered in a gray sweater and dark denim jeans with the ease of a satiated man. But his smile is all edges and corners. He's the one who broke through my defenses, who peeled back layers of flesh and fear to lay bare the truth at the heart of me.

Bastard.

But a talented one.

"Quite the picture we make, don't you think?" Kaspian drawls, condescension shading his gaze.

There's something else there too—an earnestness that clings to the fringes of his slanted smirk, as if he's glimpsed something on me that's more precious than the coveted ruby necklace.

"I'm so glad my intimidation, kidnapping, and torture amuses you," I challenge, my voice steadier than I feel.

Kaspian tilts his head, regarding me as a cat would a fish

flapping helplessly on land. "Everything about this situation amuses me, Elara."

His eyes hold mine, and in them, I see a flicker of genuine curiosity—a rarity for someone who usually views people as codes to be cracked and files to be encrypted.

"Even your resilience," he adds in a low voice.

I jolt at the compliment. It's as if he recognizes the strength it takes to sit here, ensnared by the desires of potent men, each with their own dark yearnings and sordid histories.

I concede, but mirror his tone, "Don't mistake your amusement for triumph, Kaspian."

His lips twitch.

They can give me tea and soft blankets, but they're bound by needs darker than the night outside these stained glass windows.

"You can go, Elara," comes a gruff voice from the far corner. "After your ... tea."

Axe lingers at the edge of the room, a silent force that pulls my gaze even as I try to resist. His posture is rigid against the windowpane, the muscles in his jaw working quietly as if he's grinding down the words he wants to say.

"You don't have to stay," he clarifies, brows taut.

I'm not supposed to want Axe, not after the way he dominated me in the depths of this estate's underbelly, but the craving is there, insistent and throbbing like a pulse.

"I think I'll wait," I say, folding my arms on the table. Threading my fingers helps to quell the shaking. "And I'd like some soup, too."

All four of them go still.

It's subtle, each one of them barely stirring the air around their bodies, but I've surprised them with my request.

"You're ballsy, beastie," Kaspian says, his smile slow and satisfied as he reclines on one of the head chairs. "Why would you ever want to lengthen your time with us?"

His stare shines like he knows exactly why.

"Because I'd like some answers. Trust cuts both ways, and I gave you access to a precious heirloom," I start, my voice gaining strength as I pull the blanket tighter around my form. "Why do you all want my necklace so badly?"

The question smolders. Their secret—that they have more reasons to seek the ruby Heart than mere greed or power—scents the air like sulfur.

I see it flicker across their faces, the hesitation, the calculation. It's unlike them to take part in *quid pro quo's*. They have no responsibility to tell me anything now that they know where the jewel they've worked so hard for is.

The power I'm using to try and convince them is only my experience in the basement. I have to believe ... to hope ... that I wasn't the only one in the thralls of different, breathtaking emotions that stripped me bare.

It wasn't simply about domination, control, and release.

To me, there was also *connection*.

"Because." Kaspian finally breaks the silence, his voice smooth but edged with something that sounds like extreme caution. "We all have our chains, beastie. And the ruby Heart... it might just be the key to breaking them."

Wilder nods, a fierce glint in his eyes that speaks of a burning need for something. "That ruby means salvation for me, a chance to rewrite a legacy smeared by dishonor. The Sovereigns will no longer punish me."

Axe adds quietly, turning away from the window to face

me, "Each of us has a debt to pay the Sovereigns, a wound to heal."

The anguish in his eyes now seems tinged with a flicker of hope, as though the ruby Heart could stitch together the frayed edges of his own fragmented mind.

Their admissions lay bare in the space between us, and for a moment, Thornhaven's opulent quarters feel like a confessional.

The tension is broken when a thin, bearded man in a chef's coat exposing his tattooed neck and forearms strides in and sets a steaming teapot in front of me.

And a bowl of split pea soup.

The sweet and savory scent of the soup wafts under my nostrils, sending a growl more bestial than Kaspian's new nickname for me through the room.

I thank the chef, my eyes not on him but cast to the ceiling, wondering where the cameras are. Did he hear my request?

Cav nods his thanks before the chef disappears, then refocuses his attention on me, that invincible smirk on his lips as he reads the suspicion on my face.

"There is no surveillance in our wing. Yet." Cav indicates Kaspian. "Well. There were. But Kasp felt the need to blind the Sovereigns from our comings and goings with a constant loop of a benign video."

"Sovereigns?" I repeat. I keep hearing the name, yet the boys never explain it. I taste the strange word in my mouth as I spoon a rather large portion of the piping-hot soup into a shallow china bowl. The scent permeates my senses, momentarily blanking my mind with its promise of nourishment.

"Sovereigns. Consider them the kings of the Cimmerian

Court," Kaspian clarifies, staring across the room and out the window in almost absent-minded boredom. "It's what we call our superiors."

Wilder adds, "The ones who pull the strings—those higher up the food chain."

His gaze remains riveted on me, a stark challenge against my questioning.

"Charming," I comment, lifting the spoon to my lips despite the tremors running through me.

The soup tastes like heaven, a rich harmony of flavors that sends warmth radiating from my core outward. I swallow more than just the food; I swallow down the uncertainty that threatens to choke me.

The Cimmerian Court. The ruby Heart. Kings and Sovereigns.

What century have I fallen into?

Kaspian reads my mind, his earlier disinterest replaced by a direct, focused stare that seems to penetrate my bones. "And just like the Medieval times, they're not exactly benevolent rulers."

"I see," I say simply.

If they think I'm going to cower because of their candid revelations, they're sorely mistaken. Then again, maybe they're counting on it.

"So, your kings are making you find my ruby because it's valuable to them, but you guys also need it to move higher in the Court's ranks? Or, no, that can't be it." I scrunch my brows over the steaming soup. "You're not initiates. You already have all the benefits of being full-fledged members in this underground medieval society of yours. So why would they need to threaten you?"

The once casual shuffle of movements now halts, as if my words have physically restrained them.

"You can mock the Court all you want," Cav says, his tone lowered to a terrifying level. "But you have no idea the violence they can unleash on you, your family, everyone you love." Cav cocks his head, as studious as an owl scouting fidgeting prey on the ground. "Or, maybe you do."

My spoon clangs into the bowl. "What is that supposed to mean?"

Cav blinks out of the strange heat coating his eyes, his pupils retracting almost voluntarily as he straightens. "We leave everything behind to become a part of the Court. We love no one. Trust none. And bow to the Sovereigns alone. That is why you are nothing but a trinket we've now grown bored with. You mean nothing. You *are* nothing. And now that I've gotten the necklace from you? You're worthless."

The chuckle that follows is a bottomless rumble that doesn't reach Cav's face. He leans on the table casually, but there's nothing casual about him.

Wilder's fist clenches on the table, a visual warning as deadly as a viper coiled and ready to strike.

But at who? Me? Cav?

Cav's words ring in my ears, but I steady my voice. "Your attempt to demean me seems rehearsed. It's not very creative." My heart pounds in my chest. "Perhaps you can insult less and explain more."

Cav peels his lips back—

"The ruby isn't just valuable—it's a test," Axe cuts in softly, immune to Cav's obvious glare to shut up. "Find it, and we prove our loyalty, our usefulness. Fail, and we're expendable...to be made examples of."

The expression on Axe's face remains unreadable, but it is clear in his body language he has become more alert when he includes Cav. "Elara endured our dungeon and survived. She deserves to know some things."

"Mm, she is shockingly clear-eyed and logical after what we did to her," Kaspian muses. "Can't say I expected that."

Cav's lips part to spit another retort, but I cut him off. "Before any of you try to belittle me again, just remember—I gave you what you wanted."

My unexpected challenge seems to catch him off-guard. Cav blinks but recovers quickly, his eyes narrowing at my audacity.

Yet the venom of Cav's verbal poison remains. It feels like a leaden weight anchoring me to the chair.

He's right, they owe me nothing, they've never owed me anything.

But I don't let it erode my resolve. I don't give them the satisfaction of seeing how much his words hurt me.

My attention turns to Wilder. Out of all of them, he's the most likely to keep talking.

"I gave you want you wanted," I repeat, "so please, tell me why an heirloom I never knew existed is now so important that you would hurt me for it."

Wilder's eyes twitch. A minute, but present, flinch.

"They may look like a bunch of self-titled monarchs playing dress-up, but the Sovereigns don't fuck around," he says. "When they say jump, we're already in mid-air asking how high on the way down. And this time, the ground's rigged with explosives."

I absorb their words, the pieces falling into place. "So, this isn't about gaining favor or securing a better position within the Court. It's about not being killed off."

Axe nods, solemn. "Exactly. And it's not just us at stake here. The Sovereigns, they have ways of making their displeasure known, reaching out far beyond just the one who disappoints them."

"Not simply that," Kaspian smoothly interjects, Cav glowering at him nearby. "They dangle this Heart in front of us as forgiveness. For the wrongs our families have caused in previous generations. We're legacies, all four of us, automatically given titles within the Court. We still undergo initiation, and if we endure it without complaint, we're guaranteed membership. These current Sovereigns, while they accepted our membership, they have very broken bones to pick with us. If we give them the Heart, those past sins will be forgiven."

I shake my head, absorbing the information. "And you believe them? What do *they* want with the necklace?"

Cav shifts in his chair, his hands clenched into fists on the table.

"I think that's enough for tonight," he says.

He stands, looking toward me with no emotion, before he abruptly turns to exit the room without another glance back.

Kaspian simply smiles, pushing back his chair. The light of the chandelier above us glints off the frost in his eyes.

"Enjoy your meal," he says with a coiled smile before disappearing into the hallway, too.

Axe raises his clouded gray eyes to mine. "Eat your soup, Elara. You'll need your strength. Once you're done, I'll get you home."

Before I can muster a response, Wilder stands abruptly

from his chair. The sudden motion startles me, breaking my train of thought. His long fingers clasp the backrest of my chair.

"Good night, all. It's been real."

In the silence that ensues after Wilder's departure, I'm left alone with Axe. He doesn't speak. His gaze fixes on a point beyond my shoulder, lost in thought. Instead, Kaspian's mockery and Cav's venomous words clang around the inside of my skull, relentless.

As I spoon the last of my soup, Kaspian's earlier words force themselves forward: *We all have our chains.*

Only then do I realize that despite their machismo and intimidation tactics, we're not as different as it seems. They're prisoners of their own circumstances just as much as I am.

Somehow knowing that makes me feel less alone.

I take a single sip of tepid tea, the honeyed sweetness a stark contrast to my experience with these men.

I am not in control here.

But maybe, just maybe, neither are they.

CHAPTER 22

AXE

The scent of sex clings to Elara as I lead her through the halls of Thornhaven, her slender form shrouded in a cloak, hood drawn over her face like a veil of privacy.

When we'd arrived with her, there was no one here. Since then, the manor has gotten more active, and we've made her appear like any other girl we bring to our private wing, invited in and escorted out completely obscured, including their eyes.

At the bottom of the immense staircase, the initiates on the first floor enjoy the privileges of the mansion, cloaks and masks tossed aside as they play billiards, take advantage of the unlimited bar, and splay out on the luxury sofas while musing over their choices of kneeling, blindfolded women lined up near the hearth.

The women made a willing choice to be here for Selection and signed non-disclosure agreements. Every one of them submits to the process of a mystery fuck with pleasure.

I notice Elara's roommate, Sasha, in the middle, her lips lifted in a glossy, trembling smile.

Sneaking a glance at Elara who is obliviously facing forward, I wonder if she has any idea what her friend gets up to.

The ladies the four of us choose never go in a line-up, and we've never perused one. Our selections are deliberate, well researched and reserved only for those willing to do one night with no questions, period.

Which is why tonight's activities with Elara were so unexpected. From any of us. Kaspian, Wilder, Cav and I aren't known to share … until now.

"Where are we? Who do all these voices belong to?"

Elara's voice is muffled, but the curiosity lacing her words is clear as the moon struggling to pierce the canopy above once we exit through the massive double doors.

"Returning you to campus, as promised," I mutter, my hands steady on her arm despite the thundering pulse in my veins.

I've successfully navigated Elara through Thornhaven's first floor, otherwise known as the Initiate's Playhouse. Not one of them turned their head towards us.

Kaspian, with Wilder by his side, has violently cemented that the four of us are never to be disturbed, especially while entertaining at home.

The thought of these freshmen or sophomores noticing Elara, even with just a curious quirk of an eyebrow, sends my vision into the black.

Potential members of the Court are rotten, spoiled souls, indulging in females like 5-star courses, rolling in seven-figure bank accounts and attending more vile, black-market auctions and events than I have the brain span to describe.

These current initiates, with all their flies down, are our future leaders, our corporate giants, our flagrant *fuck you* to democracy.

It's been happening for centuries, yet it never ceases to amaze me just how much power is given to pasty, weak-chinned, rancid rich boys.

We trek further away, where the wrought-iron gates stand like sentinels, their arrowheads reaching out like fingers ready to snatch Elara away from me.

It's here, far from prying eyes, that I finally remove the hood, her hair cascading around her shoulders, her amber eyes reflecting the wildness of a cat.

"Better?" I ask, my voice betraying nothing of the storm raging inside me.

"Much."

She blinks, her vision adjusting, unaware of how the sight of her fuels the fire within me.

"Does Sasha have to sign for me?" she asks.

I pause, staring at Elara with confusion.

Her forehead smooths, and she allows a quick smile. "You're saying you're taking me back to the dorms like I'm a package to be returned."

"Oh." I hold her by the elbow again and start forward in the direction of the steep, rocky incline that skirts the manor's outer boundaries. "No, I don't mean it like that."

I just need to get you out of here before the initiates notice you.

Loose stones and hidden roots make the descent treacherous, requiring my unwavering focus to guide Elara's steps, my hand firm on her arm.

She stumbles over the hem of her cloak and I swoop in to catch her before she crushes her skull on a jagged rock.

"Oh my—!" Elara clutches onto my shoulders like I'm the ledge keeping her from descending into Hell. "Wow, you're quick on the reflexes, Axe."

The warmth that follows my name, said with her voice, is like a large swallow of whiskey—heat, fire, pleasure.

"I do this all the time," I manage to say.

Oh, yeah. Great one, Axe. Maybe next time you can tell her you do good at good things.

Elara doesn't seem to mind my dumb response. She smiles, closed-mouthed but genuine, her hands squeezing my shoulders.

If I let myself, I could happily be encased in amber for eternity.

She blinks against my stare. "Um. You can let me go now."

"Shit," I mumble, righting her, then resuming my gentlemanly hold on her elbow.

"Is there any possibility I can take off this robe?" she asks.

"No."

Her lips tense at my blunt denial, but she doesn't argue. We've made clear she's to obey if she wants to get through us unscathed, but now it's just me.

I thought I couldn't wait to get her alone again. But now that she's not naked and tied down, I'm … fuck, I'm *nervous*.

"So you do this all the time, huh?" Elara gamely takes a wide step over a cluster of stones as we continue our descent.

"Thornhaven Manor is deliberately impossible to find unless you know exactly where to step."

There. That's a much better response.

"But didn't we arrive by car?"

"Yes."

She pauses in our careful strides for long enough that I realize I'm supposed to say more.

"The Sovereigns might not honor any implicit agreement to leave you unharmed. I'm taking you back on foot to avoid detection because we suspect the Sovereigns might have the manor and its surroundings under surveillance, especially the more obvious routes like the road used for vehicles."

Her brows jump. "Oh. Okay. You know, for a second there, I thought I was being escorted through the woods by Axe 3000—the latest in woodland navigation and technology."

I stare at her.

Then she lets out the most miraculous, dazzling laugh I've ever heard.

How can she laugh that way after meeting the Court? Enduring the four of us? How is that possible? No one finds lightness in us. Ever.

Elara's joy quickly cuts off, like I've choked it out of her once she realizes my answering expression isn't changing.

Her smile falls. "It's … it was a joke."

Her words strike a chord in me, and I find that her laughter, so unexpected and radiant, sends warmth across my body, like a campfire's heat on a snowy night.

My lips twitch into a smile at the fact that Elara seems capable of finding mirth in grim reality.

But the moment is fleeting.

"No more jokes," I say with a frown.

The knit between her brows tells me she expected that response.

The descent becomes steeper as we journey further from the manor. The cloak trailing behind Elara snags on a protruding root. I pull her back just in time before she trips over it.

"Careful," I warn, but there's no fear in her eyes, just fortitude and something else that I can't fathom.

"If you weren't tied to the Court, what would you be doing right now?" she suddenly asks.

My grip spasms against her elbow, the width of it fitting in my entire hand. "Huh?"

"Your Sovereigns like to dictate and rule over you, right? So if you could, what would you be doing instead?"

"That's a pointless question."

She doesn't falter. "Then, what's something you've always wanted to do but never had the chance?"

I frown. "That's the same question, just phrased differently."

"Fine. Is there a place you feel most at peace?"

Pulling at her arm, I force her to a stop. "What are you doing right now?"

Elara meets my unflinching glare. "Passing the time."

"I don't like this line of questioning."

"I can stop," she says lightly. "If you answer one question."

My gaze narrows, wondering what she's up to.

Instead of agreeing outright, I say, "You get one question."

She doesn't hesitate. "What do you wish people knew about you that they don't?"

"Why do you want to know?"

"That's not an answer."

"You didn't say I couldn't ask a question of my own."

Her lips pinch, caught in her own trap. "All right. I assume you know everything there is to know about me." She nods toward my hip. "Especially with that phone of yours and what you told me in the basement. The four of you had full access to my body and know my history better than even I knew. I figure I deserve to know a few things about you."

If the other three were with me, Elara's reasoning would be met with a swift *not in your lifetime, sweetheart.*

But they're not.

And I like her question.

After a moment of heavy silence, I answer, my voice low and tinged with bitterness. "Most people see me and think I'm slow, an idiot, because I have to repeat things to myself to remember them. It's like I'm constantly fighting to keep the fog at bay, to latch onto something solid in my mind. What they don't get ... what I wish they understood is that this struggle doesn't define my intelligence. Behind this face they've labeled as forgetful or dim, there's a mind that's always working overtime, trying to piece together fragments of every moment, every order, every face."

Her lashes lower, and she folds her arms, but her voice is gentle. "I already knew that about you, Axe."

My brows rise. At no point did I think she'd take the time to see behind my manipulations and orders to break her.

"Try again," she prompts.

So I do.

"There's more to me. Choices I've never been able to make, words I've swallowed, dreams I've had to bury. I've been a pawn for so long, fighting not to lose myself completely in the underworld the Court has pushed me into. Since I was a kid, they see the punching bag, then the tool, the weapon... not the man who craves a single moment of real freedom, not from the physical chains, but from the ones in here"—I tap my chest over my heart—"crafted by a lifetime of being told I'm nothing more than damaged goods."

Elara's brows come down and her face takes on an expression I can only describe as heartbroken. "Is that why you have memory lapses? You were abused so badly as a child, you experienced head trauma?"

Acid rises from my gut, scalds my throat. "One question. One answer. You got both. Let's go."

"Axe—"

She reaches for my arm as I twist away, my vision blinded with memories, screams, broken pleas. For a terrible moment, her hand becomes my foster parent's and I wrench away like I am that five-year-old again, and he is the undefeated giant.

And she falls.

"*Elara!*" I bellow as my heart leaps into my throat.

Time snaps and shatters into shards of frozen moments. I'm plunged into another section of my mind, one where I'm screaming the name, "*Mariana!*" and reaching out for somebody, my hands small like a child's.

I wrench out of it on a choked breath and into Elara's wide eyes, the startled gasp lodged in her throat, her fingers clutching at thin air thrusting into my vision.

Me, rushing to catch her, but not soon enough.

A ragged scream rips from her as she plummets down the rocky incline.

I lunge after her, my palm scraping against craggy rock,

but the pain barely registers in the surge of adrenaline and blind panic. I skid on loose stones, momentum hurling me towards her.

In between blinks, I am at her side with agility born from harsh training drills and instinctual preservation. My hand meets her shoulder, halting her descent inches before a dangerously sharp drop. The gasp that escapes her mouth is filled with relief and incredulous terror—mirroring the emotions that live in my chest.

"Hold on!"

My command mixes with the chill night air. I pull her against me as we slide further down the incline. The cloak that had been a nuisance now proves its worth as it shields both of us from nature's indiscriminate wrath.

When we finally come to an abrupt halt at the base of the slope amidst a pile of fallen leaves and underbrush, any breath I had left is stolen away by Elara's trembling form pressed against mine—agitated whimpers slipping past her gritted teeth.

My fingers probe gently around her skull, ensuring she hadn't suffered any serious injury during our calamitous descent.

When my explorations yield no alarming discovery, relief floods me like a tsunami, leaving me quaking with its aftermath.

"Jesus fucking Christ." My voice is rough, fringed with remnants of fear I refuse to acknowledge. "Are you hurt anywhere?"

Her gaze finds mine in the darkness, the moonlight seeping through the canopy above us giving her an unearthly glow.

She shakes her head, lips quivering as she tries to form words, but only manages a snagged breath.

The sigh that leaves me is shaky—my fingers tracing her cheekbone in a bizarre display of tenderness I never knew I was capable of.

Elara blinks at the unexpected touch, surprise flickering in her eyes before waning and surrendering.

I help her sit up, hands carefully avoiding any possible injury.

The silence that falls between us resonates with everything unsaid—every apology I'd never dare voice out loud.

I'm sorry I pulled away from you. I'm sorry you're with me.

For now, the words remain buried beneath the tremulous beats of my racing heart.

"I think," Elara says, her voice feeble but steady, "you guys need to hire a better landscaper."

I grumble a barely audible agreement.

But as I pull her closer against me for warmth, every cell in my body screams one word over and over with a fervor that could light the blackest corners of my soul.

Safe.

CHAPTER 23

ELARA

Axe Devereaux shouldn't affect me, not when there's active danger lurking behind him like Peter Pan's shadow. And definitely not when his "interrogation" a few hours ago twisted into something sexual and brutal.

But Axe isn't just any college guy. He's a paradox, a hazardous blue flame, and I am merely the stupid moth fluttering nearby.

My mind's in overdrive as we move off that horrific, rocky incline and into a dense, ancient forest, where the canopy above is so thick it swallows the moonlight, plunging us into the black.

Axe turns on his phone's flashlight, though I doubt it's for his benefit.

He leads with confidence, navigating the forest's natural obstacles with ease—an ease born of countless nocturnal journeys, I'm sure.

"Thank you for protecting me," I say quietly, breaking the synchronization of our breaths as we walk.

"Always," he replies without looking over.

It's more of a vow than a response. I press my lips together at his tone.

The urge to touch him is overwhelming, to trace the line of his jaw, to feel the warmth of his skin against the coldness I've long accepted as my constant companion tonight. But the way he recoiled at my attempt, the damage that clearly mars his soul, holds me back.

I stumble again, and Axe steadies me, his other hand reflexively brushing my waist. I shiver under his touch, and I know he feels it, and it's like a spark to dry tinder.

I want Axe to pull me against him again, to shield me from a perilous fall—and yet it's *him* I should want protection from.

"I swear I'm not normally this clumsy," I say with embarrassment. "Though, maybe it's because I'm not usually on makeshift paths of exposed roots and dead branches and … is that a dead bunny?"

Axe doesn't stare in the direction of a sad, fluffy lump, instead barreling me forward by the arm, his heat seeping into my sad excuse for arm muscles as he drags me along.

"Your hands," I say suddenly, hesitant but curious, "they're always so warm, even out here in the cold."

"Body's way of coping," he says tersely.

It's obvious he's done with talking, but I'm not about to relent, not when I'm so bewildered and confused by pretty much *everything* lately.

I ask, my breath fogging up in the frigid air, "Does the Court always put you in places like this? Forests in the dead of night?"

Axe is silent for a moment, but I've learned enough about

him to discern that he's not ignoring me. He's weighing his words, choosing them carefully.

"Life isn't too kind when you're branded a freak," he mutters eventually, his face hidden in the darkness.

One warm hand still clutches my arm, the heat from his skin combating the chill penetrating my clothes.

"I find solace here," Axe adds after some time, his voice barely more than a whisper carried by the wind.

The forest swallows his confession, and it feels oddly intimate, like an admission few people get to hear.

A sudden rustling of leaves startles us both, and Axe's grip tightens momentarily around my arm before relaxing again.

A fox darts out from a bush nearby, its eyes reflecting the flashlight before it disappears into the undergrowth.

A few minutes later, we've reached our destination—a clearing before the stone walls of campus where the moonlight at last filters down through the trees, mixing with street lamps and bathing the campus in a silver luminescence.

I stop dead in my tracks.

At first, I don't know why. I should race away from him, making my escape, packing up my things in my room and going ... where?

To a mother who barricades herself against her daughter? Or to a grandmother who would rather cling to the past than embrace a future with me?

"Look, Elara..." Axe says behind me.

His voice is rough, like when he screamed out my name as I was falling, it hurt. "When I pushed you away earlier. It wasn't—there are things about me I don't enjoy remembering —bad things."

My eyes, hot with concern and something fiercer, meet

his. "I have my own darkness, Axe. Maybe not like yours, but..."

"Elara, I—" The words catch in his throat, and he struggles to release them. "My memories, they're fragmented because of what I've been through. As a kid. You were right. It's not just forgetfulness."

It's a confession that brings a metallic taste to my mouth.

"Thank you for trusting me with that part of you," I whisper, holding his stare. "It helps, considering how … intimately you know me."

It's like we both tumble into the flashback at the same time. Me, strapped to a table with him above me, his fingers, his face, so rabid for me, and he contained it all within, refusing to allow it to escape.

But I saw it. I saw it—

"Fuck, Elara..." he growls, his barriers crumbling.

His hands, shaking, cradle my face and draw me towards him.

Axe's lips hover mere inches from mine. The faint light from his phone shoved in his pocket captures him; his furrowed brows, his clenched jaw, his high, almost royal cheekbones. I see him not as the quiet lurker he is to everyone else but as the man he hides beneath the enclosed surface.

He lowers his gaze, lips parting slightly. Time seems to hang in the balance, as if waiting for my response.

But before words can spill from my mouth, his fingers dig into my cheeks.

"Elara," he whispers. This time, it's not a warning.

His lips crash against mine in a way that ignites every nerve ending in my body. My shocked moan fuels the fire, our tongues entwining.

My arms wrap around him, my fingers trailing down his spine with a gentleness belying our fierce kiss.

He reacts by groaning as if in pain, then sinking his teeth into my lower lip, cutting into the tissue. I yelp and he tears away, wincing and bowing over.

"Did I hurt you?" he asks.

There's panic in his voice, so different from the man who happily told me to strip so he could tie me down, and it's a reflection of the panic that's rising in me.

I hold my fingers to my lip, pulling them back and seeing the splash of red there. My mouth throbs where he bit me.

"What happened?" I ask, still staring at my bloody fingers. "What did I do?"

Axe twists away from me, blowing out an exhale and shaking out his arms before turning back around.

"No, it's not you," Axe answers bitterly. "There's just... you touched some fresh injuries. On my back."

I let it all sink in. Axe's protective body language, his consistent recoil when I get too close, the battle clearly waging within his expression.

"Show me."

My tone leaves no room for argument.

Axe gives a sharp shake of his head, agony etched in the lines of his face as if in an attempt to figure out what he's supposed to do. "You don't want to see it."

I utter a single syllable, a command that's been building within me ever since I put the pieces together. "Turn."

Slowly, Axe obliges.

Because he's used to being told what to do.

It should satisfy me to locate his weakness, but *goddammit*, all I can feel is heartache.

His shoulders are rigid when he swings around. I can hear the tension in his breath as it slides in and out of his chest.

The fabric of his shirt conceals most of what there is to see, but what little skin is left bare by the collar appears tender, marred.

"Take off your shirt."

The words sting my ears as I say them, stark and uncomfortable in the otherwise quiet clearing.

I rarely bark orders. I smile and participate and try to be friendly to everyone. *This isn't me.*

Except … who was the girl in the Court's basement, desperate to be fucked by all four of the men who've been harassing me for days?

Axe doesn't react at first, but eventually he pulls his shirt over his head and discards it on the ground.

Then, the moonlight illuminates his back, violent slashes spread before me.

Scars web across his pale skin. They twist and curl like vines on a trellis, each one holding a story of brutal lessons.

Some are fresher than others, the cuts raw and angry.

A gasp clings to my lips, but I swallow it down until it's a ball of nausea in my stomach.

This isn't a spectacle for me to cringe at. It's a man bearing the weight of past atrocities.

Reaching out with trembling hands, I hesitantly trace my fingertips along the raised lines of his older scars.

Axe remains silent as I map out each one.

His breath holds steady, as if steeling himself against an expected pain by the person standing behind his exposed skin.

"Who did this to you?"

My voice breaks, and I know he hears the tears I'm fighting back.

"It depends which ones you're asking about. But ultimately, they're from people who should have protected me."

The admission is stark, an open wound.

On closer inspection, I notice the pattern. Squinting, I angle my head.

Symbols? Letters? Circles, stars, punctures, X's...

"What are these supposed to say?" I ask. My voice wavers under the weight of anguish threatening to choke me.

"The newer ones are from the Sovereigns," Axe answers in an undertone. "They believe the glyphs control me, make me theirs."

"What?" I rasp. I can hear his words, but processing it is an entirely different thing. "Do Cav, Wilder and Kaspian have these, too?"

"No. Their torture is different."

A moment more and I pull my hand back, the feel of his raised, puckered skin lingering on the pads of my fingers.

Axe turns to face me, his eyes searching mine for any sign of revulsion.

There's none.

Instead of drawing out what clearly humiliates him, I reach for his discarded shirt on the ground beside us. Handing it to him wordlessly, I turn away to protect his dignity.

I can hear the *whoosh* of fabric as he pulls it over his head.

The sound fills me with a strange sort of relief—the relief of knowing that I was not wrong to ask, and he was not wrong to show me.

"You asked why the Sovereigns want the ruby Heart so badly."

Axe's voice draws my head up. His words make me turn to face him.

"The Sovereigns, they're not like the ones before. They're involved in certain practices. The occult. They indulge in rituals that make them see us—Cav, Wilder, Kaspian and me—not as legacies, but as curses."

I stare at him with a mixture of confusion and foreboding. "Don't tell me they're trying to cure you with black magic?"

Axe takes a step closer, his voice dropping. "They've tormented Cav with it so much that he believes—"

Behind us, branches crack under weight. My senses spike, heart pounding at the sudden prospect of another threat.

Axe tenses, instinctively moving in front of me. His hand goes to something concealed under his jacket, his eyes scanning the bushes.

A figure barrels out of the dense tree line, and I stand in shock as the forest seals itself around us in an envelope of terror.

The last thing I feel is a brush of frantic wind as Axe launches himself forward.

CHAPTER 24
CAV

Concealed within a cluster of trees, I observe them from my secret vantage point, my heart racing with a tumultuous mix of fury and longing.

Elara, with hair that glimmers like embers in the moonlight, has Axe slumped before her. He is a formidable figure, his muscular frame regularly standing tall and proud, as if to offset the complications going on in his mind. But here, with her, he's submitted, curving his spine and exposing his mutilated back.

The sight is a blade twisting in my gut. Those scars are stark reminders of brutal orders I executed under the Sovereigns' command. Each welt is a map of agony I inflicted on Axe, my brother-in-arms.

As I watch them, conflicting emotions surge. Fury at the reminder of the agony I carved into Axe, desperation to fix what a brotherhood should be, acceptance that my life will never change, and … the illicit thrill of *her*.

My breath stops altogether as Elara's delicate fingers trace the ridges of Axe's scars, her touch laden with unexpected poignancy.

It is a tenderness that should not exist in our world, a show of compassion that stirs something deep within me.

A guttural moan escapes my chest, unbidden, as my body responds to the sight of her.

Her golden eyes hold the type of mercy that could shatter the cold edifice of the Cimmerian Court.

You can't save him, butterfly.

I watch her, every movement, every flutter of her eyelashes, every gentle sweep of her gaze over Axe's damaged flesh.

"Who did this to you?" I hear Elara ask Axe, her voice breaking under the weight of her sorrow.

"It depends on which scars you're asking about," Axe replies, his voice tinged with bitterness. "But ultimately, they are from people who should have protected me."

Axe's words wrap around me like a noose, tightening their grip on my conscience. He speaks the truth, a truth I am all too familiar with. But to hear him say it, to hear him acknowledge the trauma I imposed upon him, it cuts deep.

I have to assure myself that I *am* protecting him.

If not me, someone worse would do it. The Sovereigns wouldn't simply choose Wilder or Kaspian, no. I wouldn't be surprised if they contacted every single one of Axe's abusive foster families, then line them up for the joy of maiming him again.

They chose me because they believe me to be the most obedient, the most discreetly brutal. And in their warped logic, they're right.

But I had foolishly thought that I would never be used

against my own brothers. The weight of that realization settles heavily upon my shoulders, threatening to crush me under its burden.

I reach into my pocket, and my fingers close around the cold metal of the ruby necklace. Elara, true to her pledge of being our good girl, revealed its hiding place. I had half-expected another lie or half-truth.

I'm almost disappointed she broke.

However, the necklace she worked so hard to hide from us glints mockingly in my hand, its jagged edge a testament to something fractured. Incomplete.

My fury reignites.

She gave us the necklace, yes, but she failed to tell us what condition it'd be in.

Elara and Axe stand out in the open, lost in a moment meant for neither rules nor eyes, especially not mine. I am The Consul, enforcer of the court's merciless laws, yet here I am, coveting that which I am forbidden from experiencing.

I'm cursed, bound by blood to a legacy of misfortune and permanent servitude to the Court that began with a wrong against Sarah Anderton.

The irony of desiring the descendant of the one we wronged isn't lost on me.

"Elara." I finally allow her name to quietly slide off my tongue, a weapon forged in the fires of my restraint.

It's time to confront them.

Even if it scorches my soul to ash, I will uphold the sovereignty of the Court, regardless of the cost.

Yet, as I shift forward, primal thoughts claw at the edges of my control.

Her delicate fingers would feel like salvation on my skin,

stirring a part of me that should remain dormant—a part that screams to be acknowledged by her loving touch.

The fantasy of her taste consumes me.

I bring my fingers to my lips, searching for any remnant of her flavor, sucking on them like a man starved.

And *fuck*, it's her openness, her warmth, that pulls Axe toward her, desperate for the light she exudes.

We're *all* desperate for it.

As I pocket the gem, the rawness of my emotions collides with the rigidity of my stance.

"Damn it," I hiss under my breath.

I burst out of my hiding place, branches snapping underfoot as I storm into the clearing.

Axe reacts with the honed training of a bloodhound, leaping first and thinking second, but I catch him mid-launch and toss him aside. He has the skill to stay on his feet rather than toppling to the ground, still snarling.

"Enjoying yourselves?"

My voice is a razor slicing through any remaining tranquility they might've had.

Axe darts in front of me, shielding Elara and tensed for battle.

Confusion and betrayal swirls in his eyes as he regards me, but there's no time for explanations—not here, not ever.

"Ease up, Cav," he growls. "We're finished with her tonight."

"Make me," I taunt, stepping closer, my grin disguising a regret I dare not fully acknowledge.

Elara weaves around him as if to shield Axe from *me*. "What gives you the right—"

"Right?" The word unfurls from my lips like smoke. "Axe

wasn't being entirely honest with you. *I chiseled those scars into his back. It gives me every right.*"

My confession detonates against her like a bullet and Elara recoils. She attempts to speak but no words come out, her voice strangled by the sickening revelation.

Axe has seen much in his life, but my unhurried confession to Elara seems to have caught him off-guard.

"Good. I should make you sick." I fling my words at Elara like a cloud of daggers. "The Court should make you want to *vomit* with disgust."

Axe's knuckles turn white. His teeth grind together with a sound akin to breaking bones.

I lift my chin and meet Axe's livid gaze head-on. It's crucial he sees no remorse in my eyes. Only a decree.

Axe holds my stare for several heartbeats before finally erupting into laughter, a hollow, mirthless sound that echoes eerily. Even Elara startles at the sound.

"You've always been great at having the last word," Axe spits out, his laughter dying down as quickly as it came.

Elara moves closer to me, her anger radiating off her in palpable waves.

"You're a monster."

A monster. Yes, perhaps that's what I've become.

I smile at her, empty and soulless. "Were you expecting a prince?"

She lunges at me, nails aiming for my face. I sidestep her charge and grab her arm, twisting it behind her back and leveraging her forward. Her pained yelp fills the night as I toss her to the forest floor with ruthless force, pinning her with my body.

Every point of contact between us is electric, and I revel in the hiss of her breath, the flush on her cheeks.

"Cav. Stop," Axe commands, his voice laced with a desperate need to protect her.

I don't heed his words. Elara struggles against me, her snarl a thing of true beauty. "Let go of me!"

I murmur into her ear, my voice low and dangerous, "Can't do that, butterfly. You're too precious to let slip away just yet."

Axe's tone hardens. "Cav, let her go."

He knows better than to intercede, but it's physically costing him. Axe absolutely *vibrates* with the need to hit me.

The sight of Elara, trembling beneath me on the forest floor, stirs something within him.

Damn it all to hell. His connection to her is worse than I thought.

I could crush him, silence him forever, but I don't.

"Elara hasn't been truthful about the necklace." I turn my attention to the half of Elara's pinched, frustrated face that isn't pressed against the ground. "You've been crafty again, haven't you?"

She arches against my hold. "I don't know what you're talking about. It's there. The necklace is behind the portrait."

"Yes. That part was true."

"Then *why* are you pinning me to the ground, asshole?"

I don't answer her question. Instead, I reach into my pocket since she's easy to subdue one-handed, and pull out the jagged ruby necklace, its crimson facets mockingly twinkling.

"Is this the necklace you had in mind to give us?"

"Yes," Elara answers tightly. My weight isn't doing her lungs any favors.

"Lovely. Your honesty is so refreshing."

Shoving the necklace back into my pocket, I fix my gaze upon her once more. "So why don't you tell me why it houses only *half* of the fucking ruby?"

"Half?" Axe queries, casting me a sideways glance.

"Half," I confirm, my tone smothered with insincere solemnity.

My words are barbed hooks, and I watch them sink deep. She doesn't understand, can't possibly comprehend the war we're all ensnared in. All she sees is the monster before her, not the protector keeping the darkness at bay.

I release Elara abruptly, vaulting to my feet and studying the storm of emotions playing across her face. Axe moves as if to help her stand, but I meet his gaze with a silent warning. He halts.

"That's the ruby," Elara says as she struggles to her feet, her voice heavy with exhaustion. "The necklace from Sarah Anderton that the Wraithwood family has been hiding for centuries. It's the only ruby I know of."

"*Where's the rest of it?*"

Elara matches my shout. "I don't know!"

I force myself to take a deep breath. "Kaspian recovered an old journal in the black market. It described the ruby in detail. *This*"—I shove the necklace in front of her again, tangled in its chains—"is not all of it. The Heart is divided. And our precious butterfly here"—I spare Elara another disdainful glance—"kept that crucial detail buried under her usual layers of feigned ignorance."

Elara's eyes widen slightly before they shutter closed with denial.

Her voice wavers when she answers, "That's...I don't know anything about that. I only just found the necklace. I thought it was ugly, but I never thought it was missing anything."

Ignoring her protestations, I regard Axe, who has remained ominously silent. He watches us with an air of warring emotions that troubles me more than I'd care to admit.

"It doesn't matter," Axe says, his voice low and filled with a weary resignation. "We can look for the other half without her."

"No."

The refusal springs from my lips without hesitation.

Elara's eyes flash as she spits out, "I don't know anything else! You got what you wanted—"

Her defense does not touch me—I am too far gone into the abyss of betrayal for any words to reach me now.

"You lied to us."

Each word drops from me like a stone into a still pond.

"Axe," I call out without tearing my gaze away from Elara.

He twitches at the sound of his name, his muscles taut as a drawn bowstring. He knows what my order is without me having to say it. It is more than just a summons—it is an ultimatum.

He comes to my side, his loyalty unwavering. Elara's expression goes slack as she watches him move towards me.

"Remember this, Elara," I say, my voice low and dangerous. "I was leading you down a dangerous path before. I'll admit that. But you lie to me again, I'm going to lead you straight to Hell." I dismiss her with a jerk of my chin. "I trust you can find your way home from here."

Without another word, I turn on my heel, Axe reluctantly trailing behind me, leaving Elara on her own, her frame small against the backdrop of towering pines.

But as I retreat, I hear her whisper, "You don't get to decide my fate."

I sneer, the poison within me snaking out from my heart, and let the threat linger, as tangible as the mist shrouding me as I leave.

CHAPTER 25
KASPIAN

My balls swell as I survey the scene: Blindfolded women on their knees, surrendering to the initiates of the Court.

Their subservient positions stir a primal hunger in my gut, a raw need that has reared up again despite my earlier encounter with Elara.

Guilt gnaws at me. I am a puppet, a marionette whose strings are yanked. The thought fills me with revulsion even as I continue to observe, drawn in by evil I can't control. There's a profound connection between power and need woven into our beings. But it's not just about physicality. It's about authority, surrender, dominance—an intricate fusion far more complex than the simplicity of flesh against flesh.

But what terrifies me most is not the intensity of these feelings—it's how intoxicating they are. Elara is a honey trap that pushes back against the boundaries I've set for myself.

My pulse quickens—not solely with respect for her ability

to not only withstand me, but also an instinctive fear—as I hand her more bricks than she takes.

Typically, we abstain from the initiates' hedonistic feasts. We prefer to observe and supervise while our selected, exclusive girl, who will never be put on display, waits in our private chamber until we are prepared.

But tonight feels different. Cav demanded the privilege of retrieving the ruby Heart from the portrait in the library, while Axe was ordered to escort Elara home. If he's smart, he'll actually fuck her this time because *good god* she was amazing.

Because our parents have left to run errands, Wilder and I are left to our own devices. There's a shine to Wilder's eyes as he scans the room for something to do—evidence of fucking Elara earlier. I know it's only a matter of time before he finds trouble. Watching freshmen fumble through their introductions to unlimited pleasure is always amusing to him.

I shift beside him, stiff-backed and aching. Elara's intoxicating presence hours before didn't satiate me at all. It heightened my craving. Elara isn't just pushing back against my borders. Just thinking about her after I've had her makes me complicit in tearing them down for her.

And therein lies the dreadful beauty of it all.

As every sense comes alive—the pungent scent of anticipation hanging heavy in the air; the soft rustle of clothing shifting over bodies; the slight taste of regret bitter on my tongue—irrationality seeks refuge behind reason. Ultimately, I know it's futile. This is part of who I am—undeniable, all-consuming—a creature of want and need.

If only it were that simple…

"That one," I snap and point.

Wilder lolls his head toward me, half-lidded and almost asleep. "Huh?"

"Her." I stand, straightening my suit. "Have her brought to my room in ten minutes."

Wilder's gaze follows to where I point, at a long-haired redhead at the front of the line-up. "Dude. Seriously? But we just had the fuck of our lives—"

"Did I ask for your opinion?"

Wilder goes silent, chewing on his cheek. "Alright, man. Coming right up."

Initiates fall away from me like a rippling wave as I carve a path to the staircase and up the stairs without looking at the girl again.

If I can't have Elara, I'll just use this one until the tight, relentless ache in my cock goes away.

Ascending the staircase, I reach my hand into the pocket of my finely tailored suit, retrieving a gold-plated key. The sound of chatter and laughter from the parlor below fades as I march along the second-floor corridor, my footsteps muffled by the plush carpet underfoot. My muscles twitch in anticipation, the pain from my arousal throbbing insistently. The notion of Elara lingers in my mind—her scent, her touch, her taste—but it's an indulgence I no longer have access to.

The room designated for me is at the end of the corridor, sequestered from the rest of the bedrooms. With a swift turn of the key, the door swings open, revealing a stark interior. A king bed is shoved against the far wall, its crisp white sheets untouched. A black entertainment center contains my computers, electronics and the like, casting the room in a bluish, blinking light.

I unbutton my suit jacket, discarding it on a nearby chair

before rolling up my shirt sleeves to my forearms and moving towards a drawer by the bedside table and retrieving a bottle of lube.

Upon opening it, a flowery scent wafts in the air, an expensive aphrodisiac oil, though price is irrelevant when in the pursuit of pleasure.

As I prep myself, coating my dick in the slippery wetness, there's a soft knock on the door. Ten minutes exactly. The girl enters entirely naked, her long-red hair cascading down her naked back and sparks of nervousness reflecting in her eyes. She is pretty in a simple sort of way, without the flash of intelligence Elara has, or that warm glow promising curiosity and delight regardless of my fetishes.

No matter. Elara isn't here. Time to get over it.

"Close the door," I order tersely while pouring more oil onto my palm.

Her lips part to utter a word, but then close abruptly as she complies with my command, shutting us off from the world outside.

This girl knows nothing of what lies ahead, but will partake in this ritual nonetheless.

Her wide green eyes meet mine for the first time since she entered this room.

Not the same luscious amber.

"Turn around," I order, one hand wrapping around my cock. I've opened my fly enough to allow it to spear forward.

She complies, her hands coming up to the wall for balance. A deep sense of satisfaction washes over me. If Elara denies me her body, I will simply take my fill from those who don't.

Grunting, I jerk off while staring at this girl's flat ass, unlike the pert little melons that round out Elara's figure. My lips twist as the lube wears off, the friction becoming painful, but I don't fix it. I just want these blue balls to end, which doesn't make sense, considering I had Elara in all the ways I wanted her mere hours ago.

It wasn't enough.

Gritting out a suppressed roar, I give up, my dick now a throbbing, angry red.

"Get out," I say, turning my back to her.

"What?"

"You heard me. Get the fuck out."

"But you…" She's silenced by the glare I toss her. "Okay. Um … sorry?"

My lips peel back to shame her so ferociously, she'll have trauma for the rest of her life for speaking to me that way, when something in her clenched hand catches my eye.

"What is that?"

"Oh—right." Her shoulders slope in relief, likely at the fact there's still an opening to please me. "My escort to your room gave me this. It's for you."

"Who was your escort?"

"I don't know. He was in a mask and hood-robe thing."

Frowning, with my pissed-off dick bobbing, I come close enough to take the piece of paper from her and unfold it.

As I read it, my forehead smooths. Blood leaves my face.

I suck in a breath, lacerating my voice when I snarl at the hovering girl, "Do *not* make me tell you three times. You will regret it."

She jumps at my tone, tears soaking her eyes as she

fumbles for the doorknob, throwing it open and running for her life down the stairs.

Good.

I go back to the old-fashioned, handwritten note:

Kaspian,

Your talents are wasted on this supernatural nonsense. An initiate's work, significant to our cause, was left incomplete. It's time for you to step beyond mere possession of the ruby Heart and into the blood it's coated in.

There's a room hidden within Thornhaven, overlooked by those uninterested in our shared goals. This initiate was onto something that could change the balance of power. His last project is there, hidden in plain sight.

You're not one for chasing ghosts, and neither am I, but consider this a test of your ability to see the bigger picture. The entrance to the study is ingeniously masked by the very history we seek to preserve. Look closer at what seems familiar. The old manor has more secrets than the Court's blueprints suggest.

Before you sneer and consider this a red herring, this isn't about keeping you busy with riddles or ancient puzzles. It's about recognizing the value of what was left behind and then hidden by the more traditional Sovereigns. Find it, understand it, and use it. That's how you honor a legacy—not with words, but with action.

Consider this your new assignment. Don't disappoint.

— a concerned party

. . .

My jaw muscles join the ache in my center as I crumple the letter in my hand, knowing that I have to do the one thing I absolutely detest having to do.

Wait.

———

Four hours later, at the ass-crack of dawn, the initiates' Selection party ends, leaving the manor wide open for my exploration without questions.

All the writer had to do to get me to jump into action was tell me I could honor my legacy by finding whatever it is they want me to uncover in this supposed hidden section of Thornhaven. Since I couldn't act right away, I spent the last hours ruminating on who it could've come from.

Not Wilder, since his knowledge of the manor comprises his bedroom, the kitchen, and the exit. Cav has nothing to do with it because he never parts with his secrets, and Axe isn't the type to write letters regarding the Court's history or a potential initiate involvement—he'd just go find it himself.

The sentence that snagged my attention was *hidden by the more traditional Sovereigns*. Meaning, out of the three, there is one with a modern view of the ruby Heart and its potential.

Could that Sovereign have penned this?

We're prohibited from learning their identities, instead following orders and reinforcing their power by training for their world with cleverness, discreetness, and killer instincts. Once unleashed from the university, we're used as power tools or weapons of destruction, depending on our talents.

I've accepted my use as an information gatherer with

aplomb, considering I'm so good at doing whatever it takes to collect it. And I always choose violence.

Perhaps that is why I'm singled out as the one who has to dick around poking holes and testing walls in order to find this fucking room.

With the note shoved in my pants' pocket, I venture into the labyrinthine manor, guided by faint rays peeking through heavy drapes.

In the stillness of slumber, Thornhaven manor reveals nothing but the sound of its own breathing, a shallow inhale and exhale that reverberates through the quiet corridors.

I traverse the halls with an analytic mind nonetheless, seeking the cracks hidden in its bones. My fingers chart a sensory map of the place, tracing every corner, every nook and cranny. I run over the contours of the estate with a lover's touch—patient, intense, deliberate—seducing sighs from its walls.

I meander down one of Thornhaven's more neglected corridors on the third floor, close to the attic. It's the kind that screams *abandoned by time and housekeepers alike*. Dust is practically a carpet here, undisturbed, a testament to the Court's indifference. I can't help but find it amusing, this solitude among the decay—it's like a breath of fresh air compared to the constant occupants in the more popular areas of Thornhaven.

That's when I spot it: an old, dust-covered painting hung on the wall where no other paintings are displayed, as forgotten as the corridor itself.

"What's this? An attempt at ancestral grandeur?"

I can't resist the sarcasm, even though the only audience is spiders and cobwebs. The painting captures a scene from the estate's so-called glorious past, but all I see is a testament to ego.

Something about it catches my eye, though, a discrepancy that's almost laughable. The west wing it depicts hasn't looked like that for centuries.

"Trying to rewrite history, are we?" I mock the long-dead artist, tracing the edge of the frame with a finger.

There's a thrill in the hunt, even if it's just a visionary artist painting something unlike the others.

My mind kicks into gear, instincts honed not just for the kill but for the chase, unraveling the secret hidden in plain sight.

The frame is a golden relic crowned with dust, making it almost blend into the faded wallpaper. The painting itself is a lush depiction of Thornhaven Estate, as it might have been if the Sovereigns hadn't gotten hold of it and converted it to their harsh standards. It's a sun-drenched summer day. Every window gleams, reflecting the clear blue sky, a stark difference from the current, weather-beaten facade.

The west wing, particularly, draws my eye. It's there, painted with such meticulous detail, yet I know for a fact it's nothing but rubble now, a victim of some long-forgotten calamity. In the foreground beside the garden, a small, solitary figure gazes up at it, an intriguing anomaly.

My gaze sharpens.

I dissect the tableau with the precision of a surgeon. There is more here than mere artistry.

My fingers itch, compelling me to touch the canvas, expecting nothing more than the brushstrokes and thick hemp under my fingertips. But as I trace the line where the vibrant garden meets the architectural marvel of the west wing, something feels off.

"Well, fuck me," I murmur.

The surface beneath my fingers shifts slightly, a panel disguised within the painting's scenery. Surprised, I press down, and the piece of canvas depresses with a satisfying click. It's clever, and I nod at the painting like it's a person who's particularly impressed me.

Encouraged, I examine the figure standing alone. It seems odd, out of place. On a hunch, I touch the figure, applying a bit of pressure, and another section behind the painting compresses.

Who would have thought?

The painting, a static relic of the past, now feels alive under my hands, a gateway.

A final shift, a soft whirring from behind, causes me to turn in time to watch a fissure emerge, slicing through the floral motifs of faded roses and creeping ivy painted on the wallpaper before it slowly widens into an open doorway.

"My, my."

I proceed without hesitation. Each step down is a stride deeper into the manor's heart, every echo of my footfall a bold challenge thrown into the cavernous void.

My favorite kind of summons.

The long, tight staircase hidden in the walls ends in what memory serves as below the first floor, below even the basement. The air is icy, yet claustrophobic. It's windowless, full of stone, and coated in soil and damp. It also coughs up a foreign chill and a pleasant cocktail of mildew and centuries-old dust.

The sight elicits no triumphant grin from me.

This could be a trap.

Senses on alert, my expression remains an impassive mask as I bring take my phone from my pocket and turn on the flashlight.

I move further into the belly of the beast until a room at the end of the corridor emerges from the semi-darkness. My other hand tightens on my pocketed switchblade as my gaze penetrates the darkness, searching for any sign of movement. I advance into the room, muscles taut, every sense heightened. My attention flicks over potential hiding places quickly and systematically.

My secret admirer said I would find a room. This isn't that. This is a fucking *cathedral* of books.

After ensuring I'm alone, I take in the room's expanse. It's a library, the vaulted stone ceiling lost in the shadows above. Shelves reach up as if trying to touch the heavens, though they are blind to it, laden with countless tomes and manuscripts.

I tread softly. This chamber, though forgotten, throbs with the lifeblood of those who have shaped our dark society from within these very walls.

Except, at least three people know of its existence.

Me, my penpal, and a nameless initiate.

"Secrets upon secrets," I mutter to myself, fingertips grazing a curious-looking globe with continents that no longer exist—or perhaps never did.

It's here, amidst the relics of power and occult, that I find them: documents marked with the seal of the Sovereign.

My pulse quickens as I unfold the aged parchment, and

one name among all the others sears across the page like a brand.

Maverick Wraithwood.

CHAPTER 26

WILDER

The night is so quiet, like it's waiting for someone to break the silence.

That's where I come in, the disruptor of peace.

I rev my bike's engine, my mind swimming with thoughts of her. *Sweetwitch.*

Elara Wraithwood has wormed her way into my mind and I can't shake her off. I've fucked her, twice, which is more than I usually care to invest in anyone, and yet here I am, obsessing over her as she walks out of the clearing and through the campus gates, head down and her hair hiding her face as she likely struggles with what went down with Cav and Axe.

I witnessed most of it after leaving Kaspian to do whatever it is Kasp does when he's not with us, getting quickly bored and leaving the manor for what I thought was an aimless ride around town.

And yet I drove straight to her.

Cav can go home and have his internal battle with the

Heart, and Axe can enter dreamland with the sugar plum memory of Elara stroking his scars.

All I know is, now that they're done with her, *I* get to have her.

She represents everything I shouldn't want: a distraction, a complication, but I can't seem to stay away.

As Elara nears her dorm, her movements betray her unease. She fumbles with her keycard like she's struggling to find stability in a world that seems intent on throwing her off balance.

A cat-like smile curls upon my lips. The engine of my bike shatters the silence, piercing through the night with its raw power, echoing like a scream in a library. Startled, Elara stumbles backward, her eyes widening as she tries to avoid the path of my front wheel. With a skillful skid, I come to a stop before her, effectively cutting off her retreat to Camden House.

Swinging off the bike, I flash her that grin I've been told is trouble. I never bother with a helmet. Rules and safety aren't really my forte. "Need a lift, sweetwitch?"

My gaze rakes over her slender form, re-envisioning rosebud nipples and a soaked, overused pussy hidden beneath the cloak she's wearing. She'd only be more enticing if she were wearing *my* jacket, but alas, she peeled off the shirt I offered her and shimmied back into that tight, black number also hidden under her cloak.

Elara glares at me, her eyes on fire. "Now is not the time, Wilder."

My eyebrow quirks, but I feign ignorance.

"I'm offering you an escape, since you look like you need one. Unless you want to hide under your covers and try to sleep us off, which, sorry to say, we're not the kind to read you bedtime stories and wish you sweet dreams."

I extend a leather-clad hand towards her and wait.

Instead of fleeing in the opposite direction, she hesitates, and I can't help the slow, upward tilt of my lips. "Scared?"

I can almost hear her thoughts, weighing the sanity of taking a midnight ride with TFU's resident adrenaline junkie. But there's that spark in her eyes, the kind that tells me she's about to do something she might regret in the morning.

And damn if that doesn't make me even hotter for her.

Elara's life has been shockingly stable since her brother's murder, but if my instincts are as on point as they always are, she's beginning to tire of living a perfect, untroubled existence.

"Trust me."

I give her my best, most gentlemanly smile, then lean against my bike and cross my arms, eyes fixed on her.

She's got that look, like she's on the edge of a cliff, wondering if the thrill of the fall's worth the impact.

Perfect.

Then, taking a deep breath, she grabs my hand, swinging a leg over the back of the bike.

"I could really fucking use some fresh air," she says on a long exhale.

"Well, fuck me. She curses, too. Keep going, baby. You're turning into my perfect woman."

Elara's cheeks flush. From insult or embarrassment, I can't tell.

I climb on and rev the engine, watching Elara's reaction from my periphery. She's trying to play it cool as she settles the helmet I stash at the back of my bike for such occasions over her head, but I can see the excitement, the fear, dancing in her eyes before she's obscured behind the visor.

It's addictive, this power to evoke such organic emotion.

The surge, the speed, it's intoxicating, and for a fleeting second, I wonder if she feels it too—the addictive rush of living on the edge, where every second pulses with life, daring you to blink.

But then I remember who I am—Wilder, the guy who chases the high, not the heartbeats of a girl who might just be rebellious enough to keep up.

As we blaze through the night, the wind is a fierce competitor, trying to outdo my velocity, but it's got nothing on me. Elara clings to me, her grip tight, a mixture of panic and exhilaration that feeds my ego.

"Scared yet?" I yell back, not really caring if she is.

My blood sings in my veins.

She doesn't scream, doesn't beg me to slow down. Instead, she clings tighter, her trust in me as reckless as the ride itself. It's a madness we share, a craving for the edge, and at this moment, flying through the darkness on twisting roads, I feel an unexpected kinship with her.

It's unsettling, this sense of closeness, as if she's not just someone I want. More than that. And damn, that's a vulnerability I'm not ready to face.

She tightens her arms around me as we approach a steep descent. I imagine her face, flushed with terror.

With expert precision, I manipulate the clutch and throttle, shifting down gears while leaning effortlessly into the downward curve. My bike responds, embracing gravity and accelerating smoothly downhill. I can feel Elara hold her breath in her chest as we rapidly plunge down.

A sharp bend approaches at the bottom of the hill. Adrenaline pumps through my veins as I prepare to tackle it head-on. The sound of rubber biting tarmac fills the air as I lean into the curve. Elara gasps audibly, her nails biting through my leather jacket.

The endorphins racing through me intensify with each passing second. As Elara clings to me, whispering a curse under her breath in awe or hatred—perhaps both—we soar through another deserted lane under the twinkling stars.

I snake an arm behind me, tentatively brushing against her thigh. Her body tenses at the contact, yet she doesn't protest nor pull away. Emboldened, I let my fingers gently graze higher up her leg.

Underneath us, the bike surges with additional horsepower, a mechanical dragon unfurling its wings and soaring into uncharted territory. The force pins Elara against me, her breasts molded perfectly to my back. I swear I can feel her taut nipples piercing through our clothes.

"Hang on!" I shout, the final warning before I push the engine beyond its limit.

The bike snarls beneath us, responding with ferocious enthusiasm as we barrel down the road at velocities that mock mortality. This ride is a dare for death, unhinged from reality's grasp and propelled by raw horsepower.

Taking a final turn, I speed the bike toward the edge of a cliff overlooking the vast forest and stop just short of the edge in a half-circle skid. As the bike comes to a stop, I prop it by grounding one foot, then exhale loudly, feeling for the first time the toll that our ride has taken on my body. There's sweat forming on my brow, and my heart pounds in my chest like a tribal drum.

Disregarding Elara's protests, I lift her off the bike and set her on the ground. Her legs wobble and she stumbles against me. Our bodies collide, and she's shaking like a baby bird.

"Well?" My voice cuts through our shared panting. "Do you still want that fresh air?"

A shaky breath delays her response, but when she finally finds her voice… "That was…"

She clocks me in the middle of my chest.

To stroke her ego, I step back, pretending to be affected by her tiny fist.

"Are you *insane*? What the hell was that? We could've been killed!"

A chuckle escapes me as I reach out to remove her helmet. Once it's off, I toss it aside and finally allow myself to take in her disheveled appearance. Flushed cheeks, tousled hair and wide eyes filled with adrenaline-induced rage.

A primitive, feral grin spreads across my face. "If I die with you wrapped around me, then kill me now."

Elara shakes her head. She takes a deep breath and looks out over the cliff. The edge leads down to a black expanse that mirrors the void above, speckled with sporadic pinpricks of starlight.

"You have some nerve," she mutters.

I shrug, a challenge lurking in the casual movement. "You didn't tell me to stop."

Her lips thin. "That doesn't mean I enjoyed the risk of dying."

"Did it feel like dying?" My eyebrows arch, my interest piqued by her response.

"No," she admits, her voice just a notch above a whisper. "It felt … alive."

I smooth my expression. I fold my arms across my chest, leaning into my bike. "That's what life should feel like, sweetwitch."

She looks at me, the moon reflected in her wide eyes adding to the depth within. Her hand comes up to push away a wild strand of hair blowing in the breeze.

The sight sends a wave of heat through me, setting off a fresh round of revving in my veins.

"I don't know how you do that," she says, gesturing vaguely at the bike. "It was terrifying, and..."

"Exhilarating."

She looks at me sidelong, her eyes still wary with disbelief at what we just did together. "I could feel the wind through my *teeth*. And I had a helmet on."

I answer with a smirk that stretches across my face.

"Will you take me back?"

Her request is simple, but behind it lingers an unspoken question—will I take her back *safely*?

I tilt my head mockingly at her. "What, you don't trust me anymore? I'm hurt. Did you ever?"

I glance down at my body before looking back up at her again and spread my arms, challenging her to deny me.

Her chin lifts defiantly at that, golden fire reigniting in her eyes. "Fuck no."

A rough laugh rips through me at that, vibrating along my chest. Right then, she's all fire and ice and damn if that isn't sexy as hell.

The scent of damp earth lingers in the air. There's a distant hoot of an owl whom I suspect mirrors my predatory instincts at this moment. My fingers twitch for contact, for the feel of her soft skin against my rough callouses. But I resist, balling them into fists at my sides to ward off the temptation.

"Say it," I challenge, daring her to admit what she really felt during our ride.

I've always found some perverse pleasure in pushing limits —in finding that boundary and smashing against it until it caves under me.

She purses her lips—an act of refusal as much as an attempt to gather her thoughts.

"You're wet, aren't you?"

I let a slow grin crawl onto my features, because I fucking *know* she is. I can damn well smell it.

I don't expect her to admit it. My eyes never leave hers as I take a step backward. Another dare.

Her gaze narrows. "Wilder."

"Tell me how wet you are for me right now." The cliff's edge is but a few steps away—a death trap hidden beneath the deceptive tranquility of nightfall.

"Wilder, stop."

I allow the corner of my mouth to curl into a mischievous grin as I continue to teeter on the very edge of the cliff, my lean torso balanced precariously over a deadly drop to the forest below. I stretch my arms out for balance, one foot dangled carelessly into open air, teetering on the precipice of oblivion.

Elara's no fool. She knows exactly what game I'm playing, that every movement of mine is calibrated to elicit a response from her.

"*Wilder.* Don't be an idiot."

Ignoring her admonition, I let my foot hang over the edge, my entire body teetering dangerously backward. A rush of air sweeps past me, carrying the threat of an imminent free fall. The cliff's jagged teeth open their welcoming maw.

"Wilder, you're scaring me." Elara's shout cuts through the wind.

"All I want is for you to be *dripping* for me, baby."

Her answer doesn't come as words, but as action. She sprints toward me, her fingers curling around my forearm and yanking me back to the relative safety of solid ground.

The force of her pull, unexpected and fierce, causes me to lose footing and we both tumble onto the gravelly soil.

The uncontrolled descent results in a twisted pile of limbs and breathless exclamations. Beneath me, Elara writhes to free herself. Every brush of her body against mine sends a sizzling jolt through my veins. My nostrils flare at her scent, a sweet blend of vanilla perfume and the high of facing death and winning that still covers her.

"Get off." Her voice is a breathless rasp in my ear.

I laugh in answer. "Do I have to check for myself?"

"You're out of your mind." She slaps my hand away as it travels between us.

The touch is a charge—a current passing from her fingers into mine through the gloves, electrifying the small spaces of air between our bodies. I pull her to a standing position, my grip lingering just a second too long for it to be casual.

"Just kidding. I don't have to feel it for myself. I know, and I remember." I give a wink to our past, delicious encounters.

With a dismissive snort, she tries to pull her hand away from mine, but I hold on.

"Let go, Wilder."

The warning in her tone does nothing to dissuade me.

I lean into her personal space, enjoying the soft pause of her breath.

"Make me," I dare her. The cliff-edge looms behind us. "Maybe this time I'll take you, too."

Instead of retreating like I expected her to, she steps forward, closing the gap between us until our bodies were are inches apart. The heat radiating from her is a tangible force that makes my blood simply *hum*.

Elara notches her chin until our lips almost touching. I smile, waiting for her surrender.

They all do, in the end.

With an unexpected surge of strength, she twists her wrist out of my grip and takes a long step back. But not before whispering in a voice so low I have to strain my ears to catch it, "You don't have to push every limit, you know."

"Why not? I'd get bored, otherwise."

Her chest rises and falls. She looks down, trying to hide her concern for me behind the curtain of her hair.

But I can see it all: the frantic rise of her chest, the pulse in her neck, the way she struggles not to stare at me.

I keep my smile as I brush dirt off my sleeves, taking my time adjusting my clothes. My eyes rake over her figure appreciatively. She's so fucking incredible in this godforsaken place that offers no escape from anyone or anything.

"You're asking for the impossible," I add. "This is who I am."

The soft mist lifts her auburn hair around her face, and as she stares back at me with desolate eyes, I actually think I may have taken it too far.

Her slim fingers are still trembling from the fall as they lift to push strands behind her ears, but they hesitate for a moment before settling on the delicate lobes pierced by small gold hoops.

I angle my head in study. "No one's ever been worried about me before. And after everything we've done to you, I did not think you'd be the one to come to my rescue."

"That suicidal game of chicken you just played may have been fun for you, but I was *terrified,* Wilder. You did that to me. I can't stand by and see someone—someone—"

She chokes, struggling to hold back tears.

And it hits me.

Oh, shit.

"Your brother." I curse. The rush of amusement that remains on my face fades behind my gaze. A sigh escapes me, the guilt piercing through my usual arrogance like a gunshot. "Fuck, sweetwitch. I wasn't thinking."

Her brows knot together, hands clasped tightly over her chest, as if trying to contain the grief that vibrates off her in waves. Her eyes glimmer with unshed tears.

Oh, no. "Please don't cry."

I don't know what to do with women who cry.

Rubbing the back of my neck awkwardly, a gesture far detached from my usual swagger, I add, "Bringing you here wasn't all for show. This overlook, this spot, is my favorite one in all of Titan Falls. No one seems to know about it but me. And now you, I guess."

Her lips part slightly as if she is about to answer, but silence stretches between us instead. The aggressive energy that usually dominates our interactions is absent now, leaving behind an unsettling void filled with an unspoken apology.

Not for her—she did nothing wrong—but for *me.*

"Do you want me to apologize?"

It's not what I meant to say, but the words slip out before I can cage them.

A sound that might have been a laugh or cry escapes her lips as she wipes her cheeks with the back of her hand. "You? Say sorry? That'd be the day."

The insult doesn't sting as much it should. Instead, it gnaws at my conscience like a rat in the cellar.

"I was just trying to..." Hell if I know what I was trying to do.

"Kill yourself?" Elara retorts instantly. The vehemence in her voice surprises me.

I feel stripped down to my core. It's an unfamiliar sensation that makes my skin crawl. Each passing second tastes like sulfur on my tongue—a taste I've been trying to swallow since I was a teen.

"No," I reply, finding myself going on the defensive. "I was trying to make you feel."

Her face alters at my words. Eyebrows furrowing, lips pursing. "Feel what?"

"Alive," I articulate slowly, carefully picking my words. "Like we're living on the edge and one false move could send us over."

She remains silent for a long moment, then breaks eye contact and looks out at the void beyond the cliff's edge. The wind plays with her hair, causing it to dance around her face like flames seeking oxygen.

"I don't need to be on the verge of death to know that I'm alive," she finally says without looking back at me.

I turn around and look at it with her, the rocky drop-off illuminated by the moonlight.

I don't fear death—never have, never will—but Elara

does. She fears it enough for the both of us. I know it's not her own death she fears but those of the people she cares about—her brother and now, perhaps against all odds, me.

After a while, she shivers slightly from the frigid mountain air against her cloak, a poor excuse for a covering. A sudden rush of disgust spreads across that beating thing in my chest. It's a hand-me-down cloak, one given to plenty of girls who are escorted in and out of Thornhaven, washed and rewashed due to the copious amounts of bodily fluids that cover it.

I'm not disgusted by the cloak. I've never cared one way or another who wears it or how many times it's used. I just don't want it on *her*. Not Elara.

Shrugging off the strange feeling in my gut, I yank the cloak off her shoulders and my jacket is on her before she can object.

She looks at me for a second, then accepts the jacket without a word, pulling it tight around herself. I turn away, facing the void beyond the cliff, and toss the offensive fabric over. I watch it billow in the wind until it's absorbed by the black.

"Wilder."

Her tone is different now. Softer. Afraid?

I urge her on with a grunt, never taking my eyes off the black expanse below.

"Cav has my ruby necklace."

"I know."

She fidgets next to me. "Then why are you here? Why do you still want to be with me?"

"I do what I want."

She's not deterred. "Why did you bring me all this way

when you should be with Cav? Especially since … it's only half of the Heart."

That gets my attention.

She jolts at my expression. "You didn't know?"

I huff a laugh. "Cav keeps his cards until he's ready to play them. I knew he'd gone to the portrait and grabbed it, saw your exchange with him in the clearing, but couldn't hear all of it. I had no idea the ruby wasn't complete." I raise my eyes to the black sky. "Fucking *figures*."

The realization of Cav withholding the full truth hits me like a punch to the ribs. It's an acute reminder of his cunning side, one I often overlook because of our shared history. Curling my fingers into my palms, I resist the urge to curse out loud, instead directing my venomous gaze towards the darkened horizon.

Elara's emboldened enough to ask, "Why is the ruby so important to you?"

I shift uneasily under her scrutiny. My heart-rate speeds up as I recall running with all my might through windowless hallways, trying to outrun the gunshots echoing behind me. I can still hear the sickening thud when they found their mark, my best friend's lifeless body falling to the ground.

The taste of copper fills my mouth when I remember looking down at her.

It's a mistake I'll never forget or forgive myself for making. A mistake that cost not only Teagan's life, but also any chance at full member status within the Cimmerian Court.

"My first name is John," I say in lieu of an answer. "John Wilder."

I cast a glance at her solemn face, taking in the fine bones of her face, the worried kink of her brows, and the timid concern lurking deep within her honey-colored eyes.

"I don't go by my first name anymore, because the last person who called me *John* was someone who died eight years ago. And she died because of this damned Court. If we find the Heart, if the four of us give it to the Sovereigns, our various debts are paid. We can avoid doing their dirty work and actually enjoy the perks of being in a secret society."

I feel her studying me despite my attempt to lighten the confession, her gaze drilling holes in my profile.

Revealing these vulnerabilities is a breach of my self-imposed code, but here, looking into the darkness at the edge of a cliff, it hardly seems to matter.

Elara doesn't press for more information. She doesn't snidely comment, *All this for the perks of being rich?*

She doesn't flinch or spit in my face. Instead, she offers something far kinder.

A gesture I haven't received in a long, long while.

She takes my hand and holds on.

CHAPTER 27
KASPIAN

"Shit."

The word escapes me like an electrical shock, and not the good kind.

Rarely, if ever, am I surprised.

With renewed fervor, I flip through the columns of names on the parchment listing all previous pledges (those vying for a formal invitation to become an initiate), and initiates dating back to 1820. I find my name a few years after Maverick's.

Maverick both pledged and became an initiate when he enrolled at Titan Falls 7 years ago, making him involved with the Court for a year before he died. Yet, there's no indication he became a full-fledged member.

The rest of the pages are etched with transactions, treaties, and covert correspondences between long-dead Sovereigns.

"Jesus, I hope this valuable database isn't one giant fire hazard. Ever heard of computers?"

It's not just the writings that tell the tale; strewn among the texts are tools of the trade for any Court member—

ciphers, seals, and instruments that speak of a legacy steeped in the supernatural and the sanctified. This room has seen more than bookish research; it's been a haven for strategic liaisons and arcane rituals.

At the Cimmerian Court's inception, the occult and immersion into dark magic was wholly accepted, even as they burned accused witches at the stake. Over the decades, belief in magic and the supernatural faded, the Court moving on to more practical tools and the study of science. With the current Sovereigns, there's been a subtle shift in their preferences, caught mainly by the four of us. I'm shocked they haven't found this section of Thornhaven. It would be such a delightful treasure goblin for them to find.

My gaze then settles on an innocuous sculpture nestled between grimoires and treatises on warfare. It's a raven, wings mid-beat as if ready to take flight. I treat the statue as I would a woman, stroking it for any special spot.

This one is a tease, however, refusing to yield any of its secrets.

When I tip the bird to the side, what lies beneath captures my attention—an encrypted hard drive, sleek and modern against the age-worn stone.

"Touché," I quip into the stuffy air.

Connecting it to my phone, I take it through a series of virus checks before allowing it to show a smattering of files labeled with dates, encrypted messages flagged with urgent markers, and digital photos capturing pages from manuscripts so old they seem to scream of curses if touched by the uninitiated.

I tap on the video dated the latest. I've learned it's always best to work backward.

"Play," I command, and a face that can't be anyone other than Maverick's fills the display. He's the male version of Elara, auburn-haired and tiger eyed, but unlike her delicate charm, he's alight with an intensity that I recognize all too well—like he's starving for something that isn't nutrition.

His voice, even in pixels, carries the weight of dread as he talks.

"Someone knows I'm close, closer than anyone has ever been," Maverick confesses to the camera, his statement causing me to squint for more detail in his expression. "If you're seeing this, trust no one."

I squint at the screen. There's no visible sign of duress in his surroundings—no gun pointed at him offscreen, no chained walls in the backdrop. Yet, the tension in his voice is unmistakable. As if he knew he was running out of time.

I close the video and begin meticulously exploring the remaining files on the drive. Dense text fills each document, encoded messages layered among pages of historical data and records. Cyphers that would take days to decode fill most of it —an array of symbols and obscure references that are as tantalizing as they are confounding.

A sudden noise behind me sends adrenaline pumping through my system like rocket fuel. Every nerve ending ignites with alertness. I turn around swiftly, knife first.

A rat scurries out from its hiding spot, white eyes gleaming and tail flicking nervously. I almost laugh at my startled reaction but keep a firm grip on the switchblade— there are certainly worse things than rats in Thornhaven Manor.

I need back-up.

Pocketing the USB securely, I begin my ascent back up the hidden staircase.

As I emerge from the abyss and into the neglected corridor, I can't help but glance back at the painting—the innocuous guardian of secrets—and the anonymous writer who led me here.

"Damn you, Maverick," I mutter under my breath. "Can't you Wraithwoods be easy for once?"

I head to my room, lock the door, and prepare for a long day at my computer.

CHAPTER 28
ELARA

The air is thick with burned rubber as we tear through the moonlit streets. Wilder chose a different route back to campus with flatter roads, but I'm still gripping his waist like it's my life preserver. He's eating up the road so fast, I doubt the motorcycle's wheels are even hitting asphalt.

As the wind whips over my helmet, carrying away my whispered prayers for safety, I cling to him, my fingers digging into the firmness of his waist.

Wilder's impassive hunch over his bike is a stark contrast to the vulnerability he'd shown earlier on the cliff, an unexpected softness that's added another layer to my complicated dynamic with these men.

Laughter bubbles from my throat, a mix of fear-induced hysteria and an inexplicable sense of anticipation.

My body's like its own person now, separate from my mind.

And I'm not sure they're friends anymore.

The chill of the night doesn't quell the hellfire exuding

from the bike's engine when Wilder finally coasts to a stop in front of Camden House.

I pull my off my helmet then slide off the bike, carefully avoiding scalding my leg. Wilder holds out his arm for leverage.

Because I don't believe he's the kind of guy who expects goodbyes, I turn for the entrance, but I'm stopped by his gloved hand on my arm.

"Let me escort you."

I pause, giving him a funny look.

He barks out a laugh. "I may not look the type to have manners, but they come out every now and again. For those that are worth it, anyway."

I fight the delighted smile on my lips. "Okay. Sure."

Wilder's already seen all of me. What's the difference in seeing where I live?

Moving for the door, Wilder's casual strides keep pace with mine. His arm comes over my head to hold it open, and as I slip through into the common room scattered with late-night studiers and snackers, the sudden hush is palpable.

All sets of eyes turn to Wilder's leather-clad frame coming up behind me.

His warm breath tickles the hair at the top of my head. "Have we arrived at a nunnery or a dorm? Have these ladies ever seen a man before?"

I send him a disapproving look over my shoulder despite the smile fighting for control of my lips. "They've seen men. They just haven't seen *you*."

One side of his mouth kicks up.

"You're right, I don't think I've ever stepped foot in Camden before," he says in a low rumble behind me as we keep moving, avoiding the girls I normally stop to chat with and the table where I'm always exchanging class notes.

Come to think of it, it's been a while since I've socialized with *anyone*.

I take the first flight of stairs, utterly conscious of Wilder one step behind. My stomach tightens at his presence, my nerves coiling around my voice.

The staircase, saturated under the harsh overhead light, gives way to the softly lit corridor. We don't have to walk far. As I search for my keys in my coat's pocket, Wilder leans against the wall next to me. His quietness fills the space between us and engulfs our surroundings.

Feeling his watchful gaze on me, my hands shake slightly as I insert the key into the lock and miss.

Why am I suddenly so nervous? I've spread my legs for this man—*twice*. It's somehow more intimate to have him close by when I'm clothed. No distractions.

"Careful there." Wilder's voice breaks through the scrape of brass against metal when I miss the keyhole again.

His tone is uncharacteristically gentle and devoid of his usual mocking lilt.

Before I can respond or protest further, he reaches out. His hand brushes mine away from the door handle as he turns the key himself. A whiff of leather and engine oil wafts towards me as he steps back.

"Door's open," he announces with a smirk that adds warmth to his hooded eyes.

My heart thumps as I take one step into my darkened room. It feels surreal to have him here in this world that has thus far been separate from him. Like mixing oil with water and expecting them to blend.

I turn around and face the hallway.

Wilder leans casually against the opposite wall, arms crossed, but his hazel eyes burn into mine, smoldering with an intensity that belies his relaxed pose.

"Want that bedtime story?" he murmurs, his voice a low growl that seems to echo in the quiet corridor.

My fingers twitch with the need to touch, to confirm that the man before me is real and not just a figment of some dark fantasy.

I lift my hand, almost as if in a trance, and move towards him, brushing my fingertips along the hard contours of his cheek. The stubble there pricks my skin, igniting a trail of fire down my arm.

Wilder's gaze darkens, growing thick with storm clouds as he grabs my wrist gently but firmly, drawing my hand down to rest on the plane of his chest. Through the thin fabric of his shirt, I feel the steady thump of his heart, the warmth of his skin through his shirt searing into me.

The sensation makes my pulse race, echoing the beat like some kind of drum announcing an impending battle.

"Sweetwitch."

He reaches out to smooth the windblown hair away from my face. I'm too stunned to step back, my eyes glued to his as they flicker with something that borders on affection.

"Wild—" His name dies on my lips as he pulls me closer, his grip on my waist insistent. The world narrows down to the space where our bodies meet, every inch of his arousal pressed against me. His other hand slides lower, cupping my ass with an appreciative squeeze that sends a bolt of desire up my spine.

Our breaths mingle, and time seems to still, waiting for us

to bridge the final gap. His lips hover just a hair's breadth from mine, our first real kiss—

"Um. Hi?" Sasha's sleepy voice cuts through the thick atmosphere, and we freeze.

I'd completely forgot the open door behind me.

Wilder steps back, a growl of frustration rumbling deep in his chest. His eyes linger on me before he turns sharply and leaves without another word, then disappears down the stairs, leaving me adrift in the sudden silence.

Sasha mumbles something unintelligible and rolls over in her bed, slipping back into slumber as if nothing happened.

Typical. Even in sleep, she's a terrible wing-woman.

But sleep eludes me.

After going through my nightly routine and sliding under my covers, I lie awake, tangled in my sheets, haunted by *them*.

Wilder's presence lingers like a ghost on my skin, a phantom ache that echoes with each stroke. And then there's Axe—quiet, enigmatic Axe, with so many scars. My mind drifts to the rugged terrain of his body, each mark a testament to Cav's cruelty. It's a morbid, awful quilt sewn on his skin that somehow draws me in.

But I can't forget Cav and Kaspian, with their polished charm and cryptic smiles. I crave their attention, too, but it's a want laced with trepidation.

They somehow seem more sinister, their presence laced with an aura of malevolence that surpasses even the likes of Axe and Wilder. Or perhaps it's because they have deliberately shrouded themselves in mystery, refusing to divulge any information about their motivations.

They guard their personal reasons for pursuing the ruby with an ironclad resolve, leaving me to speculate. There's

Wilder, who's haunted by guilt, seeking solace in proving his friend actually died for something, and proving his worth to a rich, elite society more cruel than compassionate. And Axe, whose lineage has been denied recognition in the Court and yearns for the respect and honor that this ruby could bestow upon him.

I'm still not sure how a gemstone can do that for them. Is it because until now, the ruby Heart was just a myth and proving that it's real will give them closure? Or do they seriously believe there's magic in it?

There's so much I don't know, and I really, *really* want to keep digging.

Cav and Kaspian's motives are out of reach, but I've seen enough during our time together that their goal extends far beyond appeasing the Sovereigns. These men demand retribution, redemption, *revenge*, exacting their own form of justice.

They want their pound of flesh, too.

My once cherished friends on campus now pale compared to these men who mark my very being with their indelible presence. A stolen glance from Wilder burns hotter than a best friend's embrace; a brush of fingers from Axe eclipses any playful touch.

The dark cavity of my room becomes a theater screen for my restless fantasies mixing with memories, showcasing scenes with these men who have somehow slipped past my defenses.

I had always sought perfection, yearned for predictability, but now I find myself craving the danger they represent, the excitement that comes with being part of their circle.

But...

As much pleasure as these boys promise, there is just as much bloodshed.

As dawn creeps across the sky, staining it with the first blush of morning, I know one thing for certain.

The heat beneath my skin is a siren call to which I'm helplessly drowned by, tethered to the mystery of the ruby and the undeniable pull of these men.

Sunlight filters through the sheer curtains, casting a golden glow across my eyelids.

I stir, reluctant to leave the world of dreams behind—a world where Wilder's arrogant gaze sets my pulse racing, Axe's careful touch ignites my skin, Cav's commanding presence controls my breaths, and Kaspian's cruel machinations draw cries from deep within me.

Sheets twist around my legs, a testament to the few hours of agitated sleep I caught.

"Hey, El."

Sasha's voice cuts through the haze.

"Was I dreaming, or did an intruder in leather try to have sex with you last night?"

She peers at me from her bed, her dark eyes disconcertingly sharp with curiosity, considering she's not a morning person.

"Definitely a dream."

My reply is automatic, seized upon as a lifeline to pull me from the depth of fantasies that threaten to consume my waking moments.

Sasha hums in thought. "Too bad. I thought you nabbed one

of the Untouchable Four. Because then you would have achieved the impossible. Every single one of us dreams of banging one of them. Hell, sometimes when I'm with a guy, I ask him to put a blindfold over me so I can pretend it's—hmm. I can't think of who I'd sleep with first. I don't even care which one it is."

"Oh, come on." I snort. "You said yourself how scary they could be."

"I'm serious," she presses on, an earnest glimmer in her eyes belying her usually nonchalant demeanor. "You need to own it, girlfriend."

"Own what?"

"You know…" She waves her hand vaguely in the air. "All that."

Her gaze sweeps over the parts of me that aren't buried in covers, from my rumpled hair to my bruised lips, from my disheveled t-shirt still carrying hints of Wilder's scent to my nose.

A blush heats my face at her frankness, and I fumble out of bed for something to do. "I don't know what you're talking about."

Sasha sighs, an exaggerated show of frustration that has me rolling my eyes. "You're in denial. You're knee deep in some heavy emotional shit and still pretending it's not happening."

I open my mouth to protest, but she cuts me off.

"I'm there for you, okay? I'll always be there. But sometimes, with your rigid schedule and your constant presentation to the world, you need to be roughed up a little. That's something you should explore rather than suppress."

My mind stutters to a halt at her words. My denial isn't

new to me; it's been biting at my heels like a rabid dog ever since I met Wilder—and the others.

"You have got to loosen up a bit." Sasha follows suit and slips out of bed. "Sooner or later, you'll have to admit that mere friendships and study groups won't satisfy you anymore."

"Maybe," I mumble.

If only she knew.

The thought makes me freeze halfway to my vanity.

I tell Sasha everything. Hasn't she just mentioned my emotional shit? Only she knows about my brother. Correction: she and the Court. And yet, I haven't breathed a word to her about what I've been doing and ... who I've been doing it with.

Multiple times.

Shame fills my cheeks as easily as a blush.

"I have an idea. You could use some fun."

Sasha smiles, but her gaze is searching, as if she senses the turmoil beneath my composed facade.

"What are you thinking?"

Sasha pulls at the hem of her oversized shirt she uses as pajamas, her long black hair tangled around her shoulders. "So, there's this exclusive kind of party I go to once in a while. I haven't told you about it because, well, I'm not really *allowed* to talk about it."

Frowning, I cock my head. "That's not like you. You spill tea over everything."

"I know, right? Which means it must be truly superb for me to actually follow instructions. Anyway, they're allowing us to bring a friend tonight. And I think..." she chews on her lip, ruminating over her next words. "I think you should be my plus one."

A beat of hesitation wavers within me. Accept the invitation or decline?

Sasha scrutinizes my expression, the shiftiness in her eyes a sure sign she expects, even hopes, for a certain response.

My decision hovers between us like another being, asking for a choice that feels weightier than it should.

Maybe she's going through something, too. I haven't been around enough to notice, and as a genuine friend, that is inexcusable.

"No strings attached," Sasha adds quickly, sensing my trepidation. She wraps her slender fingers around her tangled hair and pulls it up into a messy bun. "Just some fun. And I mean, *really good* fun."

Intrigue gnaws at me. This is as good an excuse as any for an escape from the turmoil between who I am and who I'm becoming. Not to mention the ruby Heart and Cav's fury when I apparently only gave him half.

It doesn't matter. My part in their treasure hunt is done. I can't offer him any more.

"Okay."

The word slips from my lips before I'm even conscious of the agreement.

Sasha grins. "Yes! I'll meet you back here at 9 tonight. And wear a black dress. This isn't your typical campus party, trust me."

CHAPTER 29
ELARA

For the rest of the day, every lecture hall feels like a furnace, stoking the fires that kindled while I slept.

Words from professors drift in and out of focus, mere background noise. I try to concentrate on the intricacies of gothic architecture, but my thoughts stray, constructing not cathedrals, but scenarios—each one starring the men who have unwittingly become the engineers of my obsession.

Even now, as I jot down notes because I forgot to charge my laptop last night, my handwriting betrays me, curving and twisting into shapes that remind me of the hard lines of Axe's body, the sharpness of Wilder's teeth. The curve of Kaspian's lips.

I shake my head, chastising myself for this distraction, and yet it's a battle I'm not sure I want to win.

"Elara?"

My neighbor, Helen, whispers under the hum of the professor's discussion. "You're missing the point about the flying buttresses."

"Oh. Sorry," I reply, swallowing down annoyance, then instantly feeling guilty. Usually, she and I compare notes even in class. Why am I suddenly protective of what I'm doing? "I'll catch up."

The day drags on, a relentless march of hours.

As much as I hate to admit it, I was hoping to glimpse them *somewhere*, but they're nowhere to be found or "accidentally" run into at the food halls, the quad, the parking lot…

Ugh. Even I disgust myself at this point.

As dusk falls and the promise of escape looms closer, I accept that I might not see them again. In their eyes, I fulfilled my role. I gave up my family heirloom, this alleged priceless ruby.

Broken.

The other half lost.

Where could it be?

No. I stare at my reflection in my vanity mirror firmly. I will not fall down that rabbit hole.

The freedom of a night out, away from campus, is just the escape I need.

And tequila. *So* much tequila.

"Ready to go?" Sasha asks, snapping me back to reality as she comes up beside me and we fix our outfits.

Sasha looks amazing, choosing a black lace dress that clings tightly to her well-toned physique. The material shimmers under our ceiling's lights.

"Definitely," I nod in response, my gaze lingering on our mirror image.

Our contrasts are stark—her raven-dark hair and brown skin against my auburn waves and fair complexion; her wiry strength against my soft curves; her fearlessness versus my habitual caution.

I'm dressed in a tight, sleeveless black dress, starting at my collarbone and ending above my knees. I feel like I'm ready for a job interview, not an invite-only party, but it's the only black dress I have other than the pleather one which has been … soiled.

Sasha's wardrobe doesn't fit me, and if I asked any of the other girls I'm friends with on the floor, they'll wonder where the hell I've been and start asking questions.

The ruby. That damned ruby necklace Gram dropped into my hands at Maverick's funeral started this all.

Recollections of its polished surface tarnished by a web of fractures that I thought was because of age sends a nauseous shudder into my stomach. Someone broke it, took half of it out of a creepy necklace and put the other half…?

"You're so naturally pretty you make me want to barf. Let's go."

Sasha yanks my arm and pulls me out the door.

The purr of an engine slices through the ambient nightlife of campus, turning my head.

A sleek, black Bentley glides forward with effortless grace, its polished exterior gleaming under the muted glow of the cul-de-sac's streetlights. Its dark windows are a bottomless black, reflecting a starless sky tonight.

When it comes to a smooth stop in front of our dorm, the silence that follows is almost palpable, broken only by the distant hum of conversation and the occasional rustle of leaves in the cool night breeze.

"Is that for us?"

My question is a mix of anticipation and doubt.

Sasha's dark eyes spark at the sight of it in front of us. "Sure is. I told you this was going to be amazing. Come on."

The door is pushed open with a soft click, revealing the plush interior. Buttery white leather beckons us inside, and I'm immediately assaulted by Wilder's scent.

It's not him. Jesus, Elara, coming across any kind of leather is not allowed *to make you wet.*

"Elara Wraithwood and Sasha Sterling?"

A man who looks to be in his late twenties bends low to stare at us from his seat. This is one of those luxury vehicles where two rows of seats face each other, creating an intimate space that adds to the air of exclusivity.

The man's voice is crisp, his suit impeccable, yet there's an edge to him I can't quite place.

"That's us," I reply, letting Sasha go in first.

I slide into the seat beside her, our eyes meeting briefly before we both face the inscrutable man.

"Good evening," he says, his manner professional but distant. He's dressed in an all-black suit.

As the mystery man closes the door, sealing us within the Bentley's elegant cocoon, he turns to us. His expression is as bland as the small packet of paper he hands to me.

I look at Sasha in confusion.

"Standard procedure," he says in answer to my expression.

Sasha leans close, her voice low. "He's right. It's just to protect the residents of the manor we're going to. They're like … super private or something."

"For a party?" My eyebrows express the rest of my dubiousness for me.

"It's not that big a deal. If you ever feel uncomfortable, you can leave, no questions asked. But trust me, it's worth it."

Sasha's reassurance is meant to comfort, but it also carries the thrill of the unknown. A thrill I'm starting to chase, if only to understand the cravings that have suddenly taken hold. It's like I buried myself along with my brother, and I've only now clawed through the dirt and seen the sky again.

Yet, my fingers tremble as I hold the pen, the cool metal a sharp reminder of the choice I'm about to make. With each stroke of my name, I feel like Ariel from *The Little Mermaid*.

What more am I getting myself into? Sasha's unruffled presence beside me is both a balm and a warning. I want to ask her if she's playing Flotsam or Jetsam in this scenario, but one look from Mystery Man tells me to take this very seriously and shut my mouth.

His suit is immaculate, his demeanor impassive as if he's seen this hesitation a hundred times before. But beneath his cool exterior, there's a sharpness, an intensity that tells me he's no mere chauffeur or assistant.

"Take your time," he says, but it's not a suggestion. It's a command thinly veiled with courtesy.

I nod, not trusting my voice, but I *do* trust Sasha.

My hand steadies, driven by a purpose that feels foreign, yet empowering.

I read the block of text, noting nothing concerning. Standard language stating I'll never breathe a word of what happens tonight to anyone unless I want to owe millions of dollars in damages.

With a flourish, I sign my name.

"Done?"

The young man's inquiry pulls me back from the precipice of my thoughts.

"Done," I affirm.

He plucks the contract from my grasp. Without missing a beat, he folds it with mechanical precision and tucks it away into an inner pocket of his blazer.

"Thank you, Miss Wraithwood," he intones, his voice devoid of any emotion that might reveal what my signature truly means.

He produces something from his other pocket. The black silk gleams ominously.

He leans towards me, spreading out the covering.

I flinch back in my seat. "Is that really necessary?"

"Procedure," he states flatly, his touch clinical as he ties the blindfold effectively plunging my world into darkness.

Losing sight sends a jolt of panic through me, but I force myself to breathe evenly, reminding myself I chose this path. I *want* this path.

"Remember, Elara," Sasha says, her voice a tether in the engulfing void. "You're not alone. I'm being blindfolded, too."

Her words are meant to be reassuring. They're really not.

"Let's begin," the young man says, a finality in his tone that makes my heart race.

The car hums to life.

CHAPTER 30
CAV

I stride toward the banister of Thornhaven's mezzanine, every step deliberate. The cloying scent of multiple perfumes intermingles with the tang of sweat clinging to the air.

From my vantage point, I gaze down at the opulent foyer below, where the girls are being presented, blindfolded and on their knees, their breaths shallow and rapid.

They resemble porcelain dolls waiting to be brought to life. Disdain curls my lip at the charade.

"Ladies," I murmur, my voice cryptic and detached above their heads. "Welcome to your downfall."

The master of ceremonies, dressed in an all-black tailored suit and an expressionless white mask, announces, "You may enter, gentlemen," marking the beginning of the third evening of Selection.

I hate this night, despise it with a ferocity that tightens my chest. Yet as I sweep my gaze across the rows of submissive figures, I can't stop remembering my own Selection two years ago.

It's an addictive game of choosing however many girls you want and what you want them to do, one that plays at the edge of villainy, teasing out one's most depraved instincts.

Recently, the rows include men, with a few peppered in throughout this evening. For an exclusively male secret society, I'd consider it progressive, though the Sovereigns abhor change about as much as I loathe supervising these rutting, over-eager initiates.

The door at the far end of the room opens, and our fresh set of initiates enters. One boy stumbles slightly on his robe, his vulnerability broadcasting a warning, and for a moment, I'm tempted to shoot him.

He doesn't have it in him to complete the trials and undergo the kind of tribulations we did.

This is why only four of us remain as current members of the Court, this ancient and brutal society, out of the initial thirty who were chosen from our graduation class. And the class before that. And all classes going back twenty years.

Where they are now, dead or alive, I couldn't say. TFU loses students the way one can lose a kitten in the wild.

However, my benevolent impulse to put him out of his misery is soured tonight, tainted by the partial victory mocking me from my pocket—the ruby Heart, only half complete. Its jagged edges press into my thigh, a constant reminder of my fuck up. How could I have failed to foresee that it might not be whole after over two centuries? How could such a critical detail have eluded me?

"Nightshade?" The First Sovereign's voice cuts through the fog of my brooding, sharp and expecting behind me. "Are you partaking in the Selection tonight? I must have missed you during the first two nights."

"Merely considering my options," I lie smoothly, turning and offering a sardonic smile that doesn't reach my eyes.

I have no interest in the Sovereigns' mind games tonight, either.

"Be sure you do," he warns, his gaze no less piercing behind his porcelain mask. His robe is bright red, lined with gold, and smelling like old blood. "We expect great things from you, and you will gain great things in return."

They always expect the absolute limit, don't they? Great things, grand sacrifices, undying loyalty.

I bow my head in mock deference, letting the shadows from the domed ceiling above cloak my expression.

If only they knew that right now, I'd trade all their expectations for the chance to shatter the chains of this cursed membership.

"Of course," I murmur, my voice edged with a bitterness I can't quite conceal.

"I'd like you to present your progress with the Wraithwood girl and the ruby to us later tonight, after you enjoy the type of rewards we offer," the Sovereign replies before moving beside me to observe the initiates lining up below. "Part of our benefit is the privilege of choosing one for yourself before the initiates do. By dawdling up here, you're risking receiving the leftovers. Don't let that be your last kind of enjoyment."

My jaw sets, determination hardening my resolve. The last appointment I want to make this evening is standing before them in their chamber and informing them of the broken shard in my pocket.

Let them wait. Let them wonder.

"Do not disappoint us," the Sovereign says, as if reading my mind.

It's a final warning before he eases away from the banister and disappears down the hallway into their private, heavily secure wing.

They probably have their own line of co-eds waiting, those old farts.

A genuine smile lifts the corners of my lips. I sound just like Wilder.

With one last glance at the blindfolded innocents, I turn on my heel, surrendering to the chaos that beckons from below rather than face a trifecta of ravenous, grueling Sovereigns up here.

I risk subjecting Axe to another monstrous carving on his body because of my failure. I *have* to find the other half before I officially face them.

I'm so consumed by thoughts of its missing piece and the supposed power the Sovereigns believe it holds (more rituals, more blood, always a sacrifice), that I almost miss her.

Almost.

There, in the sea of anticipation, kneels Elara Wraithwood, her hair a dead giveaway.

My heart stutters, jolting possessive fury through my veins.

What the fuck?

She shouldn't be here.

She's not one of them.

"Elara."

Her name is fire on my breath, barely audible, but swooping through the foyer with savage precision.

How dare they include her?

She. Is. Mine.

I go rigid at the vow torpedoing through my mind.

As the speaker's voice drones on into hallowed rules of submission and expectation, I descend the stairs, each step a hammer blow.

The speaker goes quiet, his masked face turning toward me, along with all the others.

Elara's head tilts ever so slightly at the sound of my footsteps, as if she hears the whisper of her name between the slams, feels the heat of my glare.

But no, she can't see me—none of them can. It's the one rule of Selection: anonymous until chosen.

"How interesting."

I hear the Third Sovereign's voice murmur his observation above me.

I ignore the lupine voice. My eyes latch onto Elara. Her breasts rise with each hurried breath, her blindfold shrouding her eyes from the truth of her surroundings.

What the FUCK *is she doing here?*

Her hands tremble where they rest on her knees, but still she sits on her haunches with a regal air, pretending she's not terrified out of her damned mind.

Oh, butterfly. Why must you get yourself ensnared in such webs?

"Nightshade, are you laying claim?"

I can sense the Third Sovereign's smugness in the question, his assumed control over me, the way he relishes in my discomfort.

Did he orchestrate this?

I won't give him the satisfaction of seeing me unravel.

Instead, I look up and let a slow, calculated smile bare my teeth.

When I notice the Silent Sovereign next to him, a glimmer of surprise quirks across my lips, though I quickly school it.

"Just appreciating the selection presented before us," I say, each word deliberate.

"Proceed then," comes the dismissive response.

My eyes never leave Elara as I take a step closer until my shadow falls over her.

She may not yet recognize my voice, as detached and empty as it becomes whenever I speak to the Sovereigns.

Elara shivers, and the sound of her quick breaths is nearly drowned out by the waves of anticipatory laughter drifting from the initiates. It's a reminder of an easier path, one where I could lose myself in hedonistic distractions for one night.

I pause when an initiate boldly steps forward. His hand extends toward Elara, fingers curling in anticipation. Blindfolded, she remains oblivious to the peril lurking inches from her face.

I seethe, my voice dripping with venom, "She's not for you."

Time seems to freeze in place and then flicker back to life as the initiate recoils.

I can feel all their gazes on me. The two Sovereigns, the initiates, every fucking soul in this room, even the blind ones.

But none of that matters. Because when it comes to Elara, there is no choice, no chance.

"Continue," I order the speaker, my voice a low growl.

He fumbles for composure before continuing on with his script, his voice melding into the background as I stand before Elara. Her breath halts for a moment at my proximity, and her fingers clench at the hem of her dress.

My hand gently cradles her chin. A soft gasp escapes her as I tilt her face up. Even beneath the blindfold, I can sense her wide-eyed surprise.

"Hello, butterfly," I say in a low rumble only she can hear.

Recognition dawns in her posture, a sudden stiffening that's visible even with her eyes obscured. I could almost see her mind racing behind that blindfold—confusion, trepidation, outrage—all warring for dominance within her.

Slowly, I remove my palm from her warmth and, as per tradition, place it lightly on top of her head, an action that signals my choice to all present.

A collective gasp echoes around the room. I haven't Selected in years.

One swift movement removes her blindfold and our eyes clash—an amber gaze meeting cerulean iris—the world around us bleeding away.

Her pupils dilate at seeing me. I can almost sense the spike in her heartbeat. I imagine our pulses sync in this moment—*thud-thud-thud*.

Her cheeks flush, not with embarrassment, but with something akin to relief.

The foul taste of unsaid threats and future interrogations over why the hell she is *here* fills my mouth. My eyes never leave Elara. The coppery taste of blood makes me grimace—an unintentional bite of my tongue.

She watches me closely, so I lean in to whisper, that one breath shaking with rage, "Stay close to me."

Her nod is almost imperceptible, but I see it all the same.

Drawing myself to full height, I take her arm to help her to her feet before turning our backs to the room.

I stop just short of dragging her out of there. I can't afford to show any reaction to her presence other than a claiming, because then the Sovereigns would know she's important to me. As important as the ruby, if not more.

They can't have her.

We calmly move out of the foyer together, leaving behind the palpable shock and whispered speculation.

The sound of the door latching behind us echoes through the hallway, like a seal to another devil's bargain I've formed with the Sovereigns.

I say nothing while I escort Elara to my bedroom. I'm so consumed by rage, I'm afraid to do more than walk. Of what I'll do to her if I get both hands on her.

When I reach my room, I slam the door behind us and whirl. Elara jumps at both the sound and the vitriol leeching off me.

"Explain yourself," I hiss.

I can't fight off the need to punish her. My hands find her waist, fingers pressing through her dress and into skin, pulling her so close, there's no space for secrets or lies.

We're toe-to-toe, her breath mingling with mine, my anger an inferno searing her lips.

"How could you offer yourself to them?"

My words come out like bullets, each one loaded with betrayal and the agony of protection unappreciated.

The Cimmerian Court—my curse, my battlefield—is no place for her.

When Elara pales and turns her head from my fury, I latch onto her jaw. *Look at me.*

My fury thrashes within like a storm on the sea, and she's the ship at its mercy.

I grip her jaw harder, nails digging into tender flesh.

She mewls in pain, but I don't care. *I don't fucking care.*

"Look at me," I command, the words tearing themselves from my throat.

Unshed tears shimmer in her eyes as they meet mine, a silent plea echoing in their depths.

"No words?" I sneer, my hands releasing her jaw to trace the contours of her face, a twisted mockery of tenderness.

Her breath stalls as my fingers brush over her lips, an unconscious shiver running through her at the unexpected gentleness.

I rasp, each word stripped and exposed, "I want to know why you would do this. Do you have any idea what sexual fetishes those initiates are allowed to unleash upon you once they summon you to the drawing room? *Do you?*"

She holds the words hostage in her throat. The trepidation in her eyes gives testament to their weight.

"Sash—Sasha," she croaks.

"Who?"

I'm honestly so focused on Elara all the time, I completely forgot she had people other than the four of us surrounding her.

"My roommate. My best friend. She's down there, too—I need to get her out of there."

I respond with deceptive calm. "And what, exactly, were you two thinking you would find when you signed a contract and submitted to a *fucking. Blindfold.*"

Without warning, her knees buckle beneath her, and she collapses onto the cold marble floor. The suddenness of it startles me, but my quick reflexes catch her before she hits the floor completely.

That brief second of holding her, feeling her mold into my chest like she belongs there, is all I the excuse I need to launch forward, lifting and pressing her against the wall, trapping her.

The stone at her back offers no comfort, nor should it. I want to underscore the severity of her predicament and make her understand that *she does not belong here.*

Elara's eyes, wide and brilliant even in the room's deliberately low lighting, finally reveal a hint of the remorse I've been expecting.

"Answer me!" I scream into her face. My demand rips through the room, a savage beast clamoring for understanding. "Did you think we would accept you? Did you think you could survive our world?"

Elara winces so deeply it's like I've slapped her. Regret curdles, but I form it into scar tissue, my soul covered in it, and pretend there's no deep wound underneath.

But Elara forces her eyes open, looking straight into my eyes. Something flickers there, a cool veil of defiance I've grown familiar with when it comes to her.

In that moment, an unexpected realization strikes me as bitterly as my certainty that I will crack her ice under the barest of pressures.

This confrontation—framed by my rage and her obstinacy—has turned us into enemies. The very thought stirs an ache deep within me, an echo of loss whispering through every fiber of my being.

With one last blistering gaze, I abruptly release her.

I turn my back on her, raking my hand through my hair.

"Cav."

Elara's voice is sandpaper against her throat.

"I'll text Kaspian. He'll get Sasha out."

"I'm sorry. I didn't know I was coming here—"

I come at her again. "Don't you fucking apologize. You knew. You *knew* what could happen. Haven't we taught you enough of a lesson to stay away? I released you. I threatened to drag you into hell if I saw you again. Why the fuck would you come back?"

"I—" She blinks, struggling with words.

Then, it's like a switch goes off.

"*You* did this to me! You ruined me! I was fine with my life before you barged in with threats and big reveals about a horrifying legacy I never asked for. And then you drag me into your damn basement—and do things—unspeakable things—that I can't stop *craving*..."

Elara's shouting halts. She grips her head like it hurts, then spins on her heel in disgust.

With herself, with me ... both.

"Your touch..." she continues while giving me her back, her voice laced with bitterness and something dangerously akin to desire. "All four of you. Every single one of you ignited something inside of me I never knew I craved. Something primal, savage and..." Her voice breaks. "Dangerous. Beautiful."

Her words carve through me, memories of her body yielding on that slab, our shared breaths filling the room. I also remember the empty victory I felt when she gave Kaspian the location of the ruby necklace and it was finally in my possession after all that hard, relentless work.

It wasn't enough. Not just an incomplete jewel, but...

That triumph paled compared to the fire of touching her, the way her skin burned against mine.

"You left me like I was nothing." Her voice is hoarse with emotion. "When you finally got the necklace, I was nothing short of trash for you to dispose of."

Each syllable sears through the layers of my carefully constructed anger, thrashing against the walls I'd painstakingly raised.

She turns to me, chin trembling, clenched fists at her sides.

"No," she chokes out, her chest heaving with the effort to bring forth that single word. "I didn't know about tonight. Sasha said it was an exclusive party she's gone to before and had a great time. She saw what was happening to me. How I was growing quieter, distracted, ignoring everything I used to love. And she wanted to bring me back. Because that's what a friend does, Cav. She wanted to shatter the shell you had encased me in, and you know what? I *like* who I'm becoming. I'm not afraid of you. Didn't I prove that in the basement? I want you, I want all four of you." She raises her arms, then brings them down in exasperation. "I don't want a life of ignorant peace anymore. *I want fucking answers.*"

A chilling realization slithers over me, its icy tendrils coiling around my charred, barely beating heart.

My chest constricts as I witness her transformation from being a pawn in our plans to a queen willing to stand her ground.

"So fuck you, Cav," she says, and it's a plea soaked in poison, a call to an abyss I've been peering into for far too long. "Fuck you for bringing me back to you."

Our breaths are ragged, the line between anger and lust blurring until we're lost in the eye of the storm we've created.

Yet as we face each other, an unwelcome truth slithers past the scar tissue. She's not just a task, not just a name on a list to be cursed by the Court.

She's become more—much more—and it terrifies me. The very thought of her in danger slices through me sharper than any blade.

"Enough people count on me," I say, my hands balling into fists at my sides. "I can't—I won't—let you be another victim I failed to save."

The admission tastes like ash in my mouth, but it's the raw, unvarnished truth. Her scent fills my senses. I remember the feel of her curves beneath my fingers, the way she imprinted herself onto my hands, permanent as ink.

"Victim?" Her voice is filled with scorn. "Is that what you think I am?"

"Isn't it?" I counter, every word heavy with an emotion I dare not name. "There's a reason we tied you down and made you unable to escape or deny us. It doesn't matter if our torture was wrapped in orgasms. Don't you get it? Pleasure is a weapon the Court uses to get what it wants. There's a reason I didn't fuck you on that slab, Elara."

"The Court." She laughs, hollow and bitter. "You throw the name at me like it should mean something, except you haven't told me *anything* about it. You may not enjoy using pleasure as a tool, but you sure as hell love using people's weaknesses against them."

"Do you really want to know?" I spit out.

Her unwavering gaze, so stable despite all the harsh realities I'm choking her with, pierces through my fortress.

"The Cimmerian Court Sovereigns," I begin with a sneer, "are monsters dressed in finery. The four of us—Axe, Kaspian, Wilder, me—we are the only ones to have ascended in decades. All the initiates who came before us didn't make it through the trials. For two years, we've watched as new initiates are consumed by this opulent evil, chewed up by a cycle of abuse and punishment. Pleasure," I spit the word out like poison, "is but a band-aid offered for the blood they bleed."

She watches me, her eyes reflecting the ghosts that haunt me. I see my reflection there—an image of a man hollowed out by years of watching innocence corroded by sadistic rituals.

"Behind these gilded doors of power, wealth, and global influence once we graduate," I tell her, my voice thick with revulsion, "lies a hierarchy that feasts on rituals of pain, masking their savagery with promises of ecstasy. But I..." I pause, my fists clenched so tight I feel my nails digging into my palms, "... I don't know what pleasure is anymore. Not true pleasure. It's been devoured."

I struggle to breathe as my confession consumes me like a disease.

Elara doesn't recoil from the perversion I've laid bare. She doesn't scream and run, though I wouldn't blame her.

Instead, she steps closer, the space between us charged with an electricity that both threatens and beckons.

"How?" I utter, my voice trembling with a painful break. "How can you stand to be near me?"

"Let me show you," she says, her voice a gentle stroke against my soul. "Let me remind you what pleasure can be."

Her audacity should enrage me further, yet all it does is pull me into her orbit, a planet doomed to crash into the sun.

CHAPTER 31
CAV

"That's what tonight is about, isn't it?" Elara asks with forced bravado. "Endless euphoria."

My hands shake as I pin her to the wall, my breath ragged.

"Is this what you want?" I snarl, but my voice betrays my pain. I want to punish her, frighten her into never daring such recklessness again. But at the same time, her proximity is maddening, the heat of her body calling to mine in a language older than words.

Elara's amber eyes lock onto mine, fierce and unyielding.

"I didn't ask for your protection, Cav," she says softly, her breath warm against my face.

"Please," I whisper, a single word carrying the weight of centuries of men who've suffered my fate. "Don't…"

The air between us shifts, charged with anger and something far more perilous.

"Elara," I groan, my resolve crumbling as I capture her lips with mine.

The kiss is merciless, a clash of teeth and tongues.

Her fingers tangle in my hair, pulling me closer, deepening the kiss until there's no space left for thoughts or curses or deaths.

I'm lost in the sensation, in the taste of her, the way her body is so pliant against my rigid cock.

I kiss her with raw savagery.

It's real—*this is real.*

She meets my lips with the same fervor. Elara doesn't see the chains that bind me, doesn't feel the grip of our ancestor's corpses around my throat.

"More," she says before biting my lower lip, a plea that shatters the last vestiges of my control.

My hands roam over her, grasping, claiming, driven by a hunger that has nothing to do with the darkness of our heritage and everything to do with the woman who challenges and captivates me in equal measure. I push her dress up, relishing the softness of her skin under my rough touch, the way she arches into me, seeking more.

"Tell me to stop," I rasp out, desperate for her to remember where we are, what I am.

But she doesn't. She looks at me with a reckless abandon that matches my own, her gaze smoldering with that provocative spark that refuses to acknowledge the prison I'm in.

"Never," she breathes, sealing her fate to mine.

Her declaration fucking unleashes me.

Clutching the collar of her dress, I rip it in half. She gasps as the ruined fabric puddles to the floor.

I press her against the wall, claiming her mouth, biting her lips until they bleed, my body flush against hers, feeling every curve and contour. I've never wanted anyone as much as I want her.

Pulling back with a low snarl, her blood wet on my chin, I kneel between her legs, my heart racing at the sight of her purple underwear. They're damp with desire, and it takes all my restraint not to tear them off her right then and there.

Instead, I slowly slide her underwear down her legs, torturing us both, but revealing the most beautiful pussy I've ever seen and have unwillingly dreamed about since I saw it last.

"Fuck," I breathe in a ravaged voice.

I lean in, taking a slow drag of her clit into my mouth, savoring the taste. She arches her back, moaning louder.

I slide two fingers inside her, feeling her walls clench. But it's not enough. I want her pussy to suffocate me.

"You're too goddamned sweet for me," I growl against her folds, a low rumble vibrating against her sensitive clit.

Elara gasps between heavy breaths, clutching at the wall for support. "Don't stop..."

Her moans fill the air, her eyes glazed over with passion as her pussy clenches around my tongue.

My cock throbs, desperate for release, but I refuse to give in.

My pleasure is hers.

That is what she can't know. Elara must never know how deeply I will fall for her if she ever brings me joy.

Instead, I remove my mouth from her clit with a *pop* of suction, rise, and head to my nightstand.

Elara whines in protest.

"Patience, butterfly," I say while sliding a drawer open and licking her taste from my lips.

I retrieve a silicone cock ring, its spiked texture promising an uncomfortable ride. A gag gift from Kaspian when he figured out my self-imposed celibacy two years ago.

Undoing my pants, I wrap it around my dick, then turn around, greeting her cock first.

Elara's luscious mouth falls open.

She whimpers softly, her body arching off the wall, her inner thighs shining.

"This is what you want, isn't it? To be fucked by a monster," I husk out.

"Yes," she moans, too lost in the promise of me to see sense.

I take one last moment to appreciate my butterfly before she loses her wings.

Then, with a decadent chuckle, I position myself at her entrance, lifting one of her legs and hooking her under her knee to spread her open.

"Beg me, Elara."

"Please…" she whimpers.

"Please what?" I tease, shaking the tip of my cock against her soaked pussy, just enough that droplets of pre-cum run down her pussy.

"Please fuck me, Cav," she moans.

Oh, I fucking love it. I love hearing my name on her lips.

I don't hesitate, don't second guess. As though driven by a force beyond my control, I plunge into her with a grunt, thrusting deep and hard.

Her cry cuts through the air, a desperate prayer that is music to my ears. She is mine in this moment.

Gripping her hips with bruising force, I set a punishing rhythm that has both our bodies rocking against the wall.

Each thrust brings with it an onslaught of marvels that leave me both salivating for more and dreading the impending climax.

Elara matches my pace, grinding herself onto me with each stroke, even though it must hurt. This ring isn't a promise of ecstasy. It guarantees hurt. Her ragged breaths echo my own.

The scent of her arousal fills the room and I lose my goddamned mind.

Jesus, she's a fucking shapeshifter. Butterfly, Siren, Succubus.

Her nails dig into my back through the fabric of my shirt, adding a touch of pain that only enhances the carnal pleasure coursing through me. She positions her lips against my earlobe and her moans vibrate against my skin.

"Fuck," she gasps as I hit a particularly sensitive spot inside her.

I pound into her over and over again, lost in the heat of her body and that addictive scent that trails from her.

As I plunge deeper each time, she arches her back further, impaling herself onto me like this is how she wants to die.

Her walls clench and release around me as if trying to draw me in, to hold me close forever. Her fingers dig into my shoulders, her nails raking down my back as if branding me.

The rough spikes of the cock ring scrape against my sensitive cock head each time we meet at the deepest point, sending electric shocks straight to my brain. Each lash of pain only intensifies the pleasure.

When she bites down on my neck, not hard enough to break skin but enough to mark, I growl, a deep rumble that seems to echo off the walls.

"Elara."

The warning is there in my tone, but she simply grins at me, her eyes gleaming with satisfaction and something more profound.

Something that shakes me to my core.

"Do your worst Cav. I'm not going anywhere."

Before I can respond to her bold declaration, she captures my lips in a fevered kiss at the same time her pussy clenches around me, her orgasm obliterating any remaining traces of self-control.

It's a testament to the power she has over me, the ability to make me lose myself in her without a second thought.

Her cry of release into my mouth triggers my own climax. My body stiffens as I flood her with the evidence of my surrender. It's a profound moment that brands itself onto my soul, forever marking me as hers, just as much as she is mine.

Breathing heavily, I rest my forehead against hers, our harsh pants mingling between us.

I remain inside her, just like a beast knotted inside his mate, as the last vestiges of pleasure fade.

Then, I pull out slowly, closing my eyes at this pocket in time where nothing else matters but her.

Elara whimpers at the loss but says nothing. The room falls silent except for our heavy breaths.

And then it hits me, the strange tranquility after an intense round of fucking.

One I can't have.

With a swift movement, I slide the cock ring off and toss it to the side, then stride away from her.

"Cav?" she asks behind me, her tone unsure.

I don't answer.

Stepping onto the balcony, I let the cold seep into my bones, freezing me from within, making it easier for me to deal with the hellfire that we have just set aflame.

CHAPTER 32
ELARA

Cav's silhouette stands between the open French doors, his form blending into the vast expanse of the night sky with only faint stars etching his edges.

There's a throbbing ache in my middle. I'm almost positive I'm bleeding between my thighs from that bestial thing around his dick, but rather than clean myself up, all I want to do is go to him.

Doubt gnaws at me as I carefully lift a soft blanket from his bed and drape it over my shoulders, joining him on the balcony.

Without a word, I use one half of the blanket to draw him closer.

Cav's gaze remains fixed on the darkness that cloaks the ancient forest surrounding our campus. He seems oblivious to my presence, numb to the world around him.

The doubt becomes permanent when I realize the warmth of my touch will never penetrate the ice encasing his heart.

Yet, against all odds, I hold on to hope even though the

wind through the trees seems to whisper warnings of our impending demise. He is not Romeo, and I'm not Juliet. Cav simply needs time. Time for his wounds to heal. Time to realize that what we share is worth fighting for.

I'll wait as long as it takes.

As the faint stars twinkle overhead, I make a silent vow. I will not let these broken, tormented men continue to shatter.

"Listen closely, Elara."

Cav's voice yanks me into the present.

"I'm only going to say this once. I don't want to, but I need you to understand the gravity of what you're toying with."

"Okay."

I stare ahead with him, uncertain what else he could possibly confess after our last conversation.

"Centuries ago, the Nightshades, my family, betrayed an innocent woman. Sarah Anderton."

My grip tightens on the blanket draped over my shoulders.

"We handed her over to the Church, watched as they screamed 'witch' and condemned her to death. All for the promise of her gold, for her blood-soaked jewels."

"What?" I whisper in disbelief.

I frantically search through what I've learned, how Sarah was paid in jewelry to poison nobles and how that fortune was lost, despite her torture and the cruelty of her daughter's death. She never confessed the location, and treasure hunters, criminals, and tourists have been looking for it in Titan Falls ever since.

Cav's ancestors are the ones who put her to death?

By all accounts, the Nightshades stopped a murderer. It's something to be proud of, yet he says it like it's a confession.

Finally, Cav turns to me, his breathing steady, unnervingly calm.

"My ancestor, Jackson Nightshade, didn't stop there. He damned many more women and girls by doing so and even stole Sarah's daughter's child."

"But…" I can't stop blinking. I'm struggling to process the information he so casually reveals. "I don't understand. What other girls? What women?"

Cav lets out a bitter laugh. "That's what you're focusing on? Not the fact that Sarah Anderton's daughter had a child who disappeared from history along with her. A child you're descended from. Ah," he says, noticing his mic drop didn't fall very far. "You already knew."

I nod.

"Then ask your Vulture friend, Tempest, about the girls and women the Andertons were trying to save."

"But that makes no sense … Sarah was a killer, not a savior."

He throws off the blanket I had carefully placed around him. "Sarah accomplished one thing before she died. She cursed my entire fucking bloodline for betraying her, and we have been paying the price ever since."

"Wait." I resist rubbing my hands across my face in an effort to keep up with him. "You believe you're cursed because of something your ancestors did?"

My words carry skepticism, challenging him in a way that seems to sting.

"Believe?" he scoffs, that torturous anger flaring anew. "It's not belief—it's fact. This family has been paying for those sins ever since. Misfortune follows us like an invincible demon."

I step toward him, closing the gap he's desperately trying to maintain. "Cav. Curses? Magic? That's the stuff of fairy tales. Your family's misfortunes... they're just that. Unluckiness, bad choices, coincidence."

"*Coincidence?*" The word explodes from him and I recoil. "There are no coincidences with Sarah Anderton—*your* bloodline. The Nightshades are bound to this monstrous court, forced into servitude because of what we did to her. The Vultures think they solved the truth about Sarah Anderton's hidden jewels and that her trove of jewelry didn't actually exist. Except, it does, because you've just presented half of the ruby Heart to me."

Just like I've given you half of my heart, I think, but don't admit.

He continues, his lips peeled back from his teeth, "And if that fucking jewel is in play, then so is my curse."

"Cav, please slow down. Let me figure this out with you."

"The Vultures uncovered a list of associates connected to Sarah during their hunt for her hidden treasure. Jackson Nightshade was one of them. He destroyed all evidence of her riches, uncaring of the consequences it would have on future generations... or on himself. And he *sold* that baby. Your ancestor. Do you have any idea what happened to her?"

"Cav, please..." My eyes follow him as he paces.

"Whether or not you believe it, Elara, the curse is real. And I won't let you be another casualty of my legacy."

"Cav..." I reach for him, the agony on his face unbearable.

"Please," he whispers, the one word he can say that can splinter my heart into irreparable pieces. "Believe me."

A knock on his door interrupts us, causing him to whirl around.

He storms toward the door, leaving me shaking under the blanket.

"*What.*"

He throws it open without waiting for an answer, revealing Kaspian on the other side.

Kaspian reacts to Cav's stark nakedness with an arched brow, but quickly notices me and raises the other.

"Apologies for the interruption," he says smoothly, stepping past Cav's smoldering frame. "I had no idea you had an Elara burrito on your balcony. Come in, beastie. You don't deserve both Cav's icy heart and his cold shoulder."

Cav snarls, but Kaspian ignores him, extending his hand for me to take as he escorts me inside.

I steal a glance at Cav, uncertain of where his emotions now lie, but all I see is his practiced apathy.

"Why are you here, Kasp?" Cav asks. "Shouldn't you be enjoying yourself downstairs?"

Kaspian hums in thought. "Tried to last night. It didn't take."

His attention shifts to me, seduction stirring behind his eyes that sends a lightning bolt into my swollen core, before he returns to Cav.

"Besides, the third night of Selection is always so brutal," Kaspian continues. "Not my cup of tea, unless I'm allowed certain delicacies."

He winks at me as if letting me in on the joke.

I shift under my blanket, uncomfortable because I'm actually willing to cause more bleeding if it means I get another round with Kaspian.

Then realization hits me. "Oh, my god. Sasha. She's down there. I have to go get her—"

Kaspian stops me from flying out of the room by taking my arm. "Don't worry. I found her and got her out before things got out of hand. She's currently enjoying my gin stash in my room."

Relief floods through me. With everything happening with Cav, I hadn't fully grasped the implications of what the initiates do downstairs.

Sasha said she had fun last night, that she wanted to do it again…

Did she expect it to be rough tonight? Is she testing the same desires that I am?

I make a mental note to talk to her about this. Perhaps understanding her perspective can shed light on my own.

"I'm here for more important matters," Kaspian says, drawing my attention back to him.

Movement in the open doorway catches my eye. As if summoned, Axe and Wilder file in.

Kaspian nods, expecting them.

Cav, usually so inscrutable, glowers and still doesn't bother to cover himself. "I assume it was important enough to include all of us. So, what is it?"

I pull the blanket tighter around me at Wilder and Axe's presence. Yes, they've all seen me naked, but to have them surrounding me in a half-circle, their tall, broad-shouldered forms overshadowing me, I can't help but feel small.

Helpless.

Kaspian clicks his tongue. "I stumbled upon some unfortunate documents hidden in this manor, likely concealed by previous Sovereigns intending to keep them away from unscrupulous individuals like myself. Unfortunately for them, I love a good chase."

"Get to the point," Cav bites out.

Wilder crosses his arms thoughtfully, his lips pressed into a thin line. Axe shoves his hands into his pockets, his eyes narrowed as if expecting a heavy blow.

"There's no easy way to say this," Kaspian says with a prolonged sigh.

The bastard's enjoying every second. I can almost taste Kaspian's satisfaction.

I tense as he turns his attention to me, pushing the guys —his brothers-in-arms—into the background.

"I believe I know who broke the ruby Heart in half," Kaspian says to me, his face more serious than I've ever seen it.

"Why are you looking at me like that?" I falter, my stomach clenching, anticipating a brutal, unforgivable punch to the gut.

"It was your brother," Kaspian says, causing Wilder to sharply inhale, Axe to jerk back in surprise, and Cav's subtle uncoiling.

Kaspian pauses, allowing regret to soften his features into the angelic guise many people assume he actually possesses, before unveiling the empty chasm that dwells within him.

I swallow hard, my eyes burning. "No. Maverick wouldn't have any clue about this. He had no connection with the Court. He was … he was…"

Good. Innocent. Loving.

My voice fades into the silence that swallows my denials and spits back tainted memories of my brother.

"He was more than involved," Kaspian continues, undaunted by my reaction, "I think he broke that priceless jewel in half and then was killed for it."

An icy wave crashes over me, making me falter back into nothingness. I take a step back, hands groping for something to ground me. It's too much—the secrets, the lies, the sins of past and present colliding.

"You're lying," I manage to hiss through clenched teeth. "Maverick... he was innocent. It was a crime of opportunity. A burglary gone wrong. Why else would anyone—?"

But any argument dies a natural death in the face of Cav's knowing gaze as he steps forward. There's a cruel finality in his eyes that hints at the depths of his collected information that will forever elude me.

He says with exaggerated sincerity, "You cannot fathom the depths of this Court's depravity, Elara. I tried to tell you."

A gust of wind blows through the open French doors of the balcony, carrying with it the scent of impending rain and something more frightening—the cries of nocturnal predators.

Wilder's eyes ignite with twin flames, fueled by his own history with the corrupt society that cost him someone he loved, too. Axe's jaw clenches, fists tightening and nostrils flaring as he struggles for control. Cav watches me closely, as if he can read my every thought, every emotion surging through me. And Kaspian...

Kaspian smiles.

The blanket slips from my shoulders as if in surrender to an unseen force.

The French doors slam shut with an ominous thud from the wind.

My brother...

My brother.

Maverick, what have you done?

"We merely guessed at your value before, beastie," Kaspian says. "But now that we know how priceless you are, we're greedier than ever."

ALSO BY KETLEY ALLISON

all in kindle unlimited

If you want more bullies and secret societies, read:

Rival

Virtue

Fiend

Reign

The Thorne of Winthorpe:

Thorne

Crush

Liar

Titan Falls:

Cruel Promise (M/F)

Broken Beauty (Why Choose)

Loyal Vows (Why Choose)

Wicked Court (Why Choose)

also writing as S.K. Allison,

contemporary romance:

If you like your bad boys and bullies as standalones (no series, one book, a happy ending), read:

Rebel

Crave

If you like a grump turned into a protector for his woman, read:

Rock

Lover

If you like your playboys with tormented hearts and scars, read:

Trust

Dare

Play

If you like small-town, angsty vibes:

You Will Want Me